To Break the Rules

Girls Who Dare, Book 3

By Emma V. Leech

****

Published by: Emma V. Leech.

Cover Art: Victoria Cooper

ASIN No.: B07PYL119X

ISBN: 9781072068464

Table of Contents

To Break the Rules

Members of the Peculiar Ladies' Book Club

Prunella Adolphus, Duchess of Bedwin – first peculiar lady and secretly Miss Terry, author of *The Dark History of a Damned Duke.*

Mrs Alice Hunt (née Dowding)–Not as shy as she once was. Recently married to Matilda's brother, the notorious Nathanial Hunt, owner of *Hunter's*, the exclusive gambling club.

Lucia de Feria - a beauty. A foreigner.

Kitty Connolly - quiet and watchful, until she isn't.

Harriet Stanhope – serious, studious, intelligent. Prim. Wearer of spectacles.

Bonnie Campbell - too outspoken and forever in a scrape.

Ruth Stone - heiress and daughter of a wealthy merchant.

Minerva Butler – Prue's cousin. Not so vain or vacuous as she appears. Dreams of love.

Jemima Fernside - pretty and penniless.

Matilda Hunt – blonde and lovely and ruined in a scandal that was none of her making.

Chapter 1

Am I foolish, to be so intent on revenge, to risk everything I have for the chance of retribution? Perhaps, but everything I have is a lie, and sooner or later the truth will find me. At least, when the inevitable happens, I will have the satisfaction of having made him pay. That will be my legacy.

—Excerpt of an entry from Señorita Lucia de Feria, to her diary.

1st July 1814. Meeting of the Peculiar Ladies, Upper Walpole Street, London.

Lucia watched in amusement as the Peculiar Ladies made a fuss of a blushing Alice. A few days earlier, the young woman had defied her parents and married Nathaniel Hunt, owner of the exclusive and notorious *Hunter's*, a gambling club frequented by the richest men of the *ton*.

That Alice, of all people, should have stood up and defied her parents was astonishing, as she was the shyest among their group. Lucia couldn't fault her choice, however. Nate was handsome and rich, and clearly besotted with his new bride. Faced with a choice between him and the *Honourable* Edgar Bindley, there was really no contest. Honourable was a word that neither Edgar nor his vile father had any concept of.

The Earl of Ulceby, Lionel Bindley, was a greedy and selfish man who cared for nothing and no one.

Lucia knew this.

Her friends did not understand her link to Ulceby. The man himself would not know her if he passed her in the street, but she knew him. Her position at the fringes of good society was tenuous at best. Beauty gave you power, and Lucia had the attention of powerful men who hoped to seduce her. So, the invitations kept coming, for now.

Her funds, such as they were, had been used in their entirety to establish herself during this one season, to make herself a well-known figure, and therefore one not easily disposed of once the truth was out.

She had no illusions she would be welcomed into society then, no matter her financial situation. People who were friends to her now would no longer receive her, and she reminded herself daily to keep them at a distance.

Every morning, as she stared at a reflection of a woman with no place in the world, she reminded herself of her objectives, of what she sought to achieve. Friends did not enter that equation.

She had given her life over to one abiding desire.

Revenge.

She had rules to abide by, to make as many acquaintances among the *ton* as she was able, whilst allowing no one close.

Today, the Peculiar Ladies were gathered in the luxurious home of Miss Ruth Stone, whose father was of the merchant class. Rich to the point of vulgarity, he sought to enter the ranks of the *ton* but found doors closed to him on all sides. They could not ignore his wealth, but they'd never overlook his lack of breeding. Now his daughter was of age he'd pinned his hopes on her snaring an impoverished nobleman.

Unbeknown to Ruth, her father had been one of the men who had pursued Lucia the most relentlessly, intent on making her his mistress. Finding him hard to dissuade—no matter how many times she refused him—Lucia had changed tack and befriended his daughter.

Ruth was no fool and had run the household since she was little more than a girl, as her bird-witted mother had nothing on her mind further than spending her husband's money. As she had hoped, staying with Ruth as her guest for a few days had shielded Lucia from Mr Stone's interest. Despite her loathing of the man, who was a manipulative creature, she'd seen enough to realise he respected and loved his daughter and would not willingly invite her censure.

A word from Lucia could make his life very uncomfortable at home.

This was what men were, though, how they worked. They saw what they wanted and did whatever they deemed necessary to get it, caring little for who might stand in their way. Only one man had ever shown any care for Lucia, and even he could not protect her when it had mattered.

Men were loathsome creatures, self-centred and unreliable at best.

At worst… they were lethal.

Men flirted with her and Lucia allowed it, drawing them into her circle, giving them hope they might have a chance, but she never let them overstep the mark. They whispered the rumours of her parentage wherever she went—that her Spanish mother had been a courtesan—and most people expected her to follow suit. In fact, the woman in question had been Portuguese not Spanish, but English men were ignorant and careless, and it was the least of the things about her that were not as they appeared.

The offers from men had become increasingly lavish, ridiculously so, and she was careful not to bruise anyone's pride as she rebuffed their advances. That was perhaps hardest of all, when she wanted to spit in their faces and tell them to go to hell. Yet it only increased her exclusivity and their desire to have her. They called her *Señorita Ciudadela* or Miss Citadel, and they laid bets as to who would be the first to breach her walls.

It disgusted her, but Lucia was playing her own game, and soon she would laugh in their faces when they realised who it was they'd been throwing themselves and their fortunes at with such abandon.

With difficulty, Lucia forced such dark thoughts away and returned her attention to the surrounding ladies. Ruth had invited Bonnie to accompany her to the Earl of St Clair's summer ball, and Bonnie was alight with pleasure at the invitation. Sadness bloomed in Lucia's chest as she watched them laughing and chattering together. She had seen friendships blossom between the ladies, and watched both Prue and Alice as they'd fallen in love and overcome the trials and tribulations of their courtships with support from the women around them. How she longed for that—to rely on an unwavering friendship—but real friendship required truth at its foundation, and that was something Lucia could not give. She was a morass of lies and half-truths and, though it would soon be at an end, she was not fool enough to believe the truth would win her any friends.

"Well, this is all well and good," Lucia said, entering the conversation at last. "But I still have not smoked a cigar nor drunk a glass of cognac." She arranged her skirts with deliberation, affecting a prim moue of displeasure expressly to make everyone laugh.

"When are you going to do it, Lucia?" Alice asked her, a glint of sympathetic warmth in her blue eyes.

"I thought at the Earl of Ulceby's ball," Lucia said, knowing that Alice would worry for her. She was a sweet girl and her limited experience of the Ulceby men had given her a healthy fear of the family.

"Oh," Alice said, her surprise and anxiety as evident as Lucia had expected. "You're going to that?"

"Do you mind, very much, Alice?" she asked, wishing the girl had been nowhere near Edgar Bindley.

Matilda had confided that Alice had almost been violated by Edgar during a visit to Vauxhall Gardens. If not for the Marquess of Montagu's intervention, things could have ended very badly. Mr Bindley had also pursued Lucia over the past weeks, and she could feel nothing but revulsion for him. She'd taken care never to be alone with him, though he was a pale imitation of his father.

"Oh, no," Alice said in a rush, shaking her head. "Not in the least, only Lord Ulceby is not a nice man, and… do watch out for his son, Edgar Bindley. He's a spiteful cad."

"With a broken nose," Matilda murmured before taking a sip of her tea. Alice glanced at her and grinned.

"I know," Lucia said. She'd only been too pleased to discover Mr Hunt had broken Edgar's nose. Her own retribution would be bloodless, but far more devastating. "That is why I chose them. I should not like to steal anything, even as silly as a cigar and a drink, from a man I esteemed."

"Do you esteem any man?" Matilda asked, the direct question rather shocking the group as everyone stilled.

Lucia considered her answer, unsurprised by Matilda's directness; it was a quality she valued highly in the woman from whom she had recently rented rooms. "No," she said.

Everyone laughed, assuming she was being amusing again, though Lucia saw nothing to laugh about. Men would use her if she let them, so she would use them before they got the chance.

"Will you go to Ulceby's ball?" Alice said, clearly a little discomposed by Lucia's answer as she turned her attention to Matilda.

"I suppose so, to keep Lucia company and out of too much trouble if nothing else," she said with a wry laugh. "I assume they won't banish me at the door for being related to Nate, as the earl owes him too much money."

Lucia's ears pricked, noting Alice lowering her voice, unaware Lucia was still listening to the conversation.

"The earl owes everyone money," Alice said. "I can't understand how he can possibly afford to hold such a lavish ball."

Lucia listened to them talk, wondering about how a man on the verge of bankruptcy could continue to throw a fortune away.

"It's a sickness, I think," Matilda said, her voice soft. "I was angry with my father, for a very long time but… but he was so sorry for what he'd done. So full of remorse. He said demons had possessed him, and… I can almost believe it."

"It is a sickness for some," Lucia said, watching both women startle as they realised she'd been listening. "But not for Lord Ulceby. He is a cruel, greedy man, and one day he will pay the price for it."

She could not keep the venom from her words and cursed herself. Alice and Matilda were staring at her.

Hold your tongue, you fool.

Heat prickled down her back and Lucia realised she must try harder to hide her animosity for the earl.

"Well, then," Ruth said, breaking the strange atmosphere with her cheery, no-nonsense voice. "These cakes will not eat themselves. For heaven's sake, tuck in, ladies."

Oohs of pleasure murmured around the group as various trays of delicate pastries passed back and forth.

"You know," Prue said, giving Lucia and Kitty a sly glance, "both Alice and I are married because of our dares. So, I think you two ladies should prepare yourselves."

The group laughed and made sounds of encouragement, but Lucia folded her arms, a scowl darkening her face.

"I would never give a man such power over me," she said, unheeding of her own advice to keep her own counsel. The idea was too unsettling for her to hold her tongue as she ought. "I shall never marry. *Never*."

Kitty, the other young lady with a dare to complete, blinked hard and scrambled to her feet. "Would… would you excuse me, please?"

She rushed from the room, leaving the other girls gaping in her wake.

"Whatever did I say?" Prue asked, perplexed. "I know I'm good at putting my foot in my mouth, but—"

"I'll go after her," Harriet said, putting down her plate and following Kitty out the door.

"I suppose we all have our secrets," Matilda said softly, turning to look at Lucia and smiling a little.

Lucia swallowed and forced a smile to her own lips, reminding herself once more to keep her mouth shut.

***

Fred Davis sighed and rubbed at his neck, turning his head back and forth to ease the ache. He'd been standing on the same spot outside a certain gentleman's club for bloody hours now, but he was damned if he'd give up. Silas Anson was a pain in the arse, but Fred had worked for his father—the late viscount—since he was a boy. Now the old man was dead, and his sense of duty would not allow him to leave the son in the lurch.

Whether the fool liked it or not.

From what Fred knew of Silas, never had there been a man more in need of a good valet, nor one less likely to take one on. As Fred straightened and looked down the road once more, that fact was illustrated so vividly that he winced with distress.

The new Viscount Cavendish was a bloody shambles.

Towering and broad-shouldered, Silas Anson had the kind of figure suited to battlefields and sword wielding heroics. He was not at home in polite company—despite impeccable breeding—and didn't bother trying to fit in. If not for the fact he disdained the *ton* more than they disdained him, he'd probably not be welcome anywhere. However, his cavalier attitude to society made him rather an intriguing figure, and one women seemed to take to like felines around a dish of cream. Strangely, Silas seemed to care little for their attentions either, and his name had never yet been linked to any woman, respectable or otherwise.

The fellow was an enigma.

Albeit a dishevelled one.

His coat was wrinkled, his shirt a long way from the pristine white it ought to be, and his cravat made Fred want to wring his hands and weep. As for his boots, they were so offensive that Fred simply couldn't look at them.

"Lord Cavendish."

Silas's head snapped around, a glint of displeasure in his face, the startling blue gaze of generations of the Cavendish family fixing on Fred. It occurred to him then that Silas was likely unused to his new title, as his father was barely cold in the ground. He and the old man hadn't spoken since Silas was a boy.

The blue eyes narrowed and then widened as recognition filled them. "Davis?"

"Yes, my lord," Fred replied, relieved that Silas recognised him. It had to be fifteen years since they had last seen each other.

"By God." Silas stared at him for a moment, apparently nonplussed, and then startled Fred by holding out his hand. "It's good to see you."

Fred stared at the proffered hand, a little taken aback. Nobility did *not* shake hands with the serving classes, but then Silas had never paid much heed to the rules.

"Still a stickler for proprieties, I see," Silas said, a rather mocking glint in his eyes as his hand remained outstretched. There was challenge in his stance and Fred knew better than to test him. He took the viscount's hand and shook it. "What brings you to this part of town?" Silas asked, a glimmer of suspicion in the blue now.

Fred took a breath, knowing Silas would likely fight him every step of the way.

"I came to see you, my lord."

"Oh?"

The suspicious look deepened and Silas folded his arms.

"I've been valet to the Viscount Cavendish for over thirty years, my lord. I know every skeleton in the cupboard and few what's buried so deep even your father didn't remember them."

"Are… are you intending to blackmail me?" Silas said, his expression somewhere between outrage and delight.

Fred tutted and rolled his eyes. "No, my lord," he said, with every ounce of dignity he possessed. "I'm intending to work for you."

Silas stared at him in astonishment. "Doing what?"

The question so took Fred aback that he gaped at the man before him for a good while before he could bring himself to answer. "As your valet, of course."

"My valet?" Silas roared with laughter, causing people on the street to turn their heads and stare. Fred shifted uncomfortably, aware the man was making a spectacle of both of them. "By God, that's a good one. I'm not some preening tulip! I don't have a bloody valet."

"No, my lord," Fred said, his tone dry as sand. "That much is evident."

Silas stopped laughing and regarded him a little more closely. "You cheeky blighter."

"I speak as I find, my lord," Fred said, folding his arms to match the viscount's. "And you're a bloody disgrace. If those boots have seen a lick of polish anytime this past month, I'll eat my hat."

"I might make you eat it anyway," Silas retorted, clearly nettled by the comment. "I've never heard such impertinence."

"And I've known you since the day you were born, my lord, I never blamed you for running off and I've been proud of all you've achieved, but you're Cavendish now. You can't run from it any longer, and I reckon it's about time someone took you to task." Fred held his ground, waiting for the eruption, knowing too well the Cavendish temperament after decades of dealing with the man's irascible father. They despised any sign of weakness; the only way to deal with them was not to back down. "The fact is we need each other."

The mystified look in Silas's eyes satisfied Fred.

"What the devil do you mean by that?" Silas demanded.

"I mean, my lord, that you don't have the faintest idea of what your position entails, seeing as how you and your father have been estranged these past fifteen years, and I'm too old and set in my ways to go and work for someone else. I'm as much a part of your inheritance as Cavendish House, and I'll be damned if I'll let you throw away all my years of loyalty."

"You make it sound as if I was tossing you in the gutter," Silas retorted, a thread of anger in his voice. "As far as I remember, I offered you a very generous retirement in light of your loyal service to my father."

"That you did, my lord," Fred admitted, his voice softening a little as he remembered the staggering amount settled upon him. He'd not expected anything like the sum the new viscount had offered him. "But the fact is, my work is my life. I never married and I've got no kin. What would I do?"

There was a note of pleading in Fred's demand that he hadn't meant to allow, but Silas heard it the same as Fred did.

A frown of consternation gathered at his brow. "I understand," he said, his voice gruff with unease. Another trait of the Cavendish men was that they'd rather die than speak of anything that smacked of sentiment or emotion. "It's true that I… I owe you a debt, Davis," Silas said, sounding increasingly awkward.

It was Fred's turn to frown now. "Whatever for?"

Silas's mouth quirked and he huffed out a laugh. "For a thousand little kindnesses when I was a boy. For not letting me starve when the fellow banished me to my room, for taking the time to notice a snot-nosed boy when you might have ignored me, and certainly for taking the blame when that bloody vase got broken. By God, man, the fellow might have dismissed you for that."

Blushing for the first time he could ever remember, Fred stuttered and shook his head. "I never meant that you owed me aught. That's not why I'm here."

Fred watched, bemused as Silas grinned, showing even, white teeth in a face that was uncompromising and hard. "I know it, and for that alone I suppose I'd best let you have your way, though I warn you now: I'll not put up with primping and fuss. I'm not a doll to be dressed up and paraded about."

"I gathered that much," Fred said, chuckling and shaking his head with dismay.

Silas gave a snort. "Oh, to the devil with it. Come along, then. It looks like you've got yourself a job."

Fred gave a deep and heartfelt sigh of relief. "Thank you, my lord," he said, meaning it. "I promise I'll not give you cause to regret it."

"Hmmm," Silas replied, though there was laughter in his eyes. "We'll see."

Fred fell into step with his new master, unable to stop his gaze from falling to the shocking state of the man's Hessians.

"There is one condition of my employment," he said, unable to restrain himself despite his good fortune. "For the love of everything holy, let me polish your boots."

"Bloody hell, I thought you said I wouldn't regret it?" Silas shook his head and sent him an accusing look.

"What possible harm could polishing your boots do?" Fred demanded.

"A great deal," Silas said, perfectly serious. "People might think I give a damn."

Chapter 2

Thank heavens for Lucia, her company has eased the transition from leaving my brother's house and stopped me feeling too sorry for myself. She is a strange young woman, so very lovely and sweet natured, yet I cannot help but feel she is adrift somehow. I have never met someone so self-contained and so full of secrets. I wish she would confide in me. I would dearly like to be her friend.

—Excerpt of a letter from Miss Matilda Hunt to Her Grace Prunella, Adolphus, Duchess of Bedwin.

1st July 1814. The evening of Lady Grasmere's ball, Mayfair, London.

Silas stifled a groan as he stared around the crowded ballroom. At least he'd sent Fred off to fetch his belongings, so he'd avoided being primped to death before he came out.

"Why did I let you talk me into this?" he grumbled, sending an impatient look towards his companion.

Jasper Cadogan, the Earl of St Clair, returned a dazzling smile.

"Because I can charm the birds from the trees, or so I'm told," St Clair replied, his handsome face showing a hint of mockery. "Winkling you out of your blasted library didn't pose too much of a challenge. Besides, there's someone here I want you to meet."

Silas did groan this time. “Damn it, Jasper, will you stop with this ridiculous urge to get me leg shackled?”

“Who said anything about marriage?” The earl looked so offended that Silas couldn’t help but laugh. “But I’ve never met a man more in need of a bit of female company. I don’t understand why you insist on living like a blasted monk.”

“Hardly,” Silas said, a little aggrieved by the comparison. “And women cause nothing but aggravation. I’ve never met one yet who wasn’t more trouble than they’re worth, and what’s more….”

Silas trailed off mid-sentence as the thread of the conversation eluded him.

“Ah, yes,” St Clair said, sounding unbearably smug. “That’s who I wanted to introduce you to.”

The woman across the ballroom was quite simply the most exquisite vision of loveliness that Silas had ever seen. Her hair was black as a raven’s wing and swept up to show a slender neck. The heavy tresses were coiled in an elaborate coiffure and studded with seed pearls that shone like tiny stars against a midnight sky. Skin the colour of gold satin made his fingers itch with the desire to discover if it was as soft as it looked, and Silas was horrified to discover his chest tight, his breath catching in his throat.

She was all curves, a dark blue silk gown encased her lovely figure, with more pearls studding the low neck of the dress, which drew the eye to her ample bosom. All at once his mouth was unaccountably dry, and Silas took a large swallow from the glass he held, never taking his eyes from her. She was searching the room, apparently looking for someone.

The largest, darkest, thickly lashed eyes turned towards him, taking a moment to look him over, and then moving on without interest.

A jolt of irritation shot through him at being so easily dismissed.

"Who is she?" he asked, unwilling to show any curiosity, but quite unable to go another moment without knowing.

"No one really knows," St Clair replied, the amusement in his voice perfectly audible. "They call her Señorita Lucia de Feria, though Miss Hunt tells me she's Portuguese, not Spanish. The rumour is her mother was Anna-Marie de Feria."

Silas dragged his gaze from the woman to regard his friend. "The Duke of Craven's mistress?"

St Clair's mouth quirked a little. "The Duke of Craven, the Earl of Davenport, the Earl of Montrose...." He waved a hand in an airy fashion. "I don't remember the rest. An expensive piece, whichever way you look at it."

"Which of them is her father?"

"That," the earl said, his eyes alight with interest. "Is the question of the day, my friend. No one knows, and the lady won't say."

"So, who is her current protector?" Silas asked against his will, feeling an ugly sensation rise in his chest at the idea of any man *owning* the rights to such a woman.

"She has none. To my knowledge, she has refused every man who has approached her, from barons to dukes to wealthy Cits. She's had offers which would make your head spin, and no one can meet her price."

Silas felt a bewildering rush of emotion as he stared at the woman. Relief that she had not yet given herself to a man's keeping, and the hot sting of jealousy at knowing that, no matter his own wealth, he'd never be able to match the offers she'd already received.

"What *is* her price?" he asked, the question out before he could think better of it.

St Clair gave a low laugh. "No one knows. The lady implies that she is not for sale, yet she is clearly illegitimate and of questionable parentage, to put it mildly, and even a beauty like that would be hard pressed to find a suitor to marry her against such a background. The rumour is that she refuses each offer only to make herself ever more exclusive. Either way, she's got the male portion of the *ton* salivating and offering their fortunes."

St Clair was watching him, he knew it and hated the fact he was so riveted by the beautiful creature across the room, but he couldn't seem to look away.

"I *can* tell you she is intelligent, charming, and a delightful companion," the earl added, grinning as Silas glanced at him with undisguised envy in his expression.

"You've met her?"

"Yes. She's one of Harriet's friends," he said with a sigh.

Silas repressed a smile at the wistful tone of the earl's remark and returned his attention to Miss de Feria. He watched as the young woman's eyes searched the room once more and this time caught his. She held his gaze for a moment, a little surprise in her expression, perhaps taken aback by the intensity of his regard. Silas felt a prickle of awareness down his spine, and a surge of desire so intense it rocked him to his bones. The woman was dangerous, he knew it with every instinct he possessed. He'd do well to stay a long, long way away from her.

"Would you like an introduction?" St Clair asked, the question sending longing surging through his blood.

Silas swallowed. "No," he said, his voice harsh.

With resolution, he tore his gaze away from her and turned his back.

***

Lucia frowned as the man who had been staring at her with such unsettling directness looked away and turned his back on her.

She had dismissed him as no one of consequence, a man who had no part in her plans, judging him by his shockingly unkempt appearance. He looked as though he'd slept in his clothes, his hair was too long and the dark shadow of beard at his jaw suggested he ought to have shaved before he'd come out. He was large and rugged, with an air of something not quite tame about him, unlike any other man here. Frankly, he looked as if he ought to be outside doing manual labour of some kind, rather than glowering at everyone at a society event like a rabid dog in a butcher's shop. Having been obviously dismissed by him when half the men here were clamouring to lavish her with everything from houses and carriages to priceless jewels, she was honest enough to admit to feeling a little miffed, and extremely curious.

"Who is that man talking to St Clair?" she asked Matilda, striving for nonchalance.

Matilda Hunt—the closest thing that Lucia had to a friend and, in recent days, her new landlady—turned with a look of mild surprise in her blue eyes. Lucia could understand her reaction as Lucia had never shown an interest in any of the men here before, treating them all with the same mixture of exasperation and tolerance she might show an overly exuberant puppy. Far from putting them off, her complete lack of interest seemed akin to waving a red flag at a bull, or in this case a ballroom full of them.

"Oh, that's Silas Anson," Matilda said, leaning closer to whisper in Lucia's ear. "He's an intriguing one. His father died recently, making him Viscount Cavendish, not that he seems to care. He despises society. I wonder what he's doing here? It's rare to see him at this kind of event. He doesn't do small talk and polite chat." Matilda laughed. "He's been known to walk away in the middle of a conversation if he finds it tedious, and he's blunt to the point of rudeness."

"He looks a surly type, to be sure," Lucia said, wondering what on earth the man was doing at Lady Grasmere's ball if he despised everyone so, but then she had her reasons; she could only assume he had his.

"Oh, he is," Matilda agreed, smiling. "Though I must say I rather like him. One knows where one stands with a man like that. He always seems to say what he thinks. There is nothing hidden, and that is rather refreshing."

"Hmmm," Lucia replied, frowning a little. There was something about the fellow which was rather disconcerting, though she couldn't figure out what it was.

"Come along, I'll get St Clair to introduce you."

"Oh, Matilda, no," Lucia exclaimed. After being cut by him it would be mortifying if he thought she was interested in him, but too late as Matilda didn't have the least difficulty in attracting the earl's attention.

Lucia cursed inwardly as Matilda summoned St Clair to come and speak with them with an imperious little gesture and a smile. To her consternation, the earl was having the devil's own job persuading Cavendish to accompany him. The viscount clearly had no desire to meet her. Indignation swelled in Lucia's chest. She knew she was hardly good *ton*, and she knew the rumours that circulated about her, but a man that looked like he'd slept in a hedge had no business being so high in the instep.

Now, of course, the dratted man would think she *was* interested in him as Matilda had summoned them both over.

"Lord St Clair," Matilda said, greeting the earl with warmth. "How nice to see you again."

"The pleasure is entirely mine, I assure you, Miss Hunt, Miss de Feria. I am delighted to spend time in the presence of such divine beauty."

Lucia could see the viscount cringe at the fulsome compliment, and her irritation climbed a notch higher.

"Ladies, may I have the honour of presenting my good friend, Viscount Cavendish? Cavendish, these ravishing creatures are Miss Hunt and Miss de Feria."

Lucia watched with interest as the glowering brute beside him inclined his head a little.

"Ladies," he said, showing not the slightest sign of interest or pleasure at the introduction.

"My lord, it is unusual to see you at such an event," Matilda said, addressing the viscount with all her usual ease and charm. "Though you are a welcome addition with such a poor ratio of men to ladies. There are simply not enough of you, and we lack for dance partners."

To Lucia's astonishment the man snorted, a disparaging sound. "There may be some ladies here lamenting that fact," he said, sneering a little. "Somehow I doubt either of you are among their numbers."

"Was that a compliment or an insult?" Lucia asked him, having had quite enough of the ill-mannered fellow after seconds in his company. "How strange that my friend here told me you were a direct man who said what he thought, and yet I can't tell."

A pair of intense blue eyes met hers and for a moment Lucia felt the impact of his regard with a sensation that prickled all the way to her toes. For a horrifying moment she feared she might blush, but she forced herself to remain calm and hold his gaze.

"What do you think?" he replied, his tone low and unsettling.

"I think you mean to insult, my lord," Lucia said, refusing to look away from him. "Though you're not quite brave enough to do the job properly."

There was a flash of something in his eyes that might have been approval, but he quickly hid it.

"I doubt that is a quality you lack, Miss de Feria," he said, and once again she could not tell if he meant it as an insult or not.

"Indeed not," Lucia replied, giving him the most dazzling smile she could manage. "If I meant to insult a man, I'd waste no time in telling him he was acting like an ignorant caveman and complimenting his ability to dress the part too, but then I have better manners than to say such things in polite company."

There was a taut silence as the air all but sizzled around them until Lucia noticed the presence of another man at her side.

"Señorita de Feria." Lucia tore her riveted gaze away from the viscount to see the lanky frame of a Mr Richards beside her. The young man beamed. "My dance, I think," he said, a flush of enthusiasm colouring his face and making him look like an eager boy.

"Oh, yes, Mr Richards," Lucia said, only to start in astonishment as Lord Cavendish took her outstretched hand.

"No," the viscount said, giving the young man a look that dared him to contradict the statement. "You're mistaken, this dance is mine."

Lucia gaped, so astonished by the arrogance of the man that words failed her. She could hardly make a scene though, so she sent Mr Richards a look of deep apology and held her tongue.

It didn't last.

"How dare you!" she exclaimed, glaring at the dishevelled excuse for a gentleman. "I refuse to dance with you."

"Then by all means leave me standing here," he replied, the light of challenge gleaming in his eyes. "It will give the old tabbies something to talk about. I'll be left off your list of possible protectors, won't I? Though I doubt I was there to begin with."

Lucia stiffened at his words, fighting to keep her face and posture calm for fear of causing the scene he was daring her to provoke. Her words were low but full of bitterness and fury. "I have no protector and never will have. I have no need nor desire for the protection of any man, *ever*. I would rather die. I am a respectable woman, no matter what the gossips tattle about, and have done nothing to provoke such an insult as you offer me."

To her satisfaction, her words seemed to have surprised him and his expression softened a little.

"No," he said, after a pause. "You have not. You have my apology. I ought not to have spoken so unjustly."

Lucia stared at him, surprised at the ease with which he'd admitted his mistake and unsure of how to deal with him. She was saved from the effort as the dance began.

It was, without a doubt, the most uncomfortable time of her life.

Cavendish was not entirely at ease on the dance floor, though for a man of his build he moved well enough, but Lucia was all at sixes and sevens.

She was furious with him for his insults, bewildered by his reaction to her own rudeness—even more so by his apology—and horribly aware of the blatant masculinity of his body. Never in her life had she been so affected by the closeness of a man, and it was a disconcerting experience.

Even as a girl, when she'd fancied herself in love for the first time, there had been nothing to compare to the quivering heat that invaded every corner of her being in response to the raw strength that this man exuded. Everything feminine in her reacted to him, despite her willing it otherwise.

She hated him for it.

The moment the dance ended, she hurried away from him without a backwards glance.

***

Silas stood on the dance floor, watching Miss de Feria run away from him as though her heels were alight. His heart was thudding in his chest, every part of him singing with awareness, like he'd been woken up for the first time in his life.

She was magnificent.

He'd been every bit the ill-mannered brute she'd accused him of being, and she'd not let him get away with it, either. Why he'd been so awful to her, he wasn't certain, but he had the lowering suspicion it was jealousy.

The way she'd so summarily dismissed him with her glance still rankled, added to the fact that there were far wealthier and certainly more charming suitors falling over themselves to win her. He was hardly a pauper, but it appeared his father's finances were in a mess and it would take months to discover whether or not the old fool had ruined himself. Taking on an expensive mistress was beyond him for the moment, though she'd certainly made it clear she was not on the market for a protector.

Whatever the reason for his bad behaviour, he'd hardly endeared himself to her.

Good, he thought savagely. The last thing he needed was to tie himself up in knots over a blasted woman, of all things. Whether or not he believed her denial of seeking a rich protector, she was looking for something, and he didn't doubt that whatever it was would spell trouble.

He'd been a fool to come here, and a bigger one for allowing St Clair to introduce them. Having her so close to him had been the sweetest torment. A delicate perfume he could not place still lingered about him, teasing his senses.

The best thing he could possibly do was put Lucia de Feria out of his mind and never see her again. Vowing to do just that, Silas stalked from the ballroom and went home.

***

Still the evening of 1st July 1814. Lady Grasmere's ball, Mayfair, London.

“Well?” Matilda asked, looking breathless with anticipation as Lucia made her way back to her.

“*Well*?” Lucia repeated. She was flustered, put out, and beyond irritated. “I have never in all my life met a more ill-mannered, rude, uncouth, surly, shabby—”

“Don’t forget shockingly arrogant,” St Clair added with a grin.

“Oh, I certainly don’t forget that,” Lucia said, still seething as she snatched the drink from Matilda’s hand and took a large swallow. “Hateful, odious, obnoxious—”

“Yes, he’s certainly made his usual impression,” the earl said with a cheerful grin. “Though, you know, he’s really a very good fellow when one gets to know him.”

“I have absolutely *no* intention of getting to know him,” Lucia replied with some force.

“Have you known him long?” Matilda asked the earl, who shrugged.

“Not that long, but I know him as well as anyone, I think. He doesn’t have many friends.”

“You astonish me,” Lucia muttered, turning the glass back and forth in her gloved hands as St Clair chuckled.

“You know, you ought to give him a chance,” he said. “He’s not an easy fellow to get along with, I admit, but he’s got a good heart under all that wrinkled cloth and scowling. He’s the sort of man you can rely on if you’re in a fix. He’d never turn away a friend.”

“Not that he has any.”

He smiled at Lucia’s terse remark.

“Cavendish doesn’t trust many people, it’s true. His father was an absolute brute,” he added, his expression sobering. “Young Silas ran away from home when he was fifteen and disappeared off the face of the earth. He was gone so long, everyone believed him dead. Yet about five years ago he surfaced again, a rich man in his own right. He lived on the streets of London for a while before he found work with a trader in Covent Garden. He learned how to buy and sell and invested in the business until he bought the fellow out. Now he's got warehouses all over the country and is rich as Croesus, if you believe the rumour mill. His father never forgave him for it, of course, which pleased Silas no end."

Lucia frowned, more than a little surprised by the man's history. No wonder he seemed so apart from the rest of the *ton*, who would rather die than admit to being in trade. She could imagine how they would ostracise him for having turned his back on his heritage and run away.

All at once she understood the contempt he felt for those around him, and the defiance of his ill-kempt appearance and refusal to conform. How bad must life have been to induce a young man raised to such privilege to subject himself to the squalor of life on the streets? Yet, despite it all, he'd overcome the odds and succeeded, returning to sneer in the faces of those who would reject him.

An unwelcome swell of pity rose in her chest at the idea and, even worse, she felt a deep sense of empathy.

She held her tongue, at a loss for anything else to add to the conversation.

"From his reaction to her, I think, Miss de Feria has rather gotten under his skin," St Clair said, his words bringing a rush of colour to her cheeks, much to her consternation.

"Yes, like a tick," she said, smiling sweetly as the earl gave a bark of laughter.

"No," he said, struggling to compose his handsome face into something grave. "Not in the least like a tick. Like a man fighting to hold back the tide, if you ask me."

Lucia frowned, bewildered by the analogy. “He quite obviously despised me,” she said, ever more incredulous as the earl and Matilda exchanged wry smiles. “What?”

“Nothing more than a suspicion,” St Clair replied, his tone soothing. “Only, it should not surprise me if you see our mutual friend again, in the not too distant future.”

“Not if I see him first,” Lucia murmured, scowling as her companions laughed at a joke she was not prepared to share in.

Chapter 3

Everyone is talking about Lucia. Do you think the things they say about her are true? That she is looking for a man to keep her? I cannot believe it. I don't care who her mother was, Lucia has been nothing but the model of propriety. She's far better behaved than I am! Just because she is beautiful, they think the worst of her. How I hate these old tabbies who gossip and tell tales about anyone they think might be having more fun than them. It's nothing more than jealousy.

—Excerpt of a letter from Miss Bonnie Campbell to Miss Ruth Stone.

4th July 1814. Bond Street, London.

"What do you think?" Matilda asked, turning this way and that and regarding the pretty chip bonnet she was trying on in the looking glass.

"I think you could put a wet hen on your head and look stylish," Lucia remarked, casting a longing glance at a pretty confection of sky-blue velvet and white ostrich feathers. She turned her back on it with resolution, lest the temptation get the better of her. She'd strained her finances to their limits and still had five more weeks to endure before things reached their inevitable conclusion, something she both longed for and feared in equal measure.

"I'll take it, then," Matilda replied, with the happy confidence of a woman who need never worry about money. Not that it had always been the case.

Matilda had confided her own sorry history to Lucia in full: every sordid detail, from her father's gambling away their entire fortune, to her brother Nate's efforts to make it back, and to the man who had ruined her reputation by merely being alone in a room with her. That the same man, the Marquess of Montagu, now sought to make her his mistress was something else Matilda had confided in her alone. Lucia knew that Matilda hoped she would return the intimacy and, indeed, she longed to do so, but her secrets were too dangerous to share.

Besides, the truth would be out soon enough.

Once Matilda had given directions for the bonnet and several sundry items, from gloves to stockings, be delivered to her home, they headed outside once again. It was a warm day, though overcast, with slumbering clouds hanging low and somnolent in an oppressive sky. The sticky heat made Lucia feel lethargic and irritable, and her temper was not the least bit improved as they saw Viscount Cavendish notice them.

For a moment the man hesitated, and Lucia was almost certain he would cut her, but at the last moment he seemed to think better of it and turned towards them.

"Miss Hunt, Miss de Feria. A pleasure to see you."

Lucia arched an eyebrow at him. "Really, my lord? It looked very much like you wished us to a place of great heat," she said, offering him a benign smile while Matilda smothered a laugh. "I felt certain you would turn tail and run away."

To her surprise the viscount's mouth twitched a little. "Not at all," he said, those blue eyes glinting with the light of challenge. "In fact, I am so delighted by your company I do hope you will do me the honour of walking with me."

To her consternation, he held out his arm, an expectant expression on his harsh features that dared her to back down.

"A pleasure, my lord," she said, batting her eyelids at him in a manner to ensure he knew she was lying, but wasn't about flee.

Lucia placed her gloved hand upon his arm, noticing his coat was rather less wrinkled than the last time she'd seen him, and that he was cleanly shaved.

"I see more effort is made for Bond Street than for the ballroom," she said, showing her teeth as she smiled up at him.

He returned her expression in full, giving her the unnerving impression of a smiling tiger. As she took in his too-long dark hair, his weather-beaten features, and rather shambolic appearance—and not to forget that wicked glint in his eyes—she decided she could imagine him at the helm of a ship, plundering and pillaging his way across the oceans. Yes, most certainly the man could be a pirate.

"I'm afraid I cannot take the credit," he said with quiet gravity, "as I have recently inherited a valet."

"A valet?" Lucia repeated, gasping and feigning astonishment. "My, my. The poor man."

"Indeed, out of the frying pan into the fire," he said with a mournful sigh. "The Cavendishes are known for their ill tempers and lack of finesse."

"Oh dear, are you expecting me to repudiate such a claim?" Lucia asked, looking up at him with a grave expression. "For I fear I cannot in all conscience do such a thing. I do so hate dissemblers."

He stared down at her and Lucia felt a frisson of alarm at the quality of his gaze. It was as though he were looking right through her.

"*Do* you?" he asked, the question little more than a murmur, but said with such a note of enquiry that Lucia felt certain he knew everything she was hiding.

It was impossible, of course, but the sensation of being found out was so unsettling that a scarlet blush seared her cheeks.

"I think that is far enough," she said, removing her hand from his arm. "I fear you will not be welcome at our next port of call. Thank you so much for bearing us company. Good day to you, my lord."

A glint of satisfaction lingered in the knowing blue of his gaze as he gave them a formal bow. "Your servant, Miss de Feria, Miss Hunt."

Lucia simmered with irritation as she watched the insolent, aggravating man stroll away from them.

"Argh, I hate him," she muttered, glaring at Matilda, who was laughing openly now.

"Why?" she asked, looking after the viscount with amusement. "I think he's rather a breath of fresh air."

Lucia looked at her friend in bewilderment. "You're not *interested* in him, surely?" she demanded as Matilda pursed her lips.

She gave Lucia a considering look and shrugged a little.

"I don't know. Maybe. He's the kind of man who might overlook my reputation, I suppose."

Lucia frowned, a strange and unsettling sensation uncoiling in her stomach at the possibility of Matilda in the arms of the overbearing lout who'd just quit their company. Distracted by a sudden burst of laughter, she turned back to Matilda, who was staring at her with a pitying expression.

"Oh, dear me," she said, her lovely eyes glittering with mirth. "No, I'm not interested in him, dear Lucia, so you can stop looking like you swallowed a wasp."

Lucia stiffened, outraged at the idea she cared. "Whatever are you implying?" she demanded, glaring at Matilda. "I couldn't care less whether or not you have an interest in him, outside of the fact I would question your sanity."

Matilda bit her lip, so obviously disbelieving and amused that Lucia felt herself flush. Unwilling to consider the question with anything resembling an open mind, she turned tail and stalked away.

***

Matilda sighed as she watched Lucia storm off in a huff. The poor girl. It had been obvious to her when Lucia and Cavendish had met that the air had crackled with the force of their attraction. She could well understand Lucia's distress at the idea; there was nothing pleasant in discovering an attraction to a man you didn't like. Though it was even worse if you loathed him. How it was even possible she could not fathom, but it was.

She knew.

Realising with a start that she was dithering outside of the legendary *Gentleman Jackson's* boxing club, and its neighbouring fencing academy, *Angelo's*, Matilda roused herself to walk on. Her reputation was tattered enough without adding the rumour that she lingered outside such places. Having momentarily lost her bearings and sight of Lucia, Matilda turned on the spot, and walked straight into someone exiting the fencing club.

She stumbled, made an exclamation of surprise, and then yelped as her ankle turned.

"Blast!"

Looking up, she was horrified, and yet somehow unsurprised, to discover the cool, impassive gaze of the Marquess of Montagu.

"Oh, really," she said, wincing as she righted herself. "It just *had* to be you, didn't it?"

"Good afternoon to you too, Miss Hunt," the marquess drawled, the slightest glimmer of amusement in his eyes. "A delight, as always."

"Speak for yourself," Matilda returned acidly. "My morning seems to have gone to the devil. *Oh*!" she cried, as she tried to walk away.

"You're hurt."

To her surprise there was something like concern in his voice as he reached out to steady her.

"If I am," she snapped, wrenching her arm from his grasp, "it's entirely your fault."

"Miss Hunt, *you* walked into me," Montagu replied, irritating her further by stating the obvious.

"Yes, I know," she muttered, glaring at him. "But if you were anything resembling a gentleman, you'd refrain from pointing that out."

To her astonishment, Montagu laughed. Matilda had often observed that the marquess never showed a reaction of any kind. He was impossible to rouse to anger—and she'd tried a time or two—and he expressed none of the softer emotions. In all the time she'd known him, she had never once seen him so much as smile. Now, however, his obvious amusement, and its effect on his austerely beautiful face, was devastating.

Matilda caught her breath.

"I apologise for allowing you to walk into me, Miss Hunt," he said, his silver-grey eyes alight with humour. "I will endeavour to fling myself from your path in the future. How is that?"

Matilda swallowed and gave a taut nod. "Better."

Eager to be out of the man's sight with as much haste as possible, she tried to walk away but found the marquess beside her once more. His hand grasped her upper arm to support her as she cursed and stumbled again.

"What are you doing, you little fool?" he asked, his normal autocratic tone evident now. "You'll make it worse. I'll have my carriage brought around to take you home."

"No, I thank you," Matilda snapped. "The last thing I need is to be seen in your company."

"Matilda?"

Matilda looked around and sighed with relief as she saw Lucia hurrying towards her.

Thank Heavens.

"What on earth has happened?" Lucia asked, glaring at Montagu. "Unhand my friend, my lord," she said, sliding her own arm about Matilda's waist.

"Nothing," Matilda said in a rush. "I simply turned my ankle. It's nothing serious, I assure you. Lord Montagu offered to order his carriage to take me home, but I have refused for obvious reasons."

"Quite," Lucia said, giving the marquess a look of disgust. "There is no need to trouble yourself further, my lord. I will see Miss Hunt safely home."

"She cannot walk on that ankle," Montagu replied, the implacable expression he habitually wore sliding into place. "So, how do you propose to do that?"

Lucia held his gaze for a moment and then looked about her.

"Oh, Mr Richards!"

Matilda followed Lucia's gaze as she hurried to the edge of the street and waved at a young man driving a rather smart curricle.

The fellow beamed with delight at seeing Lucia, and drew his carriage to the side of the busy thoroughfare.

"Why, Señorita de Feria," he exclaimed. "What a pleasure to see you. How may I be of service?"

"Oh, Mr Richards," Lucia said, holding her hand to her heart and turning pleading eyes on the besotted young man. "Could you please help us? My friend, Miss Hunt, has turned her ankle, and I must escort her home."

"Why of course, of course!" Mr Richards exclaimed, all solicitousness as he threw the reins to his tiger and climbed down from his perch. "I'd be honoured to help."

At this point the young man spotted the marquess, and the hectic colour in his cheeks that Lucia's presence had wrought drained away in dramatic fashion.

"M-My Lord Montagu," the fellow said, suddenly stiff and awkward.

"Richards," Montagu replied, an expression of extreme displeasure in his eyes which made the young man look quite terrified. Turning back to Matilda, the marquess inclined his head a little.

"It seems my services are not required. I bid you good afternoon, Miss Hunt, Miss de Feria."

Matilda let out an uneven breath as he turned and walked away from them.

"There," Lucia said with obvious satisfaction. "We don't need him when we have such a charming companion to escort us."

Mr Richards flushed once more and stood rather straighter, and Matilda gave the young man a grateful smile.

"Indeed not," she agreed, and didn't give the marquess a backwards glance.

***

6th July 1814. South Audley Street, London.

Lucia knocked on Matilda's bedroom door and entered as she heard her friend call out in reply.

"Come in."

Lucia admired the picture of Matilda before her dressing table, putting the finishing touches to her appearance with the addition of a lovely sapphire necklace that brought out the blue in her eyes.

"How beautiful you look," Lucia said, regarding Matilda's ivory skin and blonde hair.

She was everything Lucia supposed an English lady ought to be: the perfect English rose. Lucia forced back an unwelcome stab of some jagged emotion she refused to acknowledge. Yet what must it be like to know exactly where you had come from, and where you belonged? Lucia had never, *would* never have that. She was part of two disparate worlds, each of which despised the other, and yet both were inextricably linked.

"Thank you." Matilda turned and then sighed as she looked at Lucia. "Well, I can only return the compliment. My word, poor Lord Cavendish will be surlier than ever when he catches sight of you."

Lucia rolled her eyes, refusing to be bated, though she was pleased with her gown. It was one of the last extravagances she'd allowed herself before the pot had run dry. It was a dramatic shade of deep purple, like the night sky before a storm.

"Will you be able to dance tonight?" she asked as Matilda got to her feet.

"Yes," Matilda said, grinning and doing a little jig on the spot to demonstrate. "See? Good as new."

Lucia laughed as a soft knock at the door pronounced the entry of Matilda's maid, a sweet-natured girl called Sarah.

"Here you go, Miss," she said, handing Matilda a large, square box of the kind jewellery parures were kept in.

"Oh, lovely. Thank you, Sarah."

Lucia frowned, wondering why Matilda needed it. "But surely you're not changing those glorious sapphires, Tilda? They look divine."

"No," Matilda said, shaking her head and opening the box. "But I thought you might like to wear these tonight. They are the perfect finishing touch for that dress."

Lucia moved closer and gasped at the exquisite amethyst and diamond set nestled upon a bed of white silk. "Oh, Tilda, I… I can't."

"Of course you can," Matilda said, laughing and taking out the necklace. "I insist. I'd have moped to death here all by myself. Your company has been just what I needed, and it would make me happy to see you wear them."

Lucia held her breath as tears prickled in her eyes. The weight of the necklace, cold and heavy, settled about her throat and she swallowed hard as saw her reflection in the looking glass. She wanted to tell Matilda everything, but she didn't dare. The young woman had proven herself kind and generous, but Lucia knew how that could change when the truth about her was revealed. She'd learned it the hard way. To survive what was coming, she must protect her heart. She had to prepare for the moment when these people who appeared to be her friends would turn their backs on her.

For now, however, there was no harm in accepting a kindness from Matilda.

"Thank you," she said, hearing the quaver in her voice.

Matilda smiled at her over her shoulder before turning to give her a brief hug. "You're welcome. Now, I believe there is a young lady with a dare to complete this evening."

Lucia forced a smile to her own lips and took a deep breath, knowing there was more to tonight's dare than Matilda realised.

"Indeed," she said, releasing the breath and gathering her courage. She was so close to her goal, there was no backing down now. "Once more unto the breach, dear friend, once more!"

Matilda grinned and grabbed hold of her arm, towing her from the room. "Or close up the wall with our English dead!" she exclaimed, finishing the quote with a flourish and laughing as they ran together down the stairs.

Chapter 4

I do hope that Lucia is careful at the Ulceby ball. Mr Bindley has proven himself to be a despicable man and the rumours about the father suggest the apple did not fall far from the tree. I have a terrible foreboding that something bad is coming.

Dearest Prue, tell me I'm worrying over nothing…

—Excerpt of a letter from Mrs Alice Hunt to Her Grace, Prunella Adolphus, Duchess of Bedwin.

6th July 1814. Cavendish House, The Strand, London.

Fred was beside himself with glee. He'd known it would take some time for his new master to get to grips with having a valet look after him. Despite being raised as a gentleman for half his life, the fellow seemed to take a perverse pleasure in dressing as if he'd lived the entirety of it in the gutter. However, something had moved him to attend the Earl of Ulceby's ball this evening, and Fred's services had not only been allowed, but requested.

To date, Fred had made great strides with the careful pressing and laundering of the viscount's clothes, and had even persuaded him into purchasing new shirts and cravats. There had been something of a tussle over the boots, but they had compromised. Silas refused to buy new ones, but would allow Fred to polish the old ones to his heart's content. However, he had, until this evening, refused to have his hair cut.

Now, the thick, dark locks—which had curled about his neck in such a profusion that it had made Fred's fingers itch with the desire to reach for some scissors—lay scattered about the floor at his feet.

"You needn't look so bloody smug," Silas grumbled, folding his arms and looking belligerent. "I'm not doing it for you."

"No," Fred replied, his grin widening. "For some fancy piece, I don't doubt, and she has my undying thanks."

Fred watched curiously as the viscount's thick eyebrows drew together, and wondered who the lady was that had wrought such a change in his master. Perhaps not a fancy piece, going by that troubled expression. To Fred's knowledge, Silas had never kept a mistress, and he certainly wasn't said to be in the petticoat line.

So… perhaps it was something more serious?

"What's she like?" Fred ventured to ask.

With any other employer, Fred would never have dared speak so freely. Indeed, the old viscount would have thrown something at him for such audacity. Yet Fred had known this man since he was a babe, and despite the fellow's fearsome temper and scowling countenance, there was an air about him that tugged at some fatherly sense of obligation in Fred's heart. God knew the poor blighter had seen little enough affection in his young life, and Fred reckoned there'd been little more since he'd run from home. If ever a man needed a confidant, it was Silas Anson.

Silas frowned harder and shifted, folding his arms.

"Who says there's a woman?"

Fred met his gaze in the mirror and raised one eyebrow.

Silas huffed. "No one you know," he muttered.

"Is she beautiful?"

Fred combed through the thick strands, ensuring the ends were all even, and waited for a reply.

"Yes," came the grudging answer. "Too beautiful for a man's sanity," he added, surprising Fred with the admission.

"Ah," Fred said with a sigh. "A dangerous proposition, then."

He removed the towel from about Silas's neck and carefully removed every tiny strand of cut hair from his shoulders and neck with a soft brush.

"I must be out of my mind," Silas said, and Fred stilled, pleased and touched by the fact the man honoured him with his private thoughts.

"Is she worth the risk?"

Fred watched as a slow smile curved over a mouth which was generally stern and uncompromising. "Yes," he said simply. "But the little devil is up to something, I'd stake every penny I own on it."

"Not a lady with a fortune at her disposal, then?" Fred guessed. For any lady of high birth and wealth the game would be obvious: catching herself a wealthy, titled husband. "You sure? She sounds like the tricksy sort that'll have you marching to the altar before you can say knife." He gave Silas a direct look, wagging the brush at him. "Going on the change she's wrought already, I reckon she'll have you leg-shackled before the season is over."

Silas glowered a little and snorted as he got to his feet, stretching and rubbing a hand over his shorter hair. "I'm hardly about to race up the aisle, Fred," he said, sounding amused. "And as for having a fortune, I would say not. She appears to be a woman of means, but there's something about her. She's all prickles and defiance, very much on her dignity."

"Sure it's not just your natural charm bringing out the worst in her, my lord?" Fred volunteered with a sly grin.

Silas snorted, his eyebrows hitting his hairline. "Why in God's name did I employ you?"

He glowered and looked thoroughly forbidding, though Fred could see the amusement in the man's eyes clear enough.

"You're an impudent scoundrel, Davis. Damned if I know why my father bore with you all these years."

"Oh, I was never rude to the old viscount, my lord," Fred said with a shrug. "He'd 'ave belted me."

"What makes you think I won't?" Silas demanded, looking somewhat affronted.

Fred grinned at him, gathering up his scissors and combs and heading for the door to make a quick exit. "'Cause, for all your denials and bluster, you're more of a gentleman than your father ever was."

***

6th July 1814. The Earl of Ulceby's ball, Hyde Park, London.

"Well, well. Here we are again."

Silas repressed a groan as the Earl of St Clair cornered him. He'd been lingering on the periphery of the grand ballroom, looking thunderous in the hope everyone would leave him alone.

So much for that idea.

"And looking remarkably dapper, too," St Clair continued, ignoring his friend's warning look as he walked a circle around him. "Not a crease or crinkle to be seen, and that cravat…! My word, Cavendish, you *almost* look like a gentleman."

That comment, coming from anybody else, would have earned the speaker a broken nose. As it was, Silas glowered at him. "Pike off, you damned coxcomb," he muttered.

"Oh, no, no, no. I'm desperate to see your face."

Despite knowing better, Silas turned to regard St Clair. "What do you mean?"

"I mean I want to see the look on your face when you see her."

They both knew St Clair didn't need to elaborate on exactly who he meant.

Feeling foolish and aggravated, Silas folded his arms and refused to say another word. Not that he could have done anyway; at that moment he caught sight of her, arm in arm with Matilda Hunt as they walked into the room. They were the midday sun and a starry midnight sky. Matilda Hunt wore a gown of sky blue, her blonde hair shimmering gold under the blaze of hundreds of candles. Lucia, by contrast, wore a deep, rich purple, the colour of ripe cherries. Her black hair shone, thick and lustrous, and Silas ached to take down the heavy locks and watch them spill around her shoulders in a wave of darkest silk.

They were probably two of the least marriageable ladies in the room, both tarnished by scandal and dubious reputations. There wasn't a soul here, however, who could have denied they were the most beautiful, the most desirable.

The most trouble.

"Yes, that's the look I was waiting for. Like a fox when the hounds have caught his scent. You poor bastard."

The earl's smug voice filtered through Silas's mind and he ignored it. He was past caring.

"Go to the devil, St Clair," he muttered, moving forward and keeping Lucia in his sights. His heart was beating too fast, and he knew he was in danger of playing the fool for this woman, but he couldn't help himself. There was such defiance in her eyes, as if she was waiting for an insult, waiting for someone to realise she didn't belong.

Having spent a fair portion of his youth in the gutter fighting for survival, he recognised that glint in her eyes. There was something not quite tame that warned you not to look too closely. It suggested she didn't give a damn about you, about anything, but Silas knew that was a lie too. She cared. She cared too damn much.

The knowledge made something fierce and protective spark to life in his heart. Silas wanted to save her, from what he didn't know, perhaps from herself, but he knew better than to ask or to offer. He'd have thrown any such gesture in the face of whoever gave it when he'd been making his way back to where he belonged. He'd done it himself, on his own terms. It was the only way he would allow it.

Lucia was the same. Pride and defiance. It shone from her like a fire blazing out of control and he wanted nothing more than to feel the heat of it.

***

Lucia smiled as Bonnie hurried up to them, looking like she might bounce on the spot. She was such a vivacious girl, all ample curves and laughter.

"Oh, my word, the two of you look simply glorious. Did you notice every man here turned to look as the pair of you walked in?"

Lucia had noticed, in fact, but she took a deal less pleasure in the fact than Bonnie seemed to. She'd felt the weight of their gazes, felt the speculation of their wondering just what her price was, how much they would need to spend to gain entry to her bed and her body. A shudder ran over her. She prayed it never came to that.

"Who else is here, Bonnie?" Matilda asked, looking about the crowds.

"I saw Ruth earlier, and Prue is supposed to be coming, though I've not seen her. I think Harriet is here… oh, yes, there she is. Harriet… helloooo! *Harriet*!"

Matilda winced as Bonnie shrieked her friend's name over the heads of the assembled company, and Lucia bit her lip to hold back a laugh. Those around them cast disparaging looks of disapproval at Bonnie, who flushed and seemed to deflate a little.

"Oops," she said with a rueful smile. "Sorry."

"Never mind, dear," Matilda said with a soothing tone. "Just, perhaps a tad less exuberance?"

"Yes, Mama," Bonnie said with a saucy grin, before hurrying away to find Harriet.

"Wretch," Matilda said, shaking her head and laughing as Bonnie ran off, dark curls bouncing as she went.

"It's how you feel, though, isn't it?" Lucia said, turning her attention to Matilda. "You're the mother hen, scurrying about after her chicks."

To her surprise, Matilda blushed a little and then gave a little laugh of acknowledgement.

"Yes," she admitted. "I… well, I always imagined I'd be married with children by now."

Lucia felt a surge of empathy for her. Matilda was twenty-five, and perilously close to being on the shelf. She had beauty, and—thanks to her brother—a generous dowry, yet the Marquess of Montagu had cast a shadow over her, and no eligible man would marry soiled goods for fear of becoming a laughingstock.

"But," Matilda continued, "my happy ever after seems to be out of my reach, so I've decided to ensure all of my friends have theirs. At least then, when I'm a faded old spinster, I shall have lots of offers to go and stay with them. Then I won't have to outstay my welcome in any one place."

She said it with laughter and a teasing note, but Lucia could hear the thread of truth—and the fear—behind the words. They both knew many would already consider her a spinster, too old to be certain of providing the necessary heir. Impulsively, she reached out and took Matilda's hands.

"It's not over, Matilda. There must be a good man out there for you. Don't give up yet."

Matilda squeezed her hands and smiled. "Dear Lucia," she said with such affection in her voice that Lucia's throat grew tight. "And here I was thinking you believed good men were the stuff of fairy stories, like unicorns and magical godmothers."

Lucia laughed at that, and nodded. "Indeed, from my point of view they are, but it's different for you."

"How so?" Matilda stared at her, looking puzzled and intrigued.

Lucia cursed her unguarded tongue. She shook her head and pasted a smile to her face. "It just is. Oh, look," she added, changing the subject before Matilda could pursue it further. "Here is Harriet."

Indeed, Bonnie seemed not to have found Harriet yet, as the young woman hurried up to them alone looking harassed and irritated. She was an earnest girl who possessed a mind that made Lucia feel inadequate and not a little envious. Lucia thought her a tad intimidating, which Matilda had found amusing when she'd confessed it, for it appeared Harriet felt the same way about Lucia, albeit for totally different reasons. Apparently, Harriet was dazzled by Lucia and often became a little tongue-tied in her presence. Now that *was* funny.

The young woman pushed her spectacles up her nose in a nervous gesture Lucia now recognised.

"Hello, Harriet. Are you enjoying yourself?"

"No," Harriet replied, sounding terse and disapproving. "That abominable man took Henry out drinking before coming here, and now he's... *foxed*."

Harriet mouthed rather than said the word, which made Lucia smile. She assumed the description of *abominable man* could only pertain to the Earl of St Clair, who was the best friend of Harriet's brother, Henry. Quite why Harriet held such animosity for him, no one seemed to know. It was clear that she, Henry, and St Clair had all grown up together, so Lucia assumed it stemmed from some historical event which Harriet found unforgivable. Yet the earl always sought her company, though often it seemed with the express intention of rattling Harriet's cage. He appeared to Lucia rather like a little boy pulling at her pigtails, but she kept such observations to herself, assuming Harriet would not welcome them.

"Really?" Matilda said, frowning a little. "He doesn't look foxed."

Lucia looked around and then followed Matilda's gaze to where Henry, St Clair, and—*oh, good heavens*—Lord Cavendish were heading their way.

"Oh, blast," Harriet and Lucia muttered in unison.

They exchanged a glance, their lips quirking in mutual sympathy.

Lucia avoided Lord Cavendish's eye as they exchanged greetings, though she could feel the weight of his gaze on her. The urge to look up was irritating, like an insect bite demanding you scratch it at once, even though you knew it was a bad idea. Inevitably, the temptation was too much to resist.

"Ah, there you are," he murmured, grinning at her, that pirate smile making something hot and wilful unfurl under her skin. "I wondered how long you could ignore me for."

"Some things are harder to ignore than others," Lucia said, sounding sullen rather than achieving the pert tone she'd been aiming for. Drat the man, always putting her on edge.

"Like the presence of someone you can't forget?" he said, a smirk in his tone that was unmistakable.

"I was thinking more like the bubonic plague," Lucia said, smiling sweetly at him.

He laughed at that, and Lucia tried to ignore her pleasure in the sound. He looked different tonight, as though he'd finally let his valet get his hands on him. Strangely, it didn't make him look a great deal more civilised, despite the crisp white of his perfectly tied cravat and the neatly cut hair. All that raw energy, the sense of something being held in check… it was still there. It gleamed in his eyes and added a delicious edge to that wicked smile. Yet there was something else, something in his expression that made her heart beat faster.

"I know I deserve that and more," he said, his voice softer than she'd ever heard it before. "But I hope perhaps you might allow me to start over. I'm afraid I'm barely civilised, as I've no doubt you've been told—as if it needed saying—but I'll do my best… for you."

Lucia's breath caught. His apology was there in his eyes, his gaze direct and unwavering and she believed he was sincere.

She'd seen the way men looked at her, looks of avarice and desire, of wanting to own and possess. It never failed to make her defensive and all on edge, to make her feel like the quarry in a room full of predators. For the moment she held the power to keep them at bay, but it might not always be that way.

There had been times, when she'd been younger and still idealistic, when she had longed for a protector. Not in the vulgar sense that the *ton* used for the man who owned a mistress, but in the real sense. Someone who would care for her and want to keep her safe, to keep her from hurt and from harm. She had dreamed of such a man, and how he might look at her… like Lord Cavendish was looking at her now.

Lucia swallowed, longing and frustration warring inside her. Lord Cavendish would be no different, she told herself. He saw her, but he didn't see *her*. He saw what he assumed was before him, but he didn't see the truth. Trusting him was impossible and dangerous, and that look in his eyes would turn to anger and disgust once he knew her for what she was. It was inevitable.

"I… I can't. If you would excuse me," she said, her voice quavering as she turned, and fled.

***

Silas watched Lucia hurry away with a frown of disappointment. His suspicion that the girl was in some kind of trouble—or at least that she was heading for it full tilt—was deepening by the second.

"You've worked your usual charm, I see," St Clair murmured, following his gaze as Lucia disappeared into the throng.

Silas glowered, itching to follow Lucia but not wanting to make it obvious.

"Did you hear that, Jasper?" Henry grinned, elbowing St Clair. "The ladies are all coming to your summer ball."

"How delightful," the earl replied. "I always look forward to it but now I shall be champing at the bit." He smiled at Miss Hunt and then turned to Miss Stanhope, who rolled her eyes and looked away.

Silas grinned inwardly, pleased to discover a woman on the earth who wasn't charmed out of her petticoats within seconds of meeting the man.

"Oh, come, Harriet," St Clair said with a wicked grin. "Don't tell me you're not looking forward to it. It will be just like old times. Don't you remember all those summers we spent together as children? You, me, and Henry here, all up to mischief of one kind or another."

Miss Stanhope gave him a look which would have shrivelled a lesser man. "I remember you and Henry getting into mischief, usually with me as your victim, from frogspawn in my boots to dropping worms down the back of my neck. I'm afraid my memories of those days are rather less rose-tinted than yours." She looked away from him, her scowl clearing as she saw someone across the room. "Oh, there's Bonnie. If you'll excuse me."

Silas watched as St Clair followed her departure, an expression in his eyes that Silas had not seen before. It looked very much like disappointment.

St Clair was ever the happy-go-lucky, good hearted libertine. Women tumbled into bed with him with very little encouragement and still spoke kindly of him even when he'd finished things between them. He was a man it was impossible to hate, someone whose good nature shone from him, yet Miss Stanhope seemed immune to his charisma.

St Clair turned back then, to discover Silas watching him.

"She hates me," he said, his lips quirking with a self-deprecating smile.

"I gathered as much," Silas replied. "Were you that vile to her as a boy?"

A frown gathered at the earl's brow as he considered the question. "She started it," he muttered, and then to Silas's surprise, stalked away.

To his relief, Henry took that moment to ask Miss Hunt to dance, and Silas was free. Following in the direction he'd seen Lucia leave, he hurried after her.

***

"Kitty!" Lucia exclaimed, sighing with relief as she spied the young woman at the edge of the ballroom. "I need your help."

"Oh, is it the dare?" Kitty asked, getting herself hushed as Lucia pressed a finger to her lips. "Sorry." Kitty sent her a rueful grin. "Bonnie and Harriet are over there, let me fetch them. Then we can stand watch and pretend we all got lost if we're caught."

Lucia fidgeted as she waited for the three friends to hurry back to her. Anxiety had tied her stomach in knots. Being here, in this of all places, was giving her chills. So far she'd not seen Ulceby, which was fine by her. The longer she could leave it, the better.

"I think the study is this way," Harriet said as the other girls followed in her wake.

She led them out of the ballroom and through a series of connected rooms, each more opulent than the next. Lucia's stomach churned, anger burning under her skin as she saw the way the man lived. To have all of this and to still need more, to have squandered so much…. Bile rose in her throat as emotion coursed through her, and she scolded herself for allowing it. She'd not come this far only to ruin everything by losing her head.

Suddenly they found themselves in a larger foyer, and Harriet grinned.

"It's that one," she said.

Lucia took a deep breath and nodded. "Well, then, you girls stay here and keep watch and I'll go and… have a drink," she said, laughing suddenly as the ridiculousness of the situation dawned on her.

"And smoke a cigar," Kitty said, looking envious at the idea.

"And smoke a cigar," she agreed, winking at Kitty.

Leaving them on the threshold of the study, she opened the huge door and peered around, just to be certain the place was empty. It was a huge room, dimly lit with only one lamp burning, illuminating a massive oak desk.

Lucia slipped inside and closed the door behind her. Quickly she noted a tantalus bearing what she suspected were decanters of cognac and port. Selecting one at random, she poured a small measure into a crystal glass with trembling hands, and carried it over to the desk. To her relief, atop sat an elaborately decorated cigar box, and the key was in the lock. Turning it, she opened the box, and then gasped at the erotic scene displayed on the inside of the lid. A large and leering man was making free with a woman who seemed less than thrilled by his attentions. Both parties were naked and illustrated with great attention to detail. Lucia shuddered at the scene, took a cigar, and slammed the box shut again.

Lucia's hand stilled on the box as she looked down and noticed the cigar cutter. Her breath caught. Delicately made of carved ivory, a memory flashed of it in her father's hands. He'd shown her how to cut the end off the cigar and toast the foot before lighting it when she was a very little girl. She'd sat on his knee, transfixed by the ritual and the curling smoke that had filled the room as he'd puffed on the cigar. He'd told her he travelled a great deal as a young man and had picked up the habit abroad. She remembered watching him with eager interest as he blew smoke rings over her head.

Her heart ached as she thought of him, though his face had grown dim and shadowy over the years. Now she recalled only green eyes, full of kindness, and the tone of his voice. She'd loved his voice, loved to hear him talk to her.

Lucia held the cigar to her nose, inhaling the sweet scent of the tobacco as tears pricked at her eyes. Setting it down, she reached for the cutter. As she held the cool, slender tusk in her hand, she felt a rush of anger that it was here, on this man's desk.

As if performing some religious rite, Lucia cut and prepared the cigar, exactly as her father had shown her, and took a deep draw. She choked and spluttered, her eyes watering for a different reason as the smoke stole her breath. Reaching for the glass, she took a sip and sighed as the smooth warmth of the brandy eased her throat. Trying once again, she took another, smaller puff of the cigar, remembering not to inhale but only hold the smoke in her mouth. She blew out a cloud that drifted about her in a haze.

Better.

Setting the cigar aside, she looked about the desk for paper and pen, and settled to her real object in being here.

Lucia smiled as she dipped the quill into the ink and began to draw.

Chapter 5

Why do I let that wretched man get under my skin? Just because he's handsome and titled, people hang on his every word. Even Lord Cavendish, who seems a sensible man, apparently esteems him. Yet he's a brainless nincompoop and ought not to have the power to irritate me. I should treat his comments like the droning of a stupid fly, a minor annoyance and nothing more. Why then do I want so badly to give him a set down?

—Excerpt of an entry by Miss Harriet Stanhope, to her diary.

6th July 1814. The Earl of Ulceby's ball, Hyde Park, London.

Silas ducked back behind a marble column as he saw the three young women huddled together. Frowning, he noted that Lucia was not amongst them.

It had been the devil's own job to track them down in the massive house, and it was only by luck that he'd stumbled upon them. One of his friends had been certain he'd seen Miss de Feria in their company, however. So… where was she? Then he realised the girls were standing guard. Lucia was inside the room they dithered beside. What were they up to?

Curiosity and anxiety stirred in his chest. If anyone discovered her, there would be a scene. At that moment, he heard a door opening and chanced another peek around the column. His mouth fell open, an astonished laugh catching in his throat as he saw Lucia, leaning against the door jamb in a nonchalant pose, with a glass of what looked like brandy in one hand and a cigar in the other. He blinked as she raised the cigar to her lips, took a drag, and blew out a cloud of smoke as the other three girls laughed and clapped their hands in delight.

"You little devil," he murmured, grinning from the seclusion of his hiding spot.

Something lit up inside him at her daring, at her desire to taste something forbidden to nice young ladies of the *ton*. For a moment he wished he'd had the chance to introduce her to such illicit pleasures, but then decided against it. From the triumphant look in her eyes it had been something she was proud of having done alone, and he couldn't take that from her.

On the heels of that thought, however, came a second: of the other kinds of pleasures to be had and enjoyed. He closed his eyes.

"*Behave*," he scolded himself.

She was not to be someone's mistress; she'd told him that much. The only way to make her his was to marry her and, after his behaviour, he knew she'd throw any offer back in his face. Not that he could blame her for that. Besides, he was a long way from knowing if that was something he wanted to consider. The certainty she was up to something lingered, and he needed to know what that something was before he got involved with her. He needed to know her better.

Silas pressed into the shadows behind the column while the girls hurried back towards the ballroom, the sounds of rustling skirts and excited murmurs of congratulations fading as Lucia and her friends departed. About to leave and make his way back himself, Silas froze when he heard quick footsteps cross the marbled floor.

Once more hugging the shadows, he held his breath, seeing the Earl of Ulceby heading towards the room Lucia had only just vacated, his son Edgar in tow. His stomach lurched as he realised how close she had been to discovery.

"If you hadn't made such a hash of things with that bloody Dowding chit, we might not be in such a damned fix," the earl said, his voice harsh and angry not waiting for his son who hurried to keep up with him. "But no, you're as bloody useless as your brother. You're both happy enough to spend my blunt, but neither of can stir yourselves if it means getting off your arses."

"B-But Father," Edgar protested. "I-I thought it was all arranged. How w-was I to know the little slut had taken that b-bastard Hunt as a lover?"

The earl turned, confronting his son and grasping him by his cravat. "You should have made certain of her, you fool. If you'd ruined her as you were supposed to, there would have been no question."

"But Montagu—"

"But nothing, you snivelling little rat. Damn, but you make me sick. Who the hell am I to get to marry you now? Heiresses don't grow on trees. I suppose it will have to be Miss Stone, though she reeks of the shop, and you'll not have such an easy time with her."

Their voices grew muffled as they entered the room and Silas let out a breath, hoping he could make his escape, but just when he went to move there was a shout of alarm, and a moment later the earl ran back out.

"Who's there?" the man demanded, the strange tenor of his voice making Silas's skin prickle with alarm, yet there was no possible way he could know Silas was there, hidden as he was. "Where are you? Come out, damn it. Come out and face me!"

There was terror in the man's voice and Silas heard Edgar demanding to know what was happening.

"Father, what is it? What's wrong?"

Silas dared another glimpse around the column, too intrigued not to risk looking. The earl was ashen, a piece of paper crumpled in his hand. Edgar took it from him, smoothing it out and staring at it. To his consternation, Silas could not see what they were looking at.

"What is it?" Edgar asked, sounding bewildered. "W-what does it mean?"

"A warning," the earl said, his voice low and breathless. "It's her. It must be. Someone knows. Someone knows what I did."

The earl and his son went back into the study, the door shutting behind them this time.

Silas moved at once, getting as far away from them as he could until he was back amongst the revellers once more. What the bloody hell was going on?

There was no doubt in his mind that Lucia was responsible for whatever had been on that paper. It was feasible that someone else had been in that room before her, of course it was, but he didn't believe it. He'd suspected she had secrets, and something told him they were dangerous ones. Well, from what he knew of the Earl of Ulceby, he'd been right. That was not a man you antagonised if you knew what was good for you. He was a nasty bastard whichever way you looked at it.

Fear slid down in his spine like ice water beneath his skin. Whatever she was playing at, it was a perilous game indeed.

Oh, Lucia, what the devil have you done?

***

6th July 1814. The Earl of Ulceby's ball, Hyde Park, London.

Lucia allowed the tension in her neck to ease. She'd done it. Not only had she completed her dare, but she'd taken the first step towards having her revenge. A smile curved over her mouth. She felt alive, more alive than she had in years. Destiny was calling her, and while she knew she was a long way from victory, she was taking the future into her own hands.

"My, don't you look pleased with yourself?"

She started, the tension that had so recently left her returning with a snap that made every sense spring to attention.

Lord Cavendish was beside her, staring down at her with such warmth in his gaze it made her breath catch.

"Do I?" she replied, striving for nonchalance even as her heart picked up speed.

"You do," he said, lowering his voice to an intimate level that made awareness of his interest and his proximity flare between them. "You look like a woman with secrets. Dangerous ones."

Lucia swallowed, the uneasy sensation that this man knew something making her chest tighten. Of course it was impossible, but still….

"Well," she said, tossing her head in an imperious style, "I suppose there are a lot of wives I could distress if they discovered how much their husbands had offered to bed me."

She held his gaze, daring him to insult her, to imply once again that she was biding her time to increase the bidding.

Instead his expression softened. "I'm sorry that you've had to suffer that. Sorry, too, that I listened to gossip like everyone else."

Lucia stared at him, wrong-footed and once again uncertain of how to deal with him. He never did what she expected him to.

"I'm afraid men, myself included, are avaricious creatures," he said, a wry set to his mouth. "We see something lovely and we feel the urgent desire to possess it, and there is nothing lovelier in all of England than you."

"Prettily said, my lord," she replied, feeling heat creeping under her skin but certain it was just another tack he was taking. Some had tried to overwhelm her with promises of money, jewels, and every kind of extravagance. Some had tried seduction, others bullying. This flattering approach was hardly new, either. "So, what is your offer?"

"No offer," he said, staring at her, his expression open. "I know there is only one offer you would consider, and I cannot promise I will make it but… I should like to know you better and see if…."

Lucia's breath caught, and she realised her hand had gone to her throat as the shock sank in. He couldn't be serious. She wouldn't believe it.

She snorted at him, dismissing the idea before he could laugh at her for believing it. "Oh, yes, because a man of your ilk is so desperate for a ruined bride. Surely you know the stories of my heritage?"

He shrugged, and she found her eyes drawn to broad shoulders. Unwillingly, she wondered what it might be like to be held in his arms, to feel the shelter of his powerful body surrounding her. She shivered.

"I know the rumours," he said, smiling a little. "But I've heard enough of those on my own account to know how wrong they can be."

Lucia stared at him. No. It was a game. It had to be a game. She just hadn't figured out his motivation yet, but she would. She pursed her lips and toyed with the lace at the neckline of her gown, watching his gaze follow the movement, watching his eyes darken. She sneered a little. Men were so easy to manipulate. Show them a little flesh and they salivated like hounds.

"And what if the truth is far worse than the rumours you've heard?" she asked, dropping her hand and turning away, the words hard and angry.

Before she could leave, he'd reached out, taking hold of her fingers. He didn't wear gloves and she stared down at a hand that was scarred and calloused as it curled about hers. His touch was gentle, and she looked up, bewildered by the concern she saw in his eyes.

"I don't care for what the *ton*, think, Lucia," he said, shocking her further by using her given name. "And I don't care for propriety in the same way as they do. Sometimes people must do things to survive, things they'd not do if they had another choice. Sometimes we don't have choices, I understand that."

Lucia's breathing picked up, her chest rising and falling so fast she felt giddy with it.

What was he saying?

What did he mean?

He stepped closer and the urge to take his words at face value—to cling to him and believe herself safe—was so overwhelming that she ached with the desire to close the distance between them. She wanted him to act on the look in his eyes.

"I know you don't trust me, not yet. I know you can't let yourself, but I will prove myself worthy." His grasp on her hand tightened a little, a smile curving over his harsh features. "You can trust me, Lucia. Let me help you, love, whatever it is."

She stared at him, unable to breathe, to think. His blue eyes were so certain, so honest, and there was such surety in his manner, in everything about him, such certainty of his own worth, his capabilities.

He was an illusion and not one she could risk believing in.

Perhaps if she truly had been what he saw before him, if she'd truly been Lucia de Feria, she could have put her trust in him, but she was as much of an illusion as he was, and he couldn't trust her any further than she could trust him.

"You don't want that," she said, ensuring the words were hard enough, cold enough to warn him off, so he'd not make the attempt again. "You don't want me. I can promise you that." She tugged her hand from his grasp, meeting his eyes. "Goodbye, Lord Cavendish."

***

Matilda watched the little scene play out between Lucia and Lord Cavendish with a frown, saddened to see Lucia so obviously warn him off. The viscount looked up and, seeing her watching, returned a bemused smile. Matilda moved towards him.

"Don't give up," she said to him, her voice low. "I… I worry for her. I…." She trailed off, unsure of what to say. There was nothing she could say, certainly not to a man she hardly knew, though there was something solid about him, something that felt inherently trustworthy.

"Yes," Cavendish said, apparently needing no further words to agree that Lucia was worth worrying about. "I agree. Though I do not understand how to help her. I'm afraid I was my usual charming self when we first met, and insulted her rather badly. She has no reason to trust me, and I can't offer her any. My own reputation is hardly unsullied."

"You're in good company here, then," Matilda remarked, laughing, though it wasn't an entirely happy sound.

"I hardly think so," Cavendish said, smiling at her. "I actually earned my reputation."

Matilda smiled, pleased to discover she'd been correct in her estimation.

"Thank you."

The viscount snorted and shook his head. "For what? Believing what was perfectly obvious to all concerned? The story was preposterous then, and so it is now. Your father was dying, for heaven's sake! Hardly the moment you'd dally with Montagu, of all men. Though," he added, a considering look to his eyes, "I've no idea what would induce any woman to dally with Montagu, if I'm honest."

Matilda laughed—a proper, mirthful laugh of surprise—at his comment.

Cavendish grinned at her, a wicked expression on a face that was harsher and far less refined than many of the men that surrounded them. It was a good face, Matilda thought. It was honest, if rather fierce.

"I suppose enormous wealth, staggering power, and those icy good looks might have something to do with it," he mused, pursing his lips. "If they can overlook the fact he's got as much warmth as the North Pole. They must need to sit on hot bricks after—"

"My lord!" Matilda spluttered, torn between hysterics and shock that he would speak so.

"I would like to believe you are about to take the man to task for maligning me, but I suppose that is too much to ask."

Matilda froze as the dry comment chased away any amusement she might have felt, and the sting of awareness seared her. She dared to turn, to find the marquess at her side, resplendent in his evening clothes, the harsh black and white ideally suited to the severity of his handsome face and the white blond of his hair.

"Montagu," Lord Cavendish said, showing a lot of teeth as he smiled and looking quite unrepentant. "We were just discussing your prowess with—"

"Indeed, *we* were not!" Matilda interrupted, flushing so hard she felt the burn of it all over.

"Oh?" Montagu said, lifting an eyebrow at her. "Are you quite certain? You seem inordinately interested in my activities. After all, it wouldn't be the first time we've discussed my, er… *capabilities*, would it, Miss Hunt?"

Matilda's hands itched with the desire to slap him, but she forced herself to remain calm, not to show her embarrassment or her discomfort.

"Indeed not, my lord," she said, pushing the words past gritted teeth. "And I'm afraid my comments were no less flattering than Lord Cavendish's. If you remember?"

Matilda glared at the marquess and found herself thoroughly discomposed at the glint in his eyes. Damn him, he was enjoying this!

"Well, after insulting me so, the least you can do to make amends is dance with me."

The words were so unexpected that Matilda gave a startled laugh. "You cannot be serious," she said, staring at him. "I'm *not* going to dance with you."

She stilled as Montagu leaned in and murmured in her ear. "Running scared, Miss Hunt?"

Though she knew all too well it was what he intended, her spine stiffened with indignation. She could not back down from a challenge, despite knowing it was a bad idea. Not because she was scared, for she wasn't. Not of him. Tension thrummed under her skin, the sensation implying that wasn't entirely true. Not that she feared he would lay hands on her against her will, or anything of that nature. She knew he believed in the rules of society, in how a gentleman should act, and laying hands on an unwilling woman would appal him. He'd proved that much by rescuing Alice. No. It wasn't his style at all.

He wanted her to want him.

It was this game he liked, cat and mouse, and he certainly believed himself the cat.

Well, Matilda was no mouse, and she had claws of her own. The realisation dawned on her slowly, she liked the game too. It soothed her ego a little to know how much he wanted her, and that she had the power to keep saying no.

He was watching her, a glittering look in his eyes that told her he knew he'd won this round.

"Come, Miss Hunt, let us set tongues wagging," he said, the words softer now, sliding under her skin as he reached out his hand to her. Matilda's mouth was suddenly dry, but the dancers were gathering on the floor and… she placed her hand in his.

***

Silas watched, bemused as Miss Hunt allowed the marquess to lead her onto the dance floor. What was going on between them?

He'd meant what he said; it was clear the *ton* based the story of Matilda's ruination on nothing but a series of unforeseen and unhappy events. There had been no affair, no scandal. That the marquess wanted her, however, that was blatant. It was also surprising.

Silas took an interest in the affairs of powerful men—such information was always useful— and the marquess was circumspect. There had been a series of willing widows, to his knowledge. The affairs had been discreetly managed and the only reason things weren't kept a secret was because the women themselves wanted the information known. To be Montagu's lover was a powerful position to hold, and one they'd flaunt if it wouldn't mean the man himself would dispense with them at once. He'd never yet shown a public interest in any woman and, to be fair, it was only one dance.

Yet, Silas suspected, it would not be the last.

He looked up as St Clair joined him, and they watched Miss Hunt and Montagu circle the room.

"A dazzling couple," the earl commented.

It was true. You would be hard pressed to find such a handsome pair anywhere.

"Why haven't you offered for her?" Silas asked, suddenly curious.

St Clair's eyebrows rose. "For Miss Hunt?" He shrugged and shook his head. "I like her well enough, but I have no desire to marry her."

"But you know the scandal is nothing but gossip. Your mother has supported the girl in the past, so I assume she would accept it. You're powerful enough to ignore such a story in any case. She's beautiful, wealthy, her brother is a close friend…. Why haven't you saved her from the mess she's in?"

St Clair flushed, anger sparking in his eyes. "Why don't you marry her? You don't give a damn for the good opinion of the *ton*. You save her."

Silas grinned, intrigued that he'd hit a nerve. "We both know why I won't marry her. I have an interest elsewhere. What about you?"

To his intense amusement, the flush on the earl's face deepened. "Mind your own bloody business, Silas," he said, glowering. "And stay the hell out of mine."

"Yes, that's the look I was waiting for," Silas said with a chuckle, echoing the words St Clair had given him not long ago. "Like a fox when the hounds have caught his scent. You poor bastard."

For a moment, Silas thought he'd get angry and deny it, or storm off, but after a moment of obvious annoyance, St Clair let out a huff of laughter. "You have no idea," he said, giving Silas a twisted smile.

He clapped St Clair on the back and sighed. "Come along, my friend. I think we both need to get drunk."

Chapter 6

Dear Alice,

Please will you speak to Matilda? The strangest thing happened at the Earl of Ulceby's ball last night. She danced with Montagu! It's set tongues wagging, I can tell you, not least because the whole way through the dance, they couldn't take their eyes off each other. What on earth was she thinking? She's supposed to be the sensible one!

—Excerpt of a letter from Miss Kitty Connolly to Mrs Alice Hunt.

7th July 1814. South Audley Street, London.

Lucia rose early the next morning, though she was tired and dispirited. The triumph she had felt had been short-lived, thanks to the aggravating Lord Cavendish.

She'd slept little, finding his words to her—and the manner in which they'd been spoken—simply would not allow her to rest. His face swam into focus every time she closed her eyes, and now she was restless and irritated. It was time she paid a visit to someone who had always supported her, always taken care of her, no matter what.

She slipped out of the house, needing to be alone and not wanting to have the curious gaze of a footman upon her as she paid her visit.

The morning was bright, the sky above so blue and promising such a lovely day to come that even Lucia's spirits lifted a little. She had come to love the vagaries of English weather. It was familiar to her now, softer and gentler than the climes she'd been born to. A sudden memory rose of heat on her skin and a burning sun far fiercer than the one above her now, blazing down on dusty earth. It scorched her skin and her eyes as the heady scent of sandalwood drifted on the heated air.

Lucia shook herself, unsettled by the force of the memory, by the longing for something long since lost to her. Hurrying away from the house, she hailed a hackney carriage at the first opportunity and gave an address in Cheapside.

A half an hour later, she bade the driver let her down as the market was in full swing and the streets too congested to go any further. She got out close to St Paul's Cathedral, on the corner of Bread Street and Friday Street, and despite the growing heat of the day, she was careful to settle the cloak about her shoulders, drawing up the hood.

The scent of fish made her nose wrinkle as she hurried through the market, batting away flies as the pungent wares attracted insects. A little further and the noise of the market subsided and Lucia sought a narrow, terraced house. She knocked three times, and then repeated it for good measure.

A young woman answered the door, her dark hair pulled back into a messy bun. "Oh, hello, miss," she said, smiling and showing teeth that were yellow and uneven. "We didn't expect you today."

"Hello, Mary," Lucia said, taking down her hood as she stepped inside the door. "How is she today?"

Mary grinned and rolled her eyes. "Same as ever, of course. Grumbling."

Lucia snorted and handed her cloak and gloves to the girl.

Taking a deep breath, Lucia smoothed her hair and opened the door into the back room. Though it was a warm day, a fire crackled in the grate and a tiny old lady sat beside it, peering down at a book with great concentration.

"*Nani maa*," Lucia said, exasperated. "Where are your spectacles?"

For a moment the old woman's wrinkled face split into a wide grin. "Aashini," she said, holding her arms open as Lucia moved forward to hug her. She pressed her lips to Dharani's cheek, the woman's skin as deep a brown as lovingly polished wood. Her hair was white now, but still thick and lustrous, and hung in a long plait over one shoulder. "Have you brought me more books?" she demanded, her dark eyes alight with anticipation.

"Yes, and I am happy to see you too, it's been too long," Lucia said, pretending affront at the sudden change of topic as she fished in her reticule and pulled out two books.

The old woman gave a chortle of glee and snatched them from her hands.

"I'm not sure I should let you have them," Lucia said, tutting as she was ignored in favour of investigating the new titles. "They're scandalous. Your poor old heart will probably explode with shock."

Dharani snorted and looked up at her, wagging a gnarled finger in Lucia's direction with obvious scorn. "You young people. You think you invented sex and scandal. Hmph. I could teach you a thing or two."

Lucia made a face and covered her ears. "Don't you dare," she pleaded. "Or I'm leaving right now."

"Come and sit down," Dharani said, chuckling and waving at the armchair opposite hers. "Tell me everything."

Lucia sighed and wondered where on earth to start. She decided to keep it simple; it seemed best not to mention Viscount Cavendish.

"I left him a message last night, as we discussed," Lucia said, feeling again a little surge of satisfaction at having done so. "With luck he'll not sleep easy again."

The old woman glowered and shook her head, rearranging the heavily embroidered silk that draped over her shoulders. It was a shocking pink, a gift from Lucia some years back. Dharani had always been fond of bright colours.

"You say that as if I agreed with it. This is madness, *bhanvaraa*," she said, using the nickname she'd had for Lucia since childhood. "You are dancing too close to the flames, you'll get burned."

Lucia rolled her eyes and Dharani smacked her palm flat on the books in her lap, the sound ringing out. "Do not give me that look. What becomes of me if this powerful man succeeds where he failed before? *Phir kyahoga*? Well?"

"But he did fail," Lucia said, even as fear swirled in her stomach, a sickening cold sensation making her skin clammy.

"Because of me!" the old woman said, striking her chest with her fist. "Me and Anna-Marie," she said with a sneer in her voice.

Lucia took a deep breath, knowing better than to argue. It was true enough. "Have you heard from her?" she asked, hoping the woman was well. Even after all the trouble she'd caused, Lucia hoped she was happy. "Is she all right?"

Dharani pursed her lips, aware Lucia was changing the subject. "Your *mama* is always all right. She's like a cat with an overabundance of lives," she said, though there was no real heat in the comment. She waved an arthritic hand with an impatient gesture. "Some Italian count is making use of her at present. She's lucky her looks have lasted this long, but she needs to settle. Finally, I think she knows it."

“They’re to marry?” Lucia asked, surprised that Anna-Marie should finally give in to the inevitable.

“She believes he will ask,” Dharani admitted, nodding. “For her sake, let us pray he does, though I hope he’s wealthy enough or she’ll ruin him.”

Lucia couldn’t help a smile as she remembered life with Anna-Marie. It had never been dull, that was for certain.

“Come here.”

Dharani’s command was imperious, one that expected obedience.

Glowering a little, Lucia shook her head. “I must go, *nani*,” she said, hoping to escape. “Miss Hunt will wonder where I’ve got to.”

Dharani’s mouth settled in a line of discontent and Lucia sighed. Getting to her feet, she moved closer to her and knelt beside the old woman’s chair. She grasped her chin, tilting her head up and searching her eyes.

“Who is he?” she demanded, her tone an accusation. “You’ve met someone, haven’t you? I told you there would be a man. I told you! Who is he?”

Lucia’s mouth went dry and she opened it to speak, but Dharani got there first.

“Don’t you dare lie.”

The words died on her tongue, and Lucia scowled. *Damn her.* The old woman was uncanny and Lucia had never been able to hide a thing from her.

“Viscount Cavendish,” she said, regretting the admission the moment the words left her.

Dharani nodded, a smile curving over her mouth. She studied Lucia, who squirmed under her scrutiny. “You’ll not escape him, *bhanvaraa*.”

The old woman grinned, a not altogether pleasant smile. "He means to have you, doesn't he? I can see it in your eyes. You're afraid you'll let him."

Lucia held her tongue, there was little point in trying to pretend she was wrong.

By the time she'd escaped further interrogation, it was late morning. The day was hot and sweltering beneath her heavy cloak was unappealing, but she slung it about her shoulders as she walked out the door all the same. She was about to pull up the hood when the strangest sensation hit her: an awareness of… of something, of someone.

She looked up, heart pounding, just as she saw Lord Cavendish across the street as he turned towards her with the same quizzical expression on his face.

Her breath caught and the desire to run was almost overwhelming, but she could not. They stared at each other, both equally shocked.

He was walking towards her now, with long, purposeful strides. Turning, she prayed that the door was shut, that Dharani had not come to wave her off, but her luck had run out after the excess of last night.

Dharani craned her neck, and Lucia knew what she saw: the tall English lord with eyes the colour of skies and oceans, and the wicked smile of a pirate set on plunder.

The old woman laughed, shaking her head. "Tread carefully, *bhanvaraa*, the flames are getting higher."

***

7th July 1814. Friday Street, Cheapside, London.

Silas blinked, not quite believing what he was seeing. After a sleepless night plagued with dreams of her, he wondered for a moment if he was imagining things, but no, there she was. Implausible as it seemed, Lucia stood on the street before him in

Cheapside, large as life and more beautiful than ever. He felt winded for a moment, the sensation overtaken by one of concern as he realised that she was alone.

A dark cloak covered her pretty summer gown, something a woman might wear to hide herself if she was somewhere she ought not be.

He moved towards her at once and alarm widened her eyes. She turned away, glancing behind her at the house she had emerged from, and Silas followed her gaze to see an old Indian woman standing in the doorway. She was incongruous against the dull greys of a London street, the startling pink of her sari like a burst of summer on a winter's day. A red dot blazed against her dark skin between her eyebrows, everything about her marking her as foreign to England's shores, and he felt a burst of curiosity. She was looking at him directly, and a shiver of something coasted over his skin. The old woman laughed, and looked at Lucia.

"Tread carefully, *bhanvaraa*, the flames are getting higher."

She closed the door, the warning—for it had been a warning—lingering on the air between them.

Silas stood before Lucia, staring at her in consternation. "What are you doing here?" he asked, knowing she'd hate it, hate him having any little piece of her secrets, but he had to ask.

The look of irritation in her eyes made him smile as she huffed out a breath.

"Visiting," she muttered, before making a face, as aware as he was that his questions would not stop there. "That was Dharani," she said grudgingly. "My old ayah."

Silas frowned a moment, trying to place the word, and then remembered a friend's family who had employed an Indian nanny to look after their children. An ayah.

"Your nanny?" he said, confirming his assumption.

Lucia nodded. “When Anna-Marie left us, Dharani was all I had. She found work looking after the children of a family in Norfolk and somehow persuaded them to allow me to be educated alongside them. I owe her everything.”

There was an earnest, reverent tone to her words that Silas heard and understood.

“Anna-Marie de Feria,” he repeated, frowning as he remembered the name of Lucia’s Portuguese mother. The famed courtesan who’d shared the beds of some of the most powerful men in the country.

Lucia said nothing. Silas imagined she did not enjoy being mentioned in the same breath. Like mother, like daughter was what most men would assume. It’s what *he* had assumed, he realised with shame.

“Must you come here alone?” he asked, holding out his arm for her, for if she thought she was going a step further unaccompanied she was sorely mistaken.

She sighed, glaring at him but apparently accepting the inevitable, as she didn’t protest.

“People have enough of my dark past,” she said, her tone brittle. “I keep what I can private. I don’t like busybodies who stick their noses in where they’re not wanted.”

Silas felt a smile tug at his mouth. “Is that set down meant for me?” he asked gently. “For I did not know you were here.”

“No,” she agreed, shrugging. “But I’m not stupid enough to believe you won’t try to ferret out the rest. You’re the kind of man who’ll leave no stone unturned once he’s decided on a course of action.”

“How very perceptive you are, Miss de Feria,” he said, grinning at her. “And I’m glad you’ve accepted the fact, as I already told you of my intentions.”

A blush stained her cheeks as she remembered what he'd said last night.

"I will prove myself worthy of your trust," he said, just to ensure she remembered clearly.

"Trust is given, not taken," Lucia said, and there was something in her voice now, something vulnerable and frightened. It took him aback. In the short time he'd known her, he had almost come to believe this vivacious spark of a woman feared nothing.

He stopped walking and covered her hand with his own. "Yes," he said. "I know that, but won't you trust me, Lucia? I…." He paused, wondering if she'd think he was odd for saying such a thing. "I have the strangest feeling whenever I look at you," he admitted. "I'm frightened for you. I feel you're in danger, that… you need me."

Lucia stared at him, her dark eyes widening. He got lost in those eyes, so wide and thickly lashed, and so wary. She wanted to trust him, he felt certain of it.

"You sound like Dharani," she said, looking away from him with a frown.

"She called you *bhanvaraa*," he said, wanting to know everything, just as she'd predicted.

Lucia rolled her eyes. "It means bumblebee," she muttered, her irritation obvious. "When I was a child I was always rushing about, *busy, busy*," she added, sounding so adorable Silas couldn't help but laugh.

"What did she mean?" he asked, still unsettled by the rest of what the old woman had said. "She said to tread carefully, the flames are getting higher."

They walked on and Lucia took a deep breath, her unwillingness to tell him palpable. "I don't know really, only sometimes it's like she *knows* things," she said, glancing at him, her expression daring him to mock her. “I’d swear she was a witch if I didn’t know better.”

Silas shook his head and smiled. “When I was a boy, there was a woman in the village who told fortunes. People said she was a witch. She once told me….” He stopped, remembering the phrase with perfect clarity, though at the time he’d not understood it. “She told me I needed to look in the gutters to find my purpose.” He shivered, unnerved all over again. “At the time I thought she was insulting me, but three years later I ran away from home. These streets *were* my home for a time, and I found my purpose there. I discovered who I was.”

Lucia nodded, and he knew she understood. “That’s everything, isn’t it? To know who you are.”

“Yes,” he said, though he frowned. It wasn’t as simple as that. “But—”

“But what?” she asked, and he smiled at the curiosity in her eyes.

“But it’s not always a comfortable realisation, or… or even what you might expect. It can take courage to see the truth, and not what you or others expect to see. More still to *be* that person, come what may.”

She looked troubled at that and they walked on a way in silence.

“What are you doing here, anyway?” she asked, watching him with interest. “Revisiting the past?”

Silas chuckled and shook his head. “Visiting the future. I have a new warehouse,” he said, gesturing back the way they’d come. “I was just ensuring everything is in order.”

“Don’t you have people for that sort of thing?” There was something in her voice, a spark of real interest that gave him hope.

“Of course.” Silas shrugged. “But I am not a man who leaves things to chance or assumptions. I built this business from the ground up. I'll not see it fail because I didn't take the time to check a few details."

"They say you reek of the shop," she said, and he knew she'd said it to gauge his reaction to the insult, though there had been no insult in her tone, only curiosity.

He laughed at that. "A viscount who works for a living? My god, the horror."

She paused then and surprised him by taking his hand, turning it over and tracing her fingers over his palm. "A working man's hands," she murmured as she gazed down at it, and pleasure slid under his skin at her touch.

"Yes," he said, feeling breathless as one gloved finger trailed over his skin.

She blushed then and dropped his hand. "I must go."

She hurried away from him.

"Lucia!"

He caught her up, holding her arm and making her stop. "At least let me get you a hackney."

To his relief, she nodded and allowed him to flag one down and see her safely inside.

"I want to see you again," he said, the words stark and honest.

Lucia shook her head, but he spoke again, refusing to let her deny him.

"You know we'll meet again, don't you?" he demanded, knowing it was inevitable, surely she felt it too.

He smiled at the stubborn glint in Lucia's eyes, knowing he was right.

"Yes, but I don't know if that's a good thing or not," she muttered, folding her arms.

"Lucia," he said, her name soft on his lips, matching the look in her eyes as she turned back to him. He reached out and took her hand, squeezing her fingers gently before letting her go. "Take care, love."

She smiled and nodded, and he closed the carriage door and watched it disappear into the distance, knowing he *would* see her again.

Chapter 7

Oh, Harriet, do stop being such a stick in the mud. So what if the garden party is hosted by St Clair? It will be a lovely day and I want you to come! I'm sure you can avoid him with the number of people going, though why you'd want to is beyond me. I think he's dreamy.

—Excerpt of a letter from Miss Kitty Connolly to Miss Harriet Stanhope.

7th July 1814. South Audley Street, London.

By the time Lucia got home, Matilda was up and about. Deciding she'd head off questions about her whereabouts this morning, Lucia went on the attack.

"Well, Miss Hunt. Explain yourself," she said with mock seriousness, folding her arms and endeavouring to look stern. "What were you thinking last night? You've got the *ton* all in a twitter, I can tell you that. Tongues were wagging before you'd even left the dance floor."

Lucia laughed as Matilda groaned and put her head in her hands. She was sitting at the breakfast table, nursing a cup of hot chocolate and looking pale and rather tired. It was no exaggeration, however. The marquess rarely danced, and to see him single out Matilda of all people….

That Matilda had agreed to it puzzled Lucia. Though she was all for spitting in the eye of those who would set one down, surely what Matilda had done was only giving them ammunition?

"I don't know what came over me," Matilda confessed, peeking at Lucia through her fingers. "But the wretched man all but dared me and—"

"Oh!" Lucia said with a sad shake of her head. "That old trick. I must confess, a dare is hard to refuse when there's some smug fellow goading you into it. However, I would have thought—"

"Oh, don't say it," Matilda retorted, holding out a hand to stop her. "I knew what he was doing, of course I did, but… it's worse than that."

Lucia's eyes grew round, and she settled herself in the chair at Matilda's side, perfectly happy to wallow in someone else's troubles for a change.

"Worse how?"

Matilda closed her eyes and took a deep breath, as if she was about to unburden herself of her darkest secret. "Don't judge me," she pleaded, as Lucia gave a little bark of laughter.

"As if I would," she said, appalled at the idea.

Matilda opened her eyes and bit her lip. "I… I *wanted* to dance with him and… I enjoyed it."

The poor young woman looked so mortified that Lucia almost laughed, but realised in time that this was perhaps not appropriate.

"That is… awkward," she said carefully.

Matilda pinched the bridge of her nose and grimaced. "Oh, believe me, awkward doesn't begin to describe it," she wailed. "I think I shall have a megrim."

Lucia did laugh now. "Yes, and a fit of the vapours while you're about it," she teased. "Come, Matilda, you're made of sterner stuff than that."

"I know, but he knew, Lucia and… and he didn't even gloat."

Matilda sounded anxious and perplexed, and it was clear she wanted advice and reassurance, but Lucia was the last person to give it to her. All she knew of men was to avoid them. Life was a deal simpler, and safer, that way.

"He wants you, Matilda," she said eventually. It was the simple truth. "He's decided to woo you rather than trying to bully you into his bed."

To her surprise, Matilda frowned. "He never tried to bully me," she said, sounding a little defensive. "He was rude, obnoxious, insulting, and unbelievably arrogant, but he never bullied me."

Lucia raised an eyebrow, and Matilda let out a sigh.

"No, it doesn't make the slightest difference. He's just trying to persuade me to be his mistress."

"It's a position half the women of the *ton* would murder their best friend for," Lucia said, pulling a face at the idea, though it was true enough. "You'd have wealth beyond imagining, power… notoriety of a kind that would open doors rather than close them."

"I know." Matilda's face was resigned. "None of which I care a fig for."

Lucia let out a breath and smiled. "Well, there you are then. Crisis averted."

Matilda laughed, and Lucia was pleased to see her looking more her old self.

"I'm so glad you're here, Lucia," she said, picking up her chocolate and then wrinkling her nose as she discovered it had gone cold.

"Me too," Lucia replied, and then noticed the correspondence Matilda had been reading. The pile in front of her clearly included a half dozen invitations. "Anything of interest?"

"Yes!" Matilda replied, eyes alight with pleasure. She snatched one gilt-edged slip of card from the pile with a grin. "St Clair has invited us to a garden party."

***

9th July 1814. The Dowager Countess St Clair's garden party, St James's, London.

Built in the previous century, the Earl of St Clair's London home was a neo-classical masterpiece. Designed with pleasure as its purpose, it was synonymous in the *ton*'s minds for lavish entertainments. The previous earl had been a well-loved figure, something of a benign rogue, a mantle his son had taken on with ease.

Today, however, the magnificent house played second fiddle to the garden, where no expense had been spared on one of the last great parties of the season. Overlooking Green Park, the gardens were not vast, but beautifully laid out in a series of intricate parterres that led around the grounds.

The dowager countess' white garden was a glorious sight to behold. The scent of roses drifted on the warm air of a perfect English summer day, and Lucia could only sigh with wonder at the glorious picture before her. Ladies in summer gowns added splashes of colour here and there, like silken butterflies flitting between the blooms. Music floated from an elegant marble rotunda that shielded the musicians from the heat of the afternoon sun, and the chatter of pleasant conversation filled the air.

"How beautiful it is," Matilda said with a sigh, as they made their way along the circuit walk which toured all around the garden, in the earl's and his mother's company. She took Lucia's arm and sounded wistful as she added, "One can almost imagine being in the heart of the countryside, rather than in the midst of the city."

"I can see my mother is thrilled with the compliment, Miss Hunt," St Clair said with a grin. "As this is her pride and joy, I have often wondered if I'd been better tended as a child if I'd been a rose, or even a gooseberry bush."

This somewhat wry observation caused his mother to roll her eyes.

"Oh, yes," she said, her tone dry as she sent her son a look of long-suffering patience. "I can imagine how much you would have liked me poking my nose into your affairs. You enjoyed splendid freedom as a child, always off adventuring and getting into mischief. I always took the view that, as long as you came home in one piece, it had been a successful day."

Lucia laughed, deciding that she liked the dowager countess.

At that moment, Kitty and Bonnie joined them, tugging a rather reluctant looking Harriet in their wake.

"Harriet, darling, how lovely to see you," Lady St Clair said, beaming at the young woman as she greeted her with the warmth of a beloved daughter. "I've asked St Clair so many times why we never see you. I miss the days when you and your brother used to run about the place like puppies." She gave a sigh and shook her head. "They were barely tame, you know, but I miss the noise and the laughter… even the squabbling when my wretched son had done something unforgivable, *again*."

Harriet blushed and mumbled a reply, looking awkward and as if she'd rather be anywhere else.

"Harriet still thinks I'm unforgivable, Mother," St Clair said lightly, though his gaze on Harriet was rather intent. "That's why she avoids us."

Lucia watched a troubled look enter his mother's eyes as Harriet's jaw tightened and she hurried to intervene. She'd seen the animosity Harriet harboured for the earl, and had no desire to see the lovely afternoon spoiled by a row. Turning to the dowager countess, she tried to move the conversation on.

"Was he often in trouble, Lady St Clair?" she asked, earning herself a groan from the earl.

His mother laughed, her concern disappearing as she sent her son a fond look. "When wasn't he in trouble?" she asked as the earl studied his toes. "It would be easier to pinpoint those times, I fear. I never knew a boy so ripe for kicking up larks and playing pranks."

"Mother," St Clair murmured, returning an exasperated expression that implored her to change the subject.

"He was thick as thieves with Harriet's brother, Henry, of course," she said with a gleeful tone, ignoring her son's discomfort. "And the two of them dragged poor Harriet everywhere. She usually ended up bedraggled and covered in mud as they took turns to capture her and hold her prisoner. There's a lake at Holbrooke House and I lost count of the times she came back sopping wet, shivering, and outraged. Poor girl," she said, sending the lady in question a look of affectionate warmth. "I wonder that you didn't murder them both."

"Oh, it crossed my mind," Harriet muttered, a tight smile at her lips. "If you would excuse me."

Lucia and Matilda shared a glance, both a little shocked by Harriet's abrupt departure. Glancing back at the earl, Lucia saw his gaze follow Harriet as she hurried away from them. She thought there was sorrow there, but perhaps he felt her scrutiny, for he looked up. At once there was a smile on his face and a twinkle of mischief in his eyes.

"Come ladies, let me give you the tour."

Later in the afternoon, servants moved between the guests bearing silver trays, laden with all manner of finger sized delicacies, from feather light savoury pastries to decadent sweet treats.

Lucia's interest was not in the food, but the presence of Mr Edgar Bindley. His father, the Earl of Ulceby, was also here, though Lucia had taken pains to keep out of his way. Not that the man would have the slightest clue who she was, but there was no point in tempting fate. Edgar, however, presented a temptation she could not resist.

Her fingers went to the pocket of her gown and the small metal symbol that lay within. She rubbed her thumb back and forth over it, smiling a little. Her smile widened as Mr Bindley looked up and met her gaze.

Though it revolted her to do so, she raised her glass to him and sent him a rather flirtatious expression. He hurried to her side with such alacrity she almost laughed.

"Miss de F-Feria, a delight, as always," he said, raising her hand to his lips in what she imagined he thought was a romantic and courtly gesture. Perhaps it might have been, had anyone else's lips been pressed to the back of her hand. Grateful that her gloves kept his touch from her skin, she nonetheless had to repress a shudder as she noticed a slightly damp mark on the pale green silk.

Striving to hide her distaste both at his presence and the way he crowded her, Lucia spent the next ten minutes pretending to laugh and hang on his every word. Forcing her expression to remain one of pleasure, she set her empty glass down on a tray and declined the waiter's offer of another with regret. It would have helped her nerves. Stiffening her spine, she returned her attention to the man beside her, who was telling a story of which she'd long since lost the thread.

"Oh, how funny you are, Mr Bindley," she said, her trill of laughter sounding false and brittle even to her own ears as she gave him a playful smack on the shoulder with her hand.

Pretending to stumble, she then grasped at his arm to steady herself with her left hand, while the right slipped the token into his waistcoat pocket where the line of the cloth suggested he kept a snuff box. "Oh!" she said, righting herself with a coy smile. "I do beg your pardon."

"N-Not at all, Miss de Feria," Mr Bindley said, taking advantage of the moment to grasp hold of her waist and taking his time releasing her. "I n-never mind b-beautiful women falling into my arms."

"Perhaps you might try releasing them in good time, however."

This voice came from behind them and held a thread of anger.

Mr Bindley released her at last, and Lucia put a little distance between her and the odious man. She flushed as she saw Lord Cavendish regarding them with curiosity, and a glint in his blue eyes that she didn't quite like.

"My lord," Mr Bindley said, an expression of disdain on his face as he regarded Lord Cavendish. "I did not realise St Clair had invited you."

"Oh, yes," Cavendish replied, returning a grin which was not altogether pleasant. "St Clair isn't as high in the instep as some. Good news for us, eh?"

Mr Bindley flushed with anger at the implied insult. It was obvious he looked down on the viscount—despite his title and lineage—for being a self-made man. How ridiculous, when Mr Bindley's father, the earl, was teetering on the brink of bankruptcy. Lucia smiled a little, awaiting with eager anticipation the day when she would push them over the edge.

"For you, perhaps," Bindley sneered, putting up his chin. He turned to Lucia and gave her a stiff and formal bow. "Take care, Miss de Feria, you will be judged by the company you keep." He paused to give Lord Cavendish a significant look, and stalked away.

Lucia waited as Cavendish watched him go and then turned back to her.

"What was that all about?" he asked, curiosity in his eyes as he stared down at her.

"I can't imagine what you mean," Lucia replied, moving away from him.

He followed her, walking at her side. "You know exactly what I mean. Whose benefit was that little exhibition for? Mine? Did you seek to make me jealous?"

With a little gasp at his audacity, Lucia stopped to glare at him. "You conceited wretch," she said, outraged at the suggestion. "I didn't even know you were here."

He frowned at her, but seemed to accept it. "I had another engagement so only arrived a few moments ago," he said, the admission grudging.

They walked on in silence until he spoke again, sounding troubled. "Lucia, what game are you playing with Bindley and his father?"

For a moment, the world seemed unsteady beneath her feet.

How could he...? What on earth...?

Questions crowded her mind and it took every ounce of self-control she had to remain calm. "Game?" she asked, blinking up at him and feigning innocence for all she was worth. "Whatever do you mean?"

He hesitated, looking as though he wanted to speak, to explain, but was unsure of what to say. "Lucia," he said after a long pause, and she shivered at the intimate tenor of his voice. "Love, if you're in trouble, won't you let me help you? Edgar Bindley and his father are a bad lot. The earl is a cruel man, and his son is a spineless coxcomb whose reputation suggests he's following in his father's footsteps. The whole damn family are...." He trailed off and shook his head, perhaps not able to find a word to describe the Ulceby bloodline.

There was such concern in his eyes, though. Lucia stared up at him, shaken by the way he worried over her, yet wanting to allow it.

"I saw you, Lucia," he said, his voice harder as he confronted her. "At the ball. I saw you come out of the earl's study, and I saw him shortly after, when he discovered what you'd left there. He looked like he'd seen a bloody ghost."

Lucia felt the colour drain from her face.

No, no, no.

She had no choice but to brazen it out.

"Oh, that," she said, laughing, though amusement was a long way from what she was experiencing. "That was… well, it was just a silly dare. My friends and I have this game you see, and…." She forced a look of embarrassed chagrin to her face, trying hard to ignore the sickening thud of her heart in her chest. "And, if you must know, my dare was to go into a man's study, and have a drink and smoke a cigar."

She saw his dark brows pull together, the desire to believe her shining in his eyes. His hair was unruly today, his coat a little rumpled, and she suspected he'd come direct from whatever appointment had delayed him without returning home. His valet would despair of him, no doubt. The longing to reach out and straighten his lapel, to smooth the disobedient curl of his hair was hard to resist.

"That's the only reason you were there?" he asked, the doubt in the question audible.

"Why ever else would I be there?" she said, laughing at him and praying he would believe her. Though it would be wonderful to put her trust in him, to unburden herself, she didn't dare. She doubted he'd be so sympathetic when he heard the truth. She believed he was a good man, but she'd put her trust in good men before, and been badly burned for her stupidity. No one would protect her. No one but herself.

Besides, she liked him. She liked him too well to involve him in something which would lead to the biggest scandal the *ton* had seen for years when it came out. No. He was best off out of it.

She watched as he let out a breath, apparently accepting her words. He held out his arm to her and she smiled, taking it as he guided her to the end of the path where Matilda and some of the others were chatting. They joined the group and Lucia tried to take part, to involve herself in the merry conversation, but her eyes were drawn to the other side of the little parterre, where the Earl of Ulceby was speaking with his son. They were having words about something. Edgar flinched as his father's face darkened, whatever he was saying making the young man pale.

With her heart in her throat, Lucia saw Edgar reach into his waistcoat pocket to retrieve his snuff box and saw the little glint of metal as it fell. Edgar frowned, bending to pick it up, holding it in his palm and turning to his father.

The earl gasped, snatching it from Edgar, his eyes widening as he stared about the gathering. Feeling outside of the event, as though she was witnessing a theatre production, Lucia watched as the man clutched at his chest, his face changing colour as he spluttered and gasped for breath.

"Help!" Edgar shrieked, doing nothing to help himself as his father sank to the ground. "Someone help him!"

Gasps and murmurs of horror carried across the garden, and Lucia's gaze went unwillingly to Lord Cavendish. He was staring at her, staring at her as though he believed she'd contrived the whole scene.

Lucia stared back, unable to look away.

She watched as he moved, hurrying to the earl and getting down beside him as everyone else just looked on. He undid the man's cravat, calling sharp commands for help, for someone to *fetch a doctor, damn it.*

It was inevitable that he should reach for the man's hand, opening the fingers that curled about the tiny silver token and staring down at it.

Before he could turn back to her, before he could look at her with accusation in his eyes, Lucia moved away.

"Matilda, do you think someone else could bring you home?" she asked in a desperate undertone. "I… I'm feeling a little faint. Too much sun, I think." Lucia did her best to smile and look tired and hot, rather than as if she wanted to hitch her skirts up and run as far and as fast as she could. "I should like to take the carriage and go home at once."

"Oh, you poor thing," Matilda said, all solicitousness. "Shall I accompany you, dear? I think the party might be over now anyway."

"Oh, no, no. I'm quite all right. I just need a lie down in the quiet and I shall be right as ninepence," she said, trying to sound reassuring.

Matilda frowned, and looked over to where Lord Cavendish and Mr Bindley were helping the earl to his feet. Ulceby looked grey and haggard, but not as if he was ready to breathe his last. Lucia could not decide if she was disappointed or relieved at that fact.

The orchestra—who had stopped when Edgar shrieked for help—picked up where they'd left off, and the party resumed now it seemed the earl was not lying dead at their feet.

"Well," Matilda said, a little doubtful. "It looks as though no one else is going. Perhaps the earl had too much sun too?"

"I'm sure it was something of the sort," Lucia said, trying not to sound impatient. "It is dreadfully hot."

Lucia watched as Matilda's gaze drifted across the garden, to where the Marquess of Montagu was speaking with the Dowager Countess St Clair. "If you're sure, then," Matilda said, looking back at Lucia.

With a sigh of relief, Lucia kissed Matilda's cheek. "Quite sure," she said, wondering if perhaps she ought to persuade

Matilda to come after all. For her own good. "Have fun, then," she said, biting her lip against the desire to say *and do be careful.*

Matilda was a big girl who could make her own decisions, just as Lucia had. She would have to live with them too, just as Lucia would.

Chapter 8

It was a lovely afternoon. The dowager countess is great fun, and St Clair such a handsome fellow. It's no wonder the women flock to him like flies to honey. Can you imagine being the Countess St Clair, married to such a man and living in such a beautiful place? I can't wait to see Holbrooke House with Harriet later this summer. It's going to be wonderful.

—Excerpt of a letter from Miss Kitty Connolly to Miss Bonnie Campbell.

7th July 1814. The Dowager Countess St Clair's garden party, St James's, London.

Silas looked at the small object in his hand. It was silver, no bigger than a sovereign and carefully wrought. It was shaped like a short, ornate trident and Silas had no idea what it represented. Tucking it into his waistcoat pocket, he felt relief flood through him as the earl took a shaky breath.

The man looked ashen—as if he'd aged a decade in as many seconds—but not, at least, as if he would turn up his toes. Thank God.

There was no doubt in Silas's mind now. Lucia was involved in this. He'd believed her explanation earlier, fool that he was. Deep down he'd known better, but he'd wanted to believe her. No longer. When he'd met her gaze, there had been something terrible there, something defiant and yet full of guilt.

Somehow, she had slipped whatever this was to Edgar during that ridiculous display earlier, where she had pretended to flirt with him. At the time, Silas had admitted to feelings ranging from anger to unfettered jealousy, and a half a dozen other emotions he didn't dare consider. Now he was terrified. He didn't know what game Lucia was playing, but she'd almost killed the Earl of Ulceby today. Whatever it was, it was beyond dangerous.

What her motivation was he could not fathom, but he intended to find out. A part of him didn't want to know, didn't want to investigate in case he discovered she was cold and ruthless, the vulnerability he'd seen in her eyes an illusion.

Yet, whatever the truth, he needed to know. The knowledge that he would protect her, no matter her motivation, was a truth on which he refused to dwell. Silas only knew he could not condemn her for being driven by avarice or revenge, or anything of the sort. He knew the power of such an ambition himself, and he understood it all too well.

Once he'd helped the earl to a quiet room and a doctor had been summoned, he searched in vain for Lucia, only to discover she had long gone. Well, she would not escape him. Not now. He'd have the truth from her, one way or another.

***

"Where did Lucia go?" Matilda looked around to see Harriet at her side. St Clair had just moved away from her to speak to guests on the other side of the garden. She doubted that was a coincidence.

"She left about ten minutes ago. Too much sun, by all accounts."

"Oh, that's a shame," Harriet replied, pushing her spectacles up her nose. She looked flushed and overheated herself, her light brown hair escaping its pins and her muslin gown clinging to her.

"I'm surprised you haven't escaped too," Matilda said, seeing a flash of guilt in Harriet's eyes. "You've hardly hidden your animosity for St Clair."

Harriet shrugged. "I can't be rude to Lady St Clair. She's always been so kind to me, so… I'll endure," she said, blowing an errant curl from her face with irritation. "How do you always look so cool and elegant, Tilda?"

Matilda smiled. "Stay in the shade."

"Too late for that," Harriet grumbled, peeling her skirts away from her legs with a grimace. "There was the most fascinating specimen over there. A new variety of rose that the countess propagated herself. She's promised to show me how she did it."

Matilda smiled at Harriet's enthusiasm. The young woman was often too serious, a little distant from the other girls, but she lit up at any new discovery. "Why do you hate him so?"

A guarded look entered Harriet's eyes, but she didn't bother asking who Matilda was speaking of.

"I wouldn't say I hate him exactly," she began, only to encounter Matilda's arched eyebrow. She blew out a breath, hesitating, and then the words tumbled out all at once. "Because he revels in his own stupidity and despises learning, he mocks anyone he feels is cleverer than him, and makes *them* feel foolish."

Matilda regarded her in surprise. Harriet had folded her arms, her brown eyes hard and angry.

"I don't find him the least bit stupid, Harriet," she said gently, aware that there was a deal more to her animosity than this, but knowing she must tread with care. "He's very entertaining, and stupid men simply aren't, you know."

Harriet's mouth compressed for a moment. "He's frivolous and a spendthrift, a flirt and a womaniser, and I doubt he's had an original thought in his head since the day he was born, but everyone thinks he's marvellous because he's so bloody handsome and he makes everyone laugh, usually at someone else's expense." The young woman blushed, apparently realising her outburst had been somewhat impassioned. "I… I think perhaps Lucia was right. It's dreadfully hot and I've had too much sun. Excuse me, Matilda."

Startled and a little nonplussed, Matilda watched Harriet go. Perhaps she should ask St Clair what was going on, she mused, toying with the idea. No, not today at least. She was too lethargic to meddle today. The heat of the afternoon was making her feel drowsy and she moved further into the shade, drawn by the lure of a dappled walkway. A bench was visible, overlooking a small ornamental pond, and Matilda moved towards it.

She sat down with a sigh of relief and took a moment to check her hair hadn't all tumbled down before leaning back and closing her eyes for a moment.

Her thoughts drifted back to the Earl of Ulceby's ball, and more precisely her dance with Montagu. He'd been scrupulously polite, a perfect gentleman in fact, which had rather unnerved her. She thought perhaps she preferred it when they were sniping back and forth.

Yet the dance had been magical. They'd not spoken a word to each other; she couldn't have done so if she'd tried. She hadn't wanted to break the spell of the moment by saying something that would lead to one of them insulting the other. There had been something between them, though, some strange sense of connection, of….

She had no idea what, but Montagu's words came back to her.

He had come upon her the afternoon after her brother had married Alice, and she'd only just recovered from a bout of sobbing and self-pity as she was still—and would likely always be—alone. The marquess had been the last man on earth she'd wanted to see that day, the day he'd offered to make her his mistress. Anger sparked again as she remembered, but now she realised he'd been right in what he'd said.

"*There is something between us. I should like to discover what it is.*"

He'd sounded mystified when he'd said it, and Matilda had sneered and laughed at the idea, of course, but now she wasn't so sure. He'd berated her for denying the truth, accusing her of cowardice. A prickle of unease worked its way down her spine as she wondered if he'd not been right.

Something out the corner of her eye made her turn, and she didn't even blink as she saw the man himself appear. Somehow, she'd known he would. He'd avoided her all day, so far, keeping his distance, never looking in her direction. It was all a game to him, she suspected. He was simply toying with her. The idea irritated her.

"Yes, yes, alone again, etcetera, etcetera," she said, waving an impatient hand before he could make the inevitable comment as he usually did. "Anyone would think you watch me, waiting for the moment I am all by myself."

He said nothing, but approached her holding out a glass which chinked slightly at the movement.

"I thought you might like this," he said, as unreadable as ever.

Matilda opened her mouth in surprise and reached for the glass, suddenly parched. "What is it?" she asked, suspicious all at once.

His mouth quirked a little. "My, my," he murmured. "You do believe me a villain."

"And this surprises you?" she retorted, staring at him.

He sighed. "It's orgeat, Miss Hunt. Quite unadulterated, I assure you."

Matilda frowned and took a hesitant sip, reassured to taste nothing more forbidden than orange flowers and almonds. There was ice in the drink, however, the sides of the glass sweating and dripping as she threw caution to the wind and drank deeply. The icy liquid slid down her throat, making her realise just how hot and thirsty she'd been.

With a sigh of bliss, she held the glass to her neck, allowing the remaining ice to cool her, and then opened her eyes with a start as she remembered she was being watched.

Montagu's gaze was intent, and Matilda felt a flush rise over her skin.

"Thank you," she said, cautiously. "Though I suppose I shall pay for it. You never do anything without an ulterior motive, do you?"

"No," he said, his expression unchanging.

"Do I owe you my soul now, then?" she asked sweetly, "Or do you already have that for saving Alice from Mr Bindley's unwelcome attentions? I recollect that debt was laid at my feet."

To her surprise he shook his head. "You repaid that already."

"I… I did?" Matilda could not hide her surprise.

"You did."

She regarded him, perplexed. He looked totally at ease, impeccably dressed as always, as though the heat didn't bother him in the least. Matilda had watched with amusement as collars and cravats had steadily wilted as the afternoon wore on, but Montagu was cool and pristine. Perhaps he really did have ice in his veins.

He leaned on an ebony cane with a heavy silver top, watching her, and looking the picture of the refined English gentleman.

Appearances could be deceptive.

"Good," she said, knowing it would annoy him if she didn't ask how she'd achieved such a feat. She stood, smoothing down her dress and giving him the impression she was about to leave.

"You danced with me," he said, apparently aware she would not ask, and giving her the answer, nonetheless.

"Ah, of course, a dance," she said, turning to look at him. "It should not surprise me that you price virtue so cheaply. You destroyed mine with ease enough."

"But your virtue is still intact, Miss Hunt," he said, and suddenly the atmosphere had changed, tension thrumming between them.

"It may as well not be," she snapped, and then cursed herself for the outburst, wishing she'd not allowed him to rile her.

If he'd smiled, she would have slapped him, but he did not. He only took a step closer to her.

"I don't believe you mean that," he said, his voice low, sending a strange sensation shivering over her skin. "But… if it *is* true, why not give it to me? You are as aware of the attraction between us as I am. Why not give into it?"

Matilda gasped, her breath coming faster as he closed the gap between them. He stood so close his scent reached her. Starched linen, leather, a hint of bergamot, and the clean heat of a male body filled her senses. For one bewildering moment she imagined it, imagined allowing him what he asked of her, and the idea made her giddy with an alluring mixture of fear and excitement.

"I would give you everything you could possibly desire," he said, his voice an invitation all its own, tempting her as he leaned in, his mouth so close to her ear that if she turned her head their mouths would meet. "Everything you could dream of."

Strangely, it was that which woke her from the trance and brought her back to reality with a snap.

Everything you could dream of.

Matilda closed her eyes and gave a little huff of laughter. "I'm sorry, my lord, but you are far and wide of the mark. My dreams hold things of such value, you could never begin to afford them."

A flash of arrogant pride was visible in those strange silver-grey eyes. "Name them. Name your price," he said, sounding strangely breathless.

Smiling, Matilda backed away from him, exhilaration singing beneath her skin. "My dreams would be a foreign country to you, my Lord Montagu, filled as they are with a home, children, and marriage to a man who loves and honours me. It's of no matter if he's a lord or a common merchant, either. I shan't care, you know. I shall love him with all my heart, and give him everything *he* could ever dream of."

With a little blaze of triumph burning in her heart, Matilda gave a defiant laugh and hurried away.

***

Still the 7th July 1814. Cavendish House, The Strand, London

Silas sat, lost in thought about the events of the afternoon as Fred made a production of pulling off his boots, and keeping up a litany of indignant remarks as he went.

It appeared the man was offended that Silas had attended the garden party looking less than perfect. Silas rolled his eyes, unable to concentrate in the face of his valet's petulance.

"What will people think? That's what I'd like to know," Fred grumbled. "I'll tell you," he carried on, apparently not needing an answer. "They'll think it's my fault you went out looking like you'd spend the night in a ditch, that's what they'll think."

With a sigh, Silas endured, whilst snatches of Fred's dark mutterings reached his ears including, "my reputation in tatters," and "never hold my head up again."

"Have you quite finished?" Silas asked, deadpan, as Fred bent to retrieve the shirt he'd just thrown to the floor.

"Quite, my lord," Fred replied with a sniff.

"Thank God." Silas gave him a stern look. "Now, then. You told me once you knew all the skeletons in the Cavendish cupboard. Was that true?"

All at once Fred looked wary and he straightened, narrowing his eyes at Silas. "True enough," he said, very much on his guard. "Why?"

Silas stared back at him, considering. "Did you never think to blackmail my father, or sell his secrets for a price? God knows the man did nothing to endear himself to you. I wouldn't blame you if you had."

The look of offended pride in Fred's eyes told Silas everything he wanted to know.

"My lord!" he exclaimed, such reproach in the words that Silas felt a stab of guilt for having asked at all. "If you are dissatisfied with my work, you need only have said so—"

"Oh, come down off your high horse," Silas said, shaking his head. "I ought not to have doubted you, and I apologise for asking. It was for good reason, though."

Fred stilled, bewildered. "My lord?"

"I need to know if I can trust you, Fred." Silas said, gentler now. "I'd like to, but I need to know if you'll take my secrets to your grave or if I ought to be circumspect."

He watched as Fred squared his shoulders, standing a little taller. "Anything you tell me goes no further. I swear it on my mother's grave, God bless her. You can rely on me."

There was sincerity in the man's eyes, and Silas did not doubt his honour. He'd met men who purported to be gentlemen, whose word wasn't worth a farthing, and he'd known villains who would die rather than break theirs. Honour was something he held dear, and he recognised it in another. Fred had it.

“Thank you, Fred.” Silas let out a breath of relief and uncurled his hand, staring down at the little silver object. “Now, then. What do you make of this?”

Fred moved towards him and studied the piece. “A trident?” he said, a little unsure.

Silas nodded. “It is, but… it’s different from anything I’ve seen before.’

“True.” Fred pursed his lips, thoughtful. “Anything to do with Neptune?”

“I wondered that,” Silas said, “but nothing obvious.”

Both men stared at it thoughtfully.

“You know, I have seen it before somewhere,” Fred mused, his eyebrows drawing together. “I just… I can’t remember.”

“Think on it, will you? See what you can dig up.”

“Of course,” Fred replied as Silas slipped the object back into his pocket. “May I ask why, my lord?”

Silas regarded the man in silence. “I need you to be very discreet, Fred, and not for my sake.”

Fred rolled his eyes, looking as though everything had just become clear to him. “I knew it. It’s a woman.”

Silas glowered a little but didn’t bother objecting; it was true, after all. Fred laughed and carried on with his work, collecting the dirty linen.

“I suppose it’s the woman you got your hair cut for. The one who was too beautiful for your sanity?”

“I suppose it is,” Silas admitted, ignoring Fred’s crow of laughter.

“Well, well. Don’t tell me she’s wielding a trident,” he quipped, chuckling at the idea. “I mean, I know I told you she sounded dangerous, but...." Fred trailed off, arrested by the look in Silas's eyes. "Not really?"

"She placed this Edgar Bindley's pocket and his father, Lord Ulceby's, nearly had a heart attack when he saw it. I believe she also left a drawing of the same symbol in his study, which produced a similar reaction."

The way Fred's eyes widened in shock didn't make Silas feel better.

"She's out for revenge, Fred. I know it. Believe me, I recognise the signs." Silas stood and ran a hand through his hair, wishing he had Lucia's trust, that she would confide in him. "I want to know why," he told his riveted valet. "I want to know Ulceby's secrets, and why that trident nearly sent him to his grave."

Fred let out a breath. "I dunno, my lord. I'll try to remember where I saw that thing before, but...." He stopped, considering. "I met Ulceby's valet once. Miserable old tosspot he was though, working for such a man, who can blame him?" he added. Silas could hardly disagree. "Don't reckon my chances of getting anything out of him, but... I'll try, if you like."

"Yes." He nodded, regarding Fred intently. "I want to know everything there is to know about the Earl of Ulceby. I want to know everyone he owes money to; every secret, every vice. Leave no stone unturned."

"You can rely on me, my lord."

"Good man, Fred," Silas said with real gratitude. "I know I can."

The glow of pleasure and pride in Fred's expression rather surprised him, until he remembered how his father had treated the man. Fred had deserved a great deal better than that. With that in mind, Silas retrieved two gold sovereigns from his coin purse. He put the first in Fred's hand. "You might need this to, er...

encourage his memories," he said with a wry smile before placing the second beside it. "And that's for your trouble."

Fred blushed and shook his head. "That's not necessary—"

"I know, but heaven knows you've earned it, and more besides. I know I'm not the easiest man to deal with, Fred. Let me show my appreciation at least, and tell me if you need more to make any of his staff talk."

He watched Fred stare at the two gold coins for a moment longer before the fellow smiled and tucked them into his waistcoat pocket. "You're wrong, as it happens. Compared to your sire, you're a doddle, though I shall deny saying that the next time you show me up by going out looking like you've been set upon by footpads."

"As you wish," Silas replied with gravity, suitably chastised.

He smiled to himself as Fred left the room whistling a merry tune.

Chapter 9

Dearest Dharani,

I wish you could have seen his face when he saw Kali's trishul. I could almost see her foot on his chest, just as you described her to me, squeezing the air from his lungs. He thought your curse had been brought down upon his head, and so it shall be, but it will be I who strikes the final blow.

—Excerpt of a letter from Miss Lucia de Feria to Shrimati Dharani Das.

9th July 1814. The Earl of Ulceby's residence, Hyde Park, London.

"If you would be so good as to wait here, my lord, I shall inform Lord Ulceby of your visit. He rarely receives callers before ten o'clock."

Silas nodded as the unsmiling butler left him alone in a lavish drawing room. Every surface dripped with gilt, and priceless ornaments adorned mantles, tables, and every other available surface. It was grandeur on an epic scale, a show of wealth and power that made Silas's skin crawl with the vulgarity of it. No wonder the fool was on the brink of ruin.

He shook his head, staring about him, and took a moment to inspect an unusual bronze. It appeared Indian in origin and depicted what he took to be a deity. The male figure had four arms, and in each hand he held an object: a large shell, a mace, a small disc, and a lotus flower.

The image of Lucia's brightly clad ayah standing against the grey of a London street returned to his mind, her piercing eyes appearing to regard him with a sense of inevitability, as if she'd known he would be there. A shiver ran down his spine, and he jumped a little as a voice pierced this thoughts.

"Barbaric, isn't it? Don't know why I keep it. Nasty heathen thing, but it's worth a pretty penny."

Silas swung around to see the earl had walked into the room. His eyes were heavy, dark circles beneath them that suggested he wasn't sleeping well, but he was straight-backed and an imposing presence. Tall and thin, the earl had steel grey hair and the kind of face that suggested he'd earned the look of jaded cynicism it bore. Nothing soft or kind had ever come from this man, and it was evident in his eyes.

"I am glad to see you are recovered," Silas said, moving to sit down at the earl's invitation.

"I am," the man said, a thin smile at his lips. "Though no thanks to any but you, it seems. I owe you a debt."

"Not at all," Silas said easily, doing his best to be amicable when every instinct told him this man was not to be trusted. "I was happy to help, and your son was there too, of course."

Ulceby snorted, a look of disgust colouring his expression. "There is nothing worse than reaching my age and realising you have sired two sons, neither of which is worth a damn. Fribbles, both of them." He stared at Silas, a calculating look in his eyes. "Your father despised you for what you did, you know," he said, the words designed to strike their mark, though Silas did not show a reaction. "But I wouldn't have done. I admire you. You're not afraid to get your hands dirty if the situation demands it. That takes guts. I think perhaps we are alike in that regard."

Privately, Silas thought if he was anything like this man he'd walk into the sea without delay, but he held his tongue and did his best to look flattered by the remark.

"Thank you for saying so. I'm afraid my father was not a man of your… worldly wisdom. He never left England in his life, never saw the need. Yet you have travelled widely, I believe?"

Ulceby shrugged, noncommittal. "I have seen more than most men, I suppose."

"Including India, I take it?" Silas prompted, gesturing to the figure on the mantelpiece.

There was a pause. "Yes, I spent some time there."

"It must have been fascinating." He leaned forward, hoping his interest would get the man to open up and let something slip. "I confess I've always harboured a love of adventure, a desire to see such far-off lands. Such a vast and remarkable country. What was it like?"

Silas watched with interest as the man grimaced. "Too damn hot and full of heathens. A godless country. I advise you to stay put. Once you've seen one elephant, you've seen them all," he added with a sneer.

Silas swallowed down his ire at the man's ability to dismiss a country and culture that he'd read about with wonder. The earl seemed more objectionable with every passing second, but he tried again.

"When was that?"

The earl waved a dismissive hand, looking rather impatient. "I have no idea. Fifteen years ago, perhaps? Why the interest?"

There was a suspicious glint in the man's eyes and Silas spoke with care, knowing he needed to tread carefully. "No reason, only… the little silver object you had in your hand yesterday rather looked Indian to my untrained eye." It was a total shot in the dark, the idea having only occurred to him at that moment, but he knew he'd struck gold before the earl even replied.

"It is," the earl said smoothly. "It's a good luck charm, a token I picked up over there and keep for sentimental reasons. It's Kali's trishul, Kali being one of their pagan gods."

It was a lie. Silas felt it in his gut. Oh, he believed the description was apt enough, and perhaps it was a good luck charm, to Lucia, but not to this man. For the Earl of Ulceby, whoever wielded that trident, or trishul, or whatever it may be… they were his enemy.

"Do you have it?" Ulceby demanded, extending his hand.

Silas hesitated, very aware of the tiny silver object nestled in his waistcoat pocket.

"I don't," he said, spreading his hands out regretfully. "I'm afraid I didn't realise its significance. I can't actually remember what I did with it. It maybe I left it at St Clair's place. Would you like me to ask?"

The earl waved his hand, dismissing his offer. "It's of no matter," he said, the look in his eyes saying otherwise. "Though, if you happen to come across it—"

"Of course," Silas said, getting to his feet. The desire to be out of the man's presence was a forceful one, the weight of gilt and belligerence in this house so palpable it made his skin prickle with unease. "I am glad to see you are in good health, Ulceby. Do let me know if there's ever anything I can do for you."

It was a calculated remark. Silas was believed to be a wealthy man and, as of yet, no rumours of his late father's uncertain finances had reached the ears of the *ton*. For all Ulceby knew, he was as rich as Croesus. Which he might well be, if ever he had the time to sort out his affairs.

They shook hands, Ulceby giving his thin fingers as though he was granting Silas a boon of great honour, and Silas made good his escape.

***

Lucia clutched at the bedclothes, her breath coming too fast, her chest tight as the nightmare dug its claws in harder, pulling her into the dark.

She'd been asleep that night, too, on the ornate four-poster, covered over with netting to keep the mosquitoes at bay, the perfumed smoke of agarbatties drifting into her dreams… until she'd been awakened in the dead of night and told to run away.

"*Dharani… Nani maa*," she called, her voice no longer her own, but that of a child, high pitched and filled with terror.

"Run, Aashini. Run and hide. Go to the indigo fields and don't look back!"

"No, *Nani maa,"* she cried, her hands clutching at the woman's sari, the material bunched in her small fists. "I cannot. I'm afraid. You must come with me."

A sob caught at her throat, as her beloved Dharani pushed her away, urging her to go on alone.

"I will come, Aashini, I will come as soon as it is safe. But you must go. Please *bhanvaraa.* Now! *Go*!"

A push to the small of her back had made her stumble forwards, made her gasp in shock, but she'd run then, run until she heard aggressive voices behind her, and she'd turned, hearing Dharani's voice, strong and angry, and the sound of a scuffle, of a hand striking flesh. For a moment she'd hesitated, wanting to return, but then Dharani's voice had travelled down the darkened hall, the power of it raising the hairs on the back of her neck as she swore revenge on the man who threatened the life of a child.

Run, Aashini.

The words echoed in her mind, and the little girl that had been Aashini, that *was* Lucia, ran as hard as she could. She ran into the night, clutching a well-loved rag doll as tightly as she could, running towards the fields where other terrors awaited a small child.

The dark had seemed a living thing, pressing down on her, promising there were snakes littering the dusty ground and tigers prowling at every turn. Too terrified to turn back, she'd had no choice but to run, to run and hide, cowering in a field of blue flowers and clutching a little cloth doll to her heart as the night lasted for an eternity.

***

Lucia sat bolt upright in the bed, a scream caught in her throat, her skin cold and damp with terror. She took a shuddering breath, trying to still her heart as the oppressive atmosphere of the dream lingered in the dim light of her bedroom. She could smell the indigo flowers even now, their scent pungent on the heated night air, her stomach clenched.

Flinging back the covers, she got up and hurried to the windows. Tugging back the heavy curtains she let the sunlight flood in to chase away the dark. She leaned against the windowsill, her forehead pressed to the cool glass as she tried to get a hold on herself.

"Courage, Aashini," she murmured, and then started as a knock at her bedroom door sounded.

"Yes?" she called out, striving for calm.

"It's me, Lucia," Matilda said. "May I come in?"

Rubbing a hand over her face and taking a moment to smooth her hair, Lucia ran and snatched up her wrap, tugging it on. "Yes, of course," she called, trying her best to sound cheerful and carefree.

Matilda hurried inside, a gleeful look in her eyes. "Lord Cavendish is downstairs," she said, her excitement palpable. "He wants to see you."

Oh, no.

The last thing she needed was to see the wretched man. She knew he suspected that she had somehow brought on the earl's attack. He'd seen Kali's trishul, she was sure, and now he'd not rest before he knew what it was, what it meant.

Damn him.

"Well, dear?" Matilda gave her a curious look, realising she was unwilling to see him. "What do I say? Will you go?"

Lucia looked up, apprehending she'd been silent, staring into space.

"I…."

The desire to send him away, to say she would not see him, was overwhelming. She didn't want to face him, didn't want to lie, but she didn't want to tell him the truth either. He wouldn't let her be. She knew it.

"Yes," she said, sounding a deal more decisive than she was feeling. Best get it over with though. "Yes, I'll see him, though he must wait for me to dress."

"Of course, I already told him that much. He didn't seem to mind," Matilda added, winking at her as she hurried away. "I'll send Sarah to help you."

Lucia forced a smile to her face and pushed down the desire to escape via the window. This had to be done. She must face him. Perhaps she could annoy him, make him so angry with her that he would leave in revulsion and forget about her. The idea had some merit, she thought, though the feeling of regret that filled her chest at giving him a disgust of her was an unsettling thing.

Fool, she cursed. *He's not for you.*

Lucia dressed with care, taking her time and refusing to rush. If he wanted to see her, let him wait until she was ready. The possibility that she was just delaying the inevitable occurred to her, but she refused to consider it. She was keeping the upper hand, that was all, and putting him in his place.

She was.

By the time she entered the front parlour, Lucia's stomach was tied in a knot, though her nerves were a little soothed by the look on Lord Cavendish's face. He wore the dazed expression of a man she could wrap around her finger and manipulate to do her bidding if she chose, no matter what it might be. If that look had been upon any other man of her acquaintance, she would have believed it.

Lord Cavendish, however, that was another matter.

She'd worn one of her best gowns, knowing she needed all the help she could get. It was a startling shade of green and made her think of an English springtime, of the first haze of leaves upon the trees and the sound of a cuckoo calling over and over from woodland filled with ancient oaks.

Such foreign sounds they'd been once, yet now, how familiar.

"Miss de Feria," he said, his blue eyes full of warmth, his voice echoing their intimacy, despite his use of her full name.

"My, Lord Cavendish, how formal you are today. I had quite grown used to you taking liberties with my name."

He smiled then, that pirate smile that made something in her stomach pitch and lurch like a ship on stormy seas.

"I was striving to be on my best behaviour," he said, looking a little sheepish, though there was a glint in his eyes. "I am happy to continue to take liberties, Lucia, believe me. I need little encouragement."

"You need no encouragement at all," she replied with a tart smile that only made him grin wider.

"True."

He chuckled and crossed the room to stand before her, taking her hand. Suddenly Lucia wasn't so sure she hadn't been right to consider escaping via the window as his large hands encompassed hers, trapping it between them. They were warm and rough, calloused from years of hard work, and they sent a shiver of pure pleasure rolling over her skin.

Winded, she looked up at him, trying to find some acerbic comment, something to cut him down to size, to make him look foolish and uncouth, but… but she got caught in eyes the colour of the indigo flowers she'd dreamed of so often.

"Lucia," he said, her name a soft breath upon his lips.

For a moment she wanted to correct him, to give him the name given her as a girl, but she didn't. Couldn't.

He reached out and one of those hands rose to her face, to trace the curve of her jaw, the featherlike touch making her shiver again, longing coursing through her.

Stop it, she told herself. *Stop wanting what you can't have. It's impossible.*

Yet it didn't seem impossible, not with him standing so close to her, touching her with such reverence. It seemed inevitable, inescapable, and she raised her head, answering the unspoken question in his eyes.

He lowered his mouth and she gasped at the first press of his lips against hers. She was unstable, her senses rocked, that fleeting touch enough to scatter her thoughts, her ambitions. It made her wonder what life might be like if she had taken another path.

His hands went to her waist, sliding around her back as he pulled her closer and she moved to him without protest. She clutched at his lapels as her balance seemed uncertain, her knees not as willing to support her as usual.

"Beautiful Lucia," he murmured, pressing kisses to the corner of her mouth, her jaw, hot little touches of his mouth against her throat as her breath became erratic. His lips returned to hers, his tongue a shocking surge of heat against her as he licked into her mouth.

She made an innocent sound of surprise but did not push him away, too intrigued to stop him, to ask what he was doing. He would show her, she thought, with a rather hysterical bubble of laughter rising in her chest.

He did show her, illustrating the delicious slide and caress she did her best to imitate as her body came alive. Well, this was the danger Dharani had always warned her of. She'd said Anna-Marie lived for this, for this feeling.

"*It's dangerous, Aashini. Men make too many promises they can't keep.*"

She'd ignored Dharani's warning once before, only to discover how right she was, but that time had been nothing like this….

Those kisses had been pale, insipid, nothing compared to his.

It was like comparing a warm day in Norfolk to the searing heat of Calcutta, a heat so intense you felt it could peel the skin from your bones like the flesh from a roasted fish.

Maybe Anna-Marie was onto something.

He kissed until she was dazed and giddy, and then he held her, saying nothing, just holding her close, as though he could do so all day. Forever. How she wanted him to!

It was the strangest thing, just being still in his arms. Her head rested on his chest, the fine cloth of his coat soft beneath her cheek. One hand still clutched at his lapel, the other lay against his chest, tracing patterns on his silken waistcoat. Just for a moment she felt safe, cherished, instead of like a fallen leaf tossed about on the breeze, always at the will of others, never settling, with nothing solid to cling to, no roots to anchor her.

"I would like you to trust me, Lucia," he said, the sincerity of his words making her close her eyes against the anguish that burned there, hot tears she refused to allow, stinging.

The moment of peace and happiness had passed, as she'd known it would. She'd not get it back again. Time to move on.

"Trust you with what?" she said with a false little laugh, giving him the benefit of a raised eyebrow as she tried to move away from him, as though he was merely flirting and not offering her more.

His arms tightened around her, his gaze on her with an expression which dared her to make light of his words.

Silly man, of course she dared.

"With my heart, perhaps?" she said with a teasing lilt. "Or were you thinking of my maidenhead? What price are you offering?"

A flash of anger and hurt heated the blue of his gaze.

"Don't do that," he said, his fingers hard upon her now. "Don't pretend you think I'm insulting you when you know I am not, *would* not. I admitted I was wrong, terribly wrong, and I wish I had never spoken so."

"Perhaps you weren't, though, my lord," Lucia said, hating herself for saying it. "My price has risen so high I'd be a fool not to consider it."

He stared at her, with such intensity that her skin seared with the force of his gaze. His jaw was rigid with tension, and then he let out a breath. "You're lying. You'd not consider it for a moment. You'd never put yourself under a man's power, unless—"

"Unless I was desperate?" she asked, giving him a sweet smile.

He moved, his hands framing her face, his touch gentle, reverent. "Is that true?"

She tried to look away from him, furious with herself for the tears that prickled behind her eyes, tears he saw. *Damn him*. He made her weak, made her doubt herself. She couldn't allow it.

His thumbs stroked her cheeks, such a tender gesture that a tear spilled over, sliding down her face.

"Lucia," he said again, her name a whisper of warmth against her lips. "Let me protect you. Marry me, love. I know you're in trouble, and I know Ulceby is at the heart of it. He's a dangerous man, darling, and one I don't doubt deserves retribution. Let me help you. Whatever it is, I swear… I *will* help you, and I will keep you safe."

Lucia's breath caught in her throat, torn between the shock of his proposal and the terror of him realising she meant to take her revenge on the earl.

If the temptation to trust in him had been tantalising, the temptation to accept his offer was doubly so. She would be safe, with the protection of his name, his wealth. Even if she failed in her goal, there would be safety. Except there wouldn't, not when he discovered the truth. He would hate her for her lies, and he'd be a source of ridicule. Likely he'd have the marriage annulled, it would be easy enough for him to do, and then she'd have that indignity to bear too. No. She could not subject either of them to that.

She stared up at him, curling her hands about his wrists. "You don't know me, my lord, and you cannot protect me."

Lucia pulled his hands away from her face, seeing the frustration in his eyes as she did so.

"You underestimate me," he said, sounding annoyed as she put space between them.

A little huff of laughter escaped her, and she smiled at him.

"No," she said gently. "You underestimate me, and exactly what it is you would be getting involved in."

"I don't care!" The words were sharp and reckless, and she felt a stab of pain at the sound because she'd heard them before, spoken in almost the exact same tone of voice.

She saw the truth in his eyes, but she thought she'd seen that same look before, too.

He was lying to himself and to her.

He would care, once he knew.

Lucia waited, wondering what he would do next, and she was not entirely surprised when he took the little silver trishul from his pocket and held it out to her.

"I know it's Indian. It represents the goddess Kali's trishul. You put it in Edgar Bindley's pocket, and when Ulceby saw it he had an apoplexy. You drew the same thing in his study the night of the ball. It means something to Ulceby, and to you. You're going to take your revenge on him, but for what, Lucia?" His voice was hard and angry now, yet filled with concern and Lucia swallowed hard, appalled that he'd already figured out so much. "You were at the ball and the garden party, you flirted with his son, but neither of them knows you, so what the bloody hell is going on?"

Lucia turned away from him, walking to the window and staring out. She trembled, sweating though her skin felt like ice.

"I would like you to leave now," she said, fighting to keep her voice calm and even.

"The hell I will!"

He crossed the room and took her arm forcing her to face him once more. She gasped at the look in his eyes.

"He'll destroy you, Lucia," he said, such pain behind the words that her throat grew tight. "Please… *please,* love. Tell me, confide in me. I won't let you down if you would only trust me."

Lucia let out a breath of laughter and closed her eyes.

“Such promises men make,” she whispered. “Promises spoken with such fervour, such love. They’re so beguiling. They make you believe.” She opened her eyes to find him staring down at her and when she spoke again, the words were cold and hard. “They’re an illusion. There is no safety, no one to protect me. Only myself. I won’t repeat the mistakes of the past, Lord Cavendish. That would be foolish.”

She strode to the door, not looking back.

“I hope you can see yourself out,” she said, and closed the door behind her.

Chapter 10

Dear Matilda,

Nate has made a list of all the most eligible men of his acquaintance. Do come and visit and look at the list, then we can arrange a series of dinner parties to introduce you to them. I just know we can find you a good man if we put our minds to it!

—Excerpt of a letter from Mrs Alice Hunt to Miss Matilda Hunt.

12th July 1814. Bond Street, London.

"Lord Cavendish! Lord Cavendish… it is you!"

Silas frowned, his hurried footsteps slowing as he turned, irritated to be accosted in the street. In truth, he'd been irritated and bad tempered for days now; ever since the beautiful and infuriating Miss de Feria had summarily rejected his proposal.

The sight of Mrs Edina Manning, society hostess and glamorous widow, hailing him with such enthusiasm, did not improve his temper. He forced a smile to his face and endeavoured to be polite. In truth, he liked Edina. She could be a bitch, but she didn't suffer fools and had a tendency towards ruthless honesty, qualities that Silas could admire.

They had dallied together on and off over the past years. Nothing serious, but an occasional physical interlude that had satisfied them both. She was an experienced woman, a little older than himself, and she knew what she wanted, and how to get it.

"Silas, darling," she purred, once she'd gotten his attention. "How lovely to see you. You're looking well."

"Edina," he replied, smiling at her. "And you look as beautiful as ever, but that goes without saying."

"Flatterer," she said, laughing, a pleasing, low and throaty sound. "Now, you wretched devil, I've invited you to two separate dinner parties and you've turned both down. I warn you now, you are about to get a third, and I shall not take no for an answer."

Silas sighed and shook his head. "You know as well as I do that I cannot abide small talk and polite conversation. I would only say something outrageous and offend everyone."

Edina's dark eyebrows rose. "Why on earth do you think I want you to come?" she demanded, making him laugh. "I adore outrageousness, as you well know. Oh, do come, Silas? I'll allow you to bring your own guests."

Silas frowned, considering that. Lucia was avoiding him, cancelling her appearance to a ball he knew she'd been going to attend, as well as several other events.

"Very well," he said, even though he knew it would give her a juicy morsel to set tongues wagging. "I'll come, if you invite Miss de Feria and Miss Hunt."

A knowing smile curved over her mouth as she looked up at him. "Ah, I see, that's how the land, lies is it? And which of the lovely young ladies is the one you are pursuing, I wonder? Or is it both?"

"I'm sure you'll figure it out," he said, winking at her.

"Wretch," she said, shaking her head and looking mournful. "I should despise you for inviting two young beauties, for how shall I compete?"

He laughed at the obvious ploy for a compliment. "Oh, take heart, Edina, you have many far more handsome beaus and more devoted ones. I don't think you require the entire male portion of the *ton* at your feet."

"Don't I?" she said with a little sniff, though laughter danced in her eyes. "That just shows what you know." She gave him a shameless wink and began to walk away. "Very well, consider it done, odious man. I'll send the invitations out and count on your attendance."

With a sigh, Silas watched her go, and then carried on his way.

***

12th July 1814. Meeting of the Peculiar Ladies, Upper Walpole Street, London.

"Are you quite well, Lucia? You're very quiet."

Lucia looked up to see Ruth watching her with concern.

"Oh, yes, quite well," Lucia said at once, striving for a smile she was not feeling. "I… I'm not sleeping well, that's all."

That was an understatement, she thought with a sigh. Thoughts of Lord Cavendish consumed her nights and her days, memories of his kiss and his proposal, his promise to keep her safe. She'd told herself to forget it, to forget him, but neither option had been successful.

"You poor dear," Ruth said, frowning and taking her hand. "Don't worry, I have just the thing in my medicine cupboard."

Lucia smiled as Ruth hurried off. She was a no-nonsense, capable young woman who seemed to manage her father's vast household with the ease of someone much more experienced. Nothing ever seemed to daunt her. She would make the perfect *ton* wife, except of course for the fact her father was of the merchant class. This alone made her quite as unmarriageable as Matilda, or any of the rest of them.

Turning her attention back to the group of young ladies, Lucia considered each one in turn. Unusually, the married ladies, Alice and Prue, were absent today, shrinking their numbers, though there was no lack of animated conversation. She felt a rush of affection for them as she looked about the remaining women. They all had their problems and peculiarities, but their friendships strengthened them.

Matilda was there, of course, and Lucia knew her story well enough. Kitty, with her Irish heritage, was an odd mixture of insecurity and outrageous courage. Prue's cousin, Minerva, had seemed a rather vacuous creature at first meeting, but Lucia sensed there was a kind and romantic heart inside her pretty and outwardly shallow exterior. Harriet, with her fierce intelligence and rather prosaic way of looking at the world, had seemed a difficult girl to like. She was something of a loner and held herself a little apart, but her attempts to befriend Kitty had shown a desire to join in and make friends.

Bonnie, by contrast, was a bundle of energy and too vivacious not to open her mouth and put her foot in it with startling regularity. She was capable of shocking lapses in judgement, as well as great warmth and kindness, and was impossible not to like.

Miss Jemima Fernside was here today, and Lucia studied her with interest. She only occasionally came to the meetings and Ruth had confided to her that the young woman's family were shabby gentility, existing on the fringes of the *ton* by their fingertips. Her gown was faded, and had quite obviously been made over several times.

What a disparate group they were, yet Lucia saw friendships and attachments all around her that she felt would stand the test of time. If only she could rely on those attachments herself.

She wondered what would happen if she stood up and told them her real name, her true heritage. Would they revile her, or accept her? She just didn't know. Believing in them and in Silas was too dangerous; it was the road to heartbreak and disappointment, and even ruin.

She was too afraid to take the risk. Not again.

Lucia sighed and tried to take an interest in the conversation. Harriet had become quite animated about a book she'd bought earlier in the week. It was called *Waverly* and was by a new and anonymous author, writing about a young man caught up in the Jacobite uprising. Although she had only read a little of the novel, Harriet was quite obviously entranced and prepared to wax lyrical about it indefinitely.

"So," Matilda said to Lucia, leaning in to whisper in her ear. "Shall we accept Mrs Manning's invitation?"

Lucia shrugged. She needed to occupy herself, it was true. It was all well and good avoiding Lord Cavendish wherever possible, but sitting at home only made her miserable and gave her far too much time to dwell. What was the point of avoiding him and then spending hours daydreaming about his kiss, his kindness… his ardent desire to keep her safe?

She sighed.

"What do you think?" she asked.

Matilda grinned. "Well, she's a rather daring woman, and she's bound to have an interesting mix of guests. Invitations are quite sort after, so… I think we should go. Better than moping about and sighing over Lord Cavendish," she added with sympathy.

"I am not moping about over Lord Cavendish," Lucia muttered, sending Matilda an outraged glare, even though she was quite correct.

"Of course not, dear," Matilda said, patting her hand so condescendingly it suggested she didn't believe a word. "So, I'll accept, then?"

Lucia huffed and reached for a cream scone, one of many such delicacies Ruth always provided for their meetings. "Oh, very well," she said, knowing she sounded ungracious.

"Excellent." Matilda beamed at her. "Just the excuse I needed to buy a new gown. That's the afternoon taken care of, then."

Looking more than pleased with the arrangements, Matilda surveyed the coffee table, which was laden with cakes and biscuits of every variety, and picked up a jam tart between thumb and forefinger.

"What do you think, Lucia?" Harriet asked, her earnest gaze fixed on her as she pushed her spectacles up her nose.

Lucia froze with the cream scone in her mouth, but didn't waste another moment to bite into it. She gave an apologetic shrug, gesturing to her full mouth as an excuse not to answer, as she didn't have the slightest clue what they'd been talking about.

"Oh, well. You, then, Matilda," Harriet went on.

Lucia almost choked on her scone as Matilda pinched her in retaliation. She smiled nonetheless, knowing how much she would miss this, this sense of belonging—of acceptance—that she had never known before in her life. Except that it was built on an illusion, on the façade that was Lucia de Feria, and she'd do well not to forget that.

***

14th July 1814. The home of Mrs Edwina Manning, Old Burlington Street, London.

Lucia looked across the carriage at Matilda and smiled. "You were perfectly correct about that gown. It looks dazzling on you."

Matilda beamed at her. "I know," she said, making Lucia snort with laughter. "Well, it does," Matilda replied, pretending to look indignant. "I'm not one for hiding my light under a bushel, dear."

"Indeed not," Lucia replied, shaking her head and smiling.

She'd had doubts about the gown when she'd seen it. Grey silk was not a colour she would have chosen under any circumstances, but she had to concede that the pale, ice grey and severe cut suited

Matilda's blonde, blue-eyed beauty to perfection. Although it had not been by design, her own sapphire blue gown complimented it quite nicely, and she thought they would make quite an entrance together.

"Have you ever met Mrs Manning before?" Lucia asked as the carriage turned onto Bruton Street. In fact, Mrs Manning only lived about fifteen minutes' walk from South Audley Street, but it wouldn't do to turn up on foot.

"Once," Matilda said, nodding. "She's quite a character. I shouldn't like to be on the wrong side of her, as she's got a sharp tongue and the wit to wield it to effect."

Lucia pondered that as the carriage rumbled on. "I wonder who else she's invited."

"Well, we are about to find out," Matilda said with a grin, as they approached their destination.

The six-storey house was an imposing building, and suggested Mr Manning had left his wife very comfortable when he'd departed the world. The impressive interior boasted a wealth of oak panelling, decorative carvings and mouldings, and the hand-carved staircase was on a grand scale.

Mrs Manning herself came to greet them, wreathed in smiles. A voluptuous woman with mahogany curls tumbling about her shoulders, she exuded the confidence and ease of a woman at home in her own skin, and well aware of her own worth.

Lucia batted down an unwelcome stab of envy and did her best to look relaxed.

"My, but don't you make an exquisite picture," Mrs Manning said, shaking her head as she stood back a little to regard them both. "Ah, I remember what it was to have the world at my feet in such a manner."

Matilda and Lucia exchanged glances, as Lucia knew neither of them thought they had anything of the sort. Mrs Manning caught the look and gave a soft laugh.

“Darlings, you can overcome any difficulty if you have beauty and brains. Make a man want you enough and he’ll move heaven and earth to give you what you want… even a ring.” She winked at them, gaining a laugh from Matilda.

“I shall bear that in mind, Mrs Manning, thank you,” she said, as the lady in question led them through to meet the other guests.

To Lucia’s relief it appeared to be a small and intimate dinner, though her ease was short lived.

“I believe you know Lord Cavendish,” Mrs Manning said, a look in her eyes that suggested to Lucia she knew damn well she was putting the cat among the pigeons.

“Indeed,” Matilda said, greeting him with a warm smile. “How good it is to see you again, my lord.”

Lucia inclined her head in greeting and tried to still her heart, which thudded uncomfortably in her chest. *Oh, good heavens.* Now she had to endure an entire evening in his company. Somehow, she just knew he’d be sitting beside her.

“This handsome young fellow is dying to make your acquaintance, too,” Mrs Manning said, bringing forward a smiling gentleman with light brown hair and hazel eyes. He was indeed handsome, with an easy-going air about him. “This is Mr David Burton. Such an interesting man! He owns half the mills in the country, you know,” Mrs Manning said, giving him a look that made the fellow blush a little. “Oh, do excuse me, I believe more guests have arrived.”

“Burton,” Lord Cavendish said, to Lucia’s intense relief turning the weight of his gaze elsewhere. “How are you? It must be a year, at least?”

"Indeed, my lord," Mr Burton replied, smiling. "Though I am happy that our business interests together seem to go on apace."

"As am I," the viscount replied dryly. "However, we must not talk business, or our company will desert us for more convivial surroundings."

"You think us uninterested in business?" Lucia remarked, with an edge to the question she knew neither of the men missed. Of course, she *ought* not to be interested in such subjects. Any woman knew the first rule of catching a man was to feign stupidity.

"No, Miss de Feria," Lord Cavendish replied, smiling at her in such a way that she felt herself heat all over. "I think you uninterested in *my* business."

"Mr Burton," Matilda said in a rush, as the atmosphere between them was becoming increasingly charged. "Do tell me about your mills…."

Lucia could not help but smile; the man was looking at Matilda as though he was in the presence of a divine being.

"I… I should be delighted to tell you anything you wish to know," he said, sounding a little breathless.

He offered Matilda his arm and Lucia watched as he escorted her about the grand room.

"A conquest has been made, I think," Lord Cavendish said, smiling.

"What's he like?" Lucia asked him, in part to keep the conversation from drifting into dangerous waters, and in part because the man looked like a devoted puppy and she hoped Matilda might have just found the good man she'd been looking for.

"Decent," he said, giving her a reassuring nod. "Intelligent and with a good heart. Wealthy. Your friend could do a great deal worse, though he's a self-made man which would make most of the women I know run screaming in the opposite direction."

"Then they're fools," Lucia said, meaning it, not realising she was being provoking until she saw the flash of jealousy in Lord Cavendish's eyes.

"You have an interest there?" he asked, and though his tone was nonchalant enough she wasn't fooled.

For a moment she toyed with the idea of taunting him, but she couldn't do it.

"No," she said softly. "I only want to see Matilda happy."

There was a taut silence before he spoke again. "And what about you, Lucia?" he asked, the words pitched low. "Have you thought any more about what I asked you?"

Words crowded in her throat. The desire to tell him that she'd thought of nothing else was almost overwhelming, but that would be as cruel as pretending an interest elsewhere.

"No," she said, though she could not disguise the sadness in her voice as she turned away from him to survey the room, just as Mrs Manning returned with the last of her guests… the Marquess of Montagu.

Chapter 11

Why must I always want more than is good for me? I ruined a perfectly happy home by falling in love with a man I ought to have known was not for me.

His promises to love me and keep me safe no matter what all crumbled to dust the moment he knew the truth. He couldn't get free of me fast enough. Why would I believe another man making the exact same promises?

Why am I such a fool as to even consider repeating the same mistake? Yet I dream of it, all the same.

—Excerpt of an entry from Señorita Lucia de Feria, to her diary.

14th July 1814. The home of Mrs Edwina Manning, Old Burlington Street, London.

There were twelve guests, and Lucia's worst fears were realised as the marquess led Mrs Manning into dinner.

Mrs Manning sat at the head of the table, with her brother—a florid man in his forties, with a jovial manner—assuming the role of host at the opposite end. The marquess naturally took the position of guest of honour to Mrs Manning's right, and the Countess Culpepper—wife of the Earl of Culpepper—sat opposite him on her left. It appeared her husband was off in the country on business. She didn't look like she minded.

Beside her sat Lord Cavendish, and beside him, Lucia. Poor Matilda was little better off and looked flushed and rather like a hen cornered by foxes at finding herself between Montagu and the adoring gaze of Mr Burton.

Well, this should be entertaining, Lucia thought, with her stomach tying itself in knots at the idea.

To her surprise, she found a Mr Henshaw on her left, who turned out to be Kitty's uncle, and Kitty herself sat beside Mr Burton. The poor girl looked anxious and out of her depth, and as if she wanted to exclaim with relief on seeing two familiar faces. The far end of the table was completed with a beaming Mr Richards—he who had so kindly rescued Matilda when she'd hurt her ankle—and a rather sour faced Miss Craven.

Something of an heiress, Miss Craven had been heralded as one of the diamonds of the season and was usually a vivacious young lady, but Lucia had heard it whispered that she had designs on catching herself a grand title—like perhaps a marquisate. Seeing Montagu at the far end of the table with Matilda at his side had to be sticking in her throat somewhat.

It was by no accident, however. The young woman had been heard a few nights ago to utter an unguarded and spectacularly stupid slight directed at Mrs Manning. She had disparaged the woman as being old and worn, and no kind of rival to her youth and beauty.

No doubt the lure of an invitation to a dinner where the marquess was to attend had been too good to refuse. Being seated as far away from him as it was possible to get, and beside Mrs Manning's good-natured bore of a brother—who would monopolise the conversation all night—was likely not what she'd had in mind. Miss Craven looked sulky and embarrassed by the arrangement, having realised too late her hostess' intent.

Mrs Manning, by contrast, looked to be thoroughly enjoying the evening.

As revenge went, it was subtle enough, but effective. Lucia felt a little sorry for the young woman, who was no doubt spoiled and indulged and didn't know better, but would bounce back and, perhaps, watch her tongue a little in the future. Besides, Mr Richards was a charming companion and—if she had any sense—one she would enjoy.

The meal began, and the table—already groaning under the weight of dazzling crystal and silver and the finest Limoges porcelain—soon looked ready to buckle as a bewildering array of dishes were brought in. Herb soup, tongue and turnips accompanied breast of veal and a platter of roast chickens, neck of venison, mutton, stewed red cabbage, and a boiled trout.

Lucia, who had felt unequal to swallowing anything from the moment she'd set eyes on Lord Cavendish, suppressed a sigh of dismay. Taking a small portion of soup and praying she'd not be accused of insulting her hostess if she didn't finish it, she hoped for the best.

"How have you been?"

Lucia looked around to find Lord Cavendish watching her.

"Fine," she replied with a tight smile, wishing her usual capacity for small talk would return to her. Under normal circumstances, she'd always been able to laugh and flirt and pretend enjoyment even when she was bored to tears. The ability seemed to have vanished ever since she'd met the infuriating and intriguing man at her side.

"You've been avoiding me."

Despite her best intentions, Lucia rolled her eyes at him. "Well, of course I have," she muttered, before sighing and softening her tone. "It's for the best."

"For whom?" he demanded, his frustration evident though the question was mild enough.

"Both of us."

"I won't give up, Lucia."

The words slid under her skin, warming her, easing the pain in her heart, which was ridiculous. He was the one causing her pain. She'd had a perfectly good plan. Make her mark on the *ton* so she was too well known to disappear without remark, and survive until her twenty-first birthday. On that day a scandal the like of which the *ton* hadn't seen in a generation would unfold, and anyone associated her would get burned.

She'd told herself she didn't care, that this was about her and no one else, but people kept insinuating themselves into her life and her affections, no matter how hard she tried to keep them at a distance.

Matilda should survive it, but only as her reputation was already tarnished. So, it would do her no good, but no serious harm. Lord Cavendish, however… people would mock him for wanting to have married her if that got about, and she cared for him too much to let that happen.

So, she would ensure it never did.

***

Matilda couldn't breathe.

Mr David Burton had wasted no time in making his admiration of her plain. He seemed to be everything she had ever hoped for in a man, as if God himself had been taking notes.

Good-looking, interesting, intelligent, wealthy, and above all… kind. You could tell all this from the look in his eyes when he spoke, she thought, the respectful way he sought her opinion and actually listened. Not only that, he seemed interested in her thoughts. He was effusive in his flattery, but in a manner that was so endearing that it was not smothering. Charming and urbane, he would make any woman—any woman with an ounce of sense—a husband she could take pride in. Of course, that excluded most of the women of the *ton*, as they could not see past the fact he worked for a living.

Yet that was something Matilda thought was in his favour.

She had suffered at the hands of the *ton*, and so would he. Perhaps it would liberate her to turn her back on it entirely, which she would effectively do if she considered marrying him.

Not that he'd asked, but from the comments he'd dropped so far it appeared he was looking for a wife—and he well knew the circumstances of her fall from grace.

It wasn't this charming, eligible man who was keeping the breath from her lungs, though.

That the instigator of her fall from grace was seated on her left….

Yes. That would do it.

She'd tried her best not to notice him, but the moment he'd entered the room she'd felt his presence. As ridiculous as she told herself that was, it had been true. The sudden shiver of anticipation over her skin, the flutter of a thousand butterflies in her stomach: Matilda had recognised the sensation before she'd even turned and seen him arrive.

He took her breath away.

Tall and lean, and as unreachable as the moon, he was like no other man in the room. The *ton* murmured of the power he held, of the influence he wielded, and that aura clung to him. There was no warmth in his expression and an indefinable air of danger clung to him, like a beautiful big cat you could only admire from a distance. Perhaps a white tiger that appeared tamed and domesticated. Get too close and he'd likely rip your throat out.

His white-blond hair and those unusual silver-grey eyes only added to the air of unattainability, as if such beauty was reserved for the gods and too perilous for mere mortals to enjoy. He carried himself with grace, and with a bearing of authority that made everyone in the room look to him as he entered, their conversations stopping.

Since they'd sat down, the marquess had been in conversation with both Mrs Manning and the Countess Culpepper, though conversation was perhaps stretching the description as both women vied to flirt with him and the marquess rarely spoke to encourage them.

He didn't need to.

Matilda tried not to notice, giving her attention over to Mr Burton. It ought to have been a good deal easier than it was.

"I understand that Miss de Feria is living with you at the moment, Miss Hunt?"

"Yes, indeed, and I was never more pleased with her company. My brother, for whom I kept house, has recently married and I swore I would not be that dreadful relation one can never get rid of, no matter how you try."

Mr Burton laughed, a warm, merry sound that made her smile. "I find it hard to believe such a description could ever be levelled at you. I'm sure they miss you."

"Oh, yes," Matilda said with an airy wave of her hand. "Because all newlyweds are so eager to have their sister underfoot at every moment of the day."

"Very well, I grant you that much, but now tell me your brother hasn't begged you to return to them."

Matilda gave him a wry smile. "He has, of course, but he is the very best of brothers and I love him too well to accept."

"He is the proprietor of *Hunter's*, I believe?"

"Yes," Matilda agreed, reaching for her wine and taking a small sip, though the temptation to drain it was strong. "Are you a member?"

There was another burst of laughter that made the corners of her mouth tug upwards.

"No, indeed. I'm afraid when one has worked as hard as I have to earn his fortune, well, it makes me in less of a rush to part with it on the roll of a dice, put it that way."

"How sensible you are," Matilda said, with genuine admiration. As her own father had sent his family to ruin with his gambling debts, that was an admirable quality to her mind.

"Oh, damned with faint praise," he said, shaking his head with a mournful expression. "That means you think me a dull dog."

"No!" Matilda protested, laughing. "I assure you it does not. If you know anything of my background, as you apparently do, then you'll know I'm sincere."

He smiled at her then, holding her gaze, his eyes warm and intent as he lowered his voice.

"As am I, Miss Hunt."

His intimate tone was full of sincerity, and she knew he would court her if she encouraged his advances. The breathless sensation only increased as panic rose in her chest.

The evening wore on and the conversation grew ever more animated as the wine flowed.

Unless you were the Marquess of Montagu.

Despite doing her level best to ignore him completely, Matilda could not help but notice he drank little and spoke less, only adding enough to the flow of chatter to ensure he wasn't insulting his hostess. When he spoke, he was charming and urbane, but he did not turn his attention to Matilda, for which she was grateful. Except she had the disquieting sense he was paying a great deal of attention to the conversation she was having with Mr Burton.

Mr Burton proved himself to be a wonderful dining companion. He was full of amusing stories but never dominated the conversation wherever possible; he spoke only to Matilda, asking her endless questions about herself, her interests, and her hopes for the future. His attention flattered and warmed her, and she found herself enjoying his company, and hating herself for enjoying even more the fact that the marquess well knew it.

Mrs Manning had suggested that their convivial little group—or at least those at her end of the table—should visit Green Park to see the Revolving Temple of Concord. The apparently impressive, though temporary, structure had been built to celebrate the victory over Napoleon and would culminate in a huge fireworks display on the first of August. As most of the *ton* would escape the heat of the city in the following weeks, retreating to their country estates, Mrs Manning proposed it would be a lovely way to bring the season to a close.

"What say you, Lord Cavendish?" she asked, turning the full force of her magnetic charisma towards him.

"I am at your disposal, naturally," he said with a charming smile, though there was no one at the table in any doubt that his attention was all for Lucia.

"It sounds a wonderful idea," Mr Burton agreed with his easy smile, as Mrs Manning sought his opinion.

At this moment, Matilda's hold on the conversation shattered, however.

She had just set down her fork, her left hand still resting upon the table top beside it, when Montagu's hand brushed against hers.

Her breath caught.

She glanced down, to see his hand was curled around the stem of his wine glass, his attention focused on the conversation. Yet his little finger moved, just enough to slide against hers in a tiny caress.

It ought to have been insignificant, so brief was the contact, yet awareness rushed over her skin in a prickling wave of heat. Her flesh seemed to tighten over her bones, as though it no longer fit her, every inch oversensitive and acutely aware of his proximity. He repeated the delicate stroke and it mortified her to feel an answering tug of desire in a place that had no business being tantalised by such a man.

She was dimly conscious of his hand moving away as the table's attention turned towards them.

"Miss Hunt?"

No. Not to them.

To her.

Matilda snapped out of the daze she'd been lost in, a scalding blush heating her cheeks.

"I-I do beg your pardon," she stammered, turning back to Mr Burton who was giving her a curious look. "I'm afraid I was wool gathering."

She was horribly aware of the marquess then, knowing he knew damn well he'd stolen her attention from Mr Burton—not to mention her wits—with such ease.

Mr Burton smiled. "I was just asking if you and Miss de Feria would do us—that is, myself and Lord Cavendish—the honour of accompanying us to Green Park for the fireworks."

"I'm afraid we've already made such arrangements."

Matilda jolted and turned to stare at Montagu in shock.

He'd never just—

He was regarding Mr Burton placidly, his expression belying the fact he was lying through his teeth. "I have already asked the ladies and will be escorting Miss Hunt and Miss de Feria. Unless perhaps you wish to change the arrangements?"

To Matilda's consternation, Montagu did not ask her, but Lucia, to confirm this outrageous statement, and she knew she was sunk.

Lucia was miserable.

Oh, she was laughing and smiling, and anyone who didn't know her would believe her in fine spirits, but there was something between her and Lord Cavendish, and she wanted to escape. Matilda could see it in her eyes.

Apparently, so could the marquess.

Lucia met Matilda's eyes for a bare moment, her expression begging forgiveness, not that any was needed. A woman like Lucia did not dare contradict Montagu in public. It would cause a scene she could ill afford and who knew how he would take it?

"Indeed not, Lord Montagu," Lucia said. "Seeing that it's all arranged."

With the exception of the marquess himself, Matilda didn't think she'd ever seen a bare-faced lie spoken with such ease. She wanted to be anywhere else but there when the devil at her side turned with a glint of amused challenge in his eyes.

"And you, Miss Hunt? Do you wish to change our arrangements?"

She swallowed, wondering why she wanted to laugh when she ought to be outraged.

"Far be it from me to upset well-laid plans," she said, relieved to hear her voice was steady when everything inside her was turning somersaults. Turning away from the marquess, she looked at Mr Burton, giving him a warm smile to ease his disappointment—and to annoy the hell out of Montagu, if she were being honest. "Another time though, I hope, Mr Burton."

He lifted his glass towards her. "You may count on it, Miss Hunt, and I hope we shall see you both there."

"Of course," Matilda agreed.

She avoided the glint of interest in Mrs Manning's eyes. The woman was clearly in no doubt there was much going on between the interested parties, but Matilda was determined not to further illustrate the fact. They were saved from further scrutiny by the obvious tension emanating from the far end of the table.

The servants were clearing ready for the next course, and Matilda could see Lucia was watching Kitty with concern. Leaning forward a little to see past Mr Burton, she could see two high spots of colour on the girl's face and a furious light in her eyes. From the smug and somewhat spiteful expression on Miss Craven's face, and the irritation emanating from Mr Henshaw, something had been said.

"Oh, wait," Miss Craven said, her sweet voice ringing about the table. "Perhaps you ought to leave the potatoes for Miss Connolly. Have you had enough, dear?"

Matilda sucked in a breath at the obvious insult to Kitty's Irish heritage. Kitty's cheeks flamed now, and Mr Henshaw threw his napkin down on the table top, looking as though he might wring Miss Craven's lovely neck.

"Miss Craven." Everyone froze, including the young lady herself as the marquess addressed her. "Are you attending the outing to Green Park?" he asked, his tone mild.

Everyone knew that those at the far end of the table had not been included among the exclusive company who had arranged the outing.

The young woman preened, blushing a little. "No, my lord, though I should like to above all things."

"A pity," Montagu murmured, and a shiver of anticipation rolled over the table as they realised where this was going. "Miss Connolly," he said, now turning his icy gaze to Kitty. "I believe Miss Hunt and Miss de Feria would be charmed to add you to our party, if you would be interested?"

Kitty swallowed, staring at the marquess in alarm, but obviously aware of the great honour he'd just allowed her. "I-Indeed, my lord," she stammered, wide-eyed with astonishment. "I… I would be very pleased to accept."

Montagu nodded and gestured for a passing servant to top up his wine, and the moment was gone, replaced by the requisite murmurs of pleasure at the appearance of the next course.

Matilda turned to look at him, finding her mouth grow dry as he moved to meet her gaze.

"Thank you," she said softly.

Montagu frowned a little. "Miss Craven is a blessed nuisance," he said with a dismissive shrug. "Her determination to catch a title is only outweighed by her tedious belief that any man should fall into her arms at the first flutter of her eyelashes. I've been awaiting an opportunity to give her a set down that would teach her some manners without utterly ruining her. Your friend merely granted me the opportunity."

She watched him for a moment, surprised he would not claim she owed him now for his act of kindness, which was not kindness at all, as he'd reminded her before. It was also on the tip of her tongue to make some acid comment about the care he'd taken in not ruining *another* female, but found she could not voice it, too in charity with him for having stepped in.

There was one thing, though, that needed saying.

"Much as I appreciate these sudden and uncharacteristic acts of kindness, I must warn you it changes nothing."

Matilda found her heart picked up speed as their eyes met again. He raised his glass, taking a leisurely sip and regarding her over the rim. Lowering the glass, he twisted the stem between long, elegant fingers, and she found her eyes drawn to them.

"I could say the same," he said at length.

She drew in a slow breath, daring to look back at him.

"I will have you," he said, his voice soft. "You know it as well as I do."

"Never."

Indignation forced the word from her lips with rather more passion than she ought to have allowed and she glanced about to see if anyone had noticed. Impossible, arrogant man.

How dare he?

Though she was forced to admit to herself alone that there was some strange and indefinable attraction that pulled her towards him, she would never allow it to overrule good sense.

She gave a laugh, a surprisingly bitter sound. "For a moment I almost allowed myself to believe there was something resembling a heart beating behind that icy façade. I am grateful to you for reminding me of the truth."

"You'd be foolish indeed to believe that," he murmured. "Almost as foolish as believing what is between us can end anywhere else but in my bed."

Matilda gasped, staring at him as her blood surged in her veins, fury and desire all in a tangle. She was giddy and angry, and she wanted to slap him so badly her palm burned with the need to do it.

Why, though?

Because he was utterly wrong?

Or because he was right?

"Sooner or later," he said, and she wasn't entirely sure if it was a question or a statement.

A slow smile curved over his mouth, and Matilda could not help but stare at it. Such a sensuous, sweet, vicious mouth, capable of both crucifying with words and kissing away the sting. The promise of wicked pleasure burned in his eyes and she looked away, before the blush at her cheeks became too vivid.

She felt of the heat of him beside her, the faint whisper of his warm breath against her skin as he leaned in and whispered in her ear.

"The clock is ticking, Miss Hunt."

Anything she might have said in return became impossible then, however, as Lady Culpepper commandeered his attention, and Matilda was left seething and unsettled at his side.

Chapter 12

Green Park, with Montagu?

What on earth was I thinking?

—Excerpt of a letter from Miss Matilda Hunt to Her Grace, Prunella Adolphus, Duchess of Bedwin.

14th July 1814. The home of Mrs Edwina Manning, Old Burlington Street, London.

After dinner, the ladies left the men to their drinks and gathered to make small talk.

"I'm so sorry," Lucia said, taking Matilda's arm. She'd felt wretched ever since she'd allowed Montagu his lie. "I panicked. I could hardly deny the arrangement without calling him a liar and making a scene, and changing it would have made me look rude and… and I just—"

"It's all right," Matilda said, giving her a warm smile Lucia did not feel she deserved. "Montagu knew damn well he'd put us in an impossible situation, and manipulating people is what he does best. Damn, but he looked smug when he asked me if I should like to change my mind. I wanted to stab him with my fork."

Lucia couldn't help but notice the odd note in Matilda's voice, however, and wondered if she was as annoyed as she pretended. Lucia still felt bad, though. Montagu was obviously set on having Matilda for himself, and marriage was not likely to be a part of the deal. That Matilda was drawn to the man despite her better judgement was not something to which Lucia was blind.

Mr Burton, was another matter, an honourable man who'd already made his interest clear. Matilda could be happy with a man like that, surely? He would offer her security and a home, family, he *could* make her happy. Perhaps she would lose her place in society, but the *ton* had already made their feelings clear about her tarnished reputation. In Lucia's view, there was little to lose and a great deal to gain.

If only her own situation was so cut and dry.

"What just happened?" Kitty demanded, hurrying to stand beside them.

"Don't ask me," Matilda replied, smiling. "Montagu is no doubt pulling all our strings, if we but knew it."

"He scares me to death," Kitty admitted. "I would never have accepted but for the fact I knew it would put that odious creature in a pelter."

"What had been going on, Kitty?" Lucia asked. "You'd all seemed to be getting on marvellously."

"And so we had," Kitty admitted, with a shrug. "I'd thought Miss Craven rather nice, until Mr Richards…."

She blushed a little and trailed off as Lucia grinned. "Until Mr Richards decided he liked you better than Miss Craven and flirted a little too openly?"

Kitty's lips twitched and she shrugged a little. "Not quite that perhaps, but… well, yes," she said, blushing and grinning all at once.

"He's a very nice young man," Lucia said, approving the match as Matilda nodded.

"Very eligible."

Kitty shrugged and looked uncomfortable, and swiftly changed the subject. "Lord Cavendish seems very taken with you, Lucia."

Lucia returned a noncommittal smile and moved away from her friends to inspect a painting a little further down the room. As if Kitty had conjured him by speaking his name, the men returned after finishing their port, and Lord Cavendish sought her out at once.

"My lord, you must stop this," she said in an undertone, deciding she must be frank with him. "People are already talking about the marked attention you show me. You might have discovered a connection between me and the earl, but you do not know my plans and I have no intention of sharing them. I can tell you, however, once they become public, you will regret this association."

He stared back at her with a smile of such placid assurance that her heart squeezed in her chest.

"I won't," he said simply.

Lucia took a breath. "Another man said that once." She saw the flash of jealousy in his eyes and allowed herself to enjoy it, just for a moment. "He said his love could endure any hardship, any test, and that he would never let me down."

"Who?" he asked, a rough note to his voice that made a shiver of pleasure run over her skin. He sounded as if he would track down any man that had hurt her and demand satisfaction of him.

"No one that matters now," she said, smiling a little. "He dropped me like a hot brick the moment he knew the truth, and he did not know of the scandal I am to bring down on Lord Ulceby."

Even though they were in company and Lucia could feel the eyes of their fellow guests on them, he stepped closer to her, lowering his voice to match hers.

"Whatever fool made such promises only to break them was not a man who could *ever* be relied on. A callow youth, perhaps, with foolish dreams and half-baked ideas, but not a man. I would marry you now, Lucia, without even knowing your secrets. I have a licence ready for the moment you agree, just tell me yes. You can depend on me, no matter what, no matter how bad the scandal, no matter how utterly it ruins us both."

"You're a fool," she whispered, staring at him in shock, too shaken to disguise her feelings or the way she trembled at his words. "Why would you do that?"

She turned and walked away from him, pretending to move along the wall to the next painting and trying to calm the tumult of her emotions. He followed close behind her, his words sliding under her skin, undermining her determination to do this all by herself, to trust no one other than Dharani ever again.

"You need me," he said, so gently her throat grew tight. "I can see how lost you are. I can see it because I know how it feels. You are adrift and you need an anchor, someone to hold on to you and give you safe harbour. I can be that anchor, Lucia. I want to, so badly. I know you don't love me, but… I think you could, if you let yourself."

She turned to look at him, caught in those indigo eyes, in the promises he was making.

It's dangerous, Aashini. Men make too many promises they can't keep.

"You could love me," he said again, not allowing her to look away, not allowing her any escape, any possibility of answering him with a lie.

"Yes," she whispered, feeling the burn of tears prickling behind her eyes. "But I can't trust you. I just… I can't…." She hurried away then, moving back to Matilda before she made a scene in front of the entire room.

***

Silas watched her go, triumph exploding in his heart, even as he knew he was a long way from making her his. She had admitted there was something between them, though, that she *could* love him, if she let herself. For the moment that was victory enough to make him feel ten feet tall. Yet his fears quickly squashed the glorious sensation. What plans did she have for Ulceby? What was their connection?

Lucia thought it damning enough to ruin her and anyone associated with her, and he didn't doubt that was true. She was an intelligent woman and he knew she resented his interference in her plans, yet he could not help himself. Every instinct told him that this woman was the one. She was the one he would regret for the rest of his days if he let her go. She was the one who would fill his heart until its last beat if he could only gain her trust and make her his.

He wouldn't give up.

Kali's trishul had led him to Ulceby and to India, and there was only one person he was aware of who really knew Lucia, who had known her all her life: her ayah, the Indian woman he had seen on Friday Street. No doubt Lucia would be furious with him, but he felt that time was running out. Whatever would happen, it would happen soon, and he had little time to gain Lucia's trust.

***

14th July 1814. Friday Street, Cheapside, London.

To his intense frustration, Silas's plans were thwarted. There was no answer at Friday Street the next day and he was kept so busy with commitments and business affairs it was four days before he saw Lucia's ayah.

Shrimati Dharani Das was a small woman with eyes of startling intensity. Feeling suddenly as though he was a wet behind the ears youth instead of a viscount, he greeted her politely and sat when she bade him do so.

She stared at him, smiling in a manner that made him uncomfortable. As before, her clothes were a splash of unexpected colour in the dim light of the parlour: a vivid emerald green which made him think of Lucia and everything that was fresh and lovely. The colour was surprising on such an elderly lady and gave her a sense of vibrancy that perhaps belied her advanced years. A plait of thick white hair fell over one shoulder and she toyed with it, sliding it between gnarled, arthritic fingers as she studied him.

His gaze was drawn to the dot of red paint between her brows, the strangest sensation rolling over him that she could see more than he would allow if he wasn't on his guard. This woman, like Lucia, protected secrets, he thought, as he did his best to hold the intensity of her gaze.

"So," she said at last, "what stories do you think you can winkle out of me that Miss de Feria has refused to allow you?"

Silas gave a soft huff of laughter, relieved by her direct approach.

"I don't know," he admitted, smiling a little. "I only know the young lady is full of secrets, and I fear for her."

"Why?" she asked, a flash of interest in her dark eyes. "You think she doesn't have courage enough? You think she needs a man to protect her?"

There was scorn behind the words, so much that he flinched a little and considered his next words with care.

"I am in no doubt of her courage, Madam, I assure you. She has a deal too much for her own good," he added with a wry smile. "I think we all need to be cared for, however, to know that there is someone at our backs, no matter what. I would be there for Miss de Feria, if she would allow it. I would like to think I could rely on her in return."

"And what would you expect from her, for your… *protection*?" There was a sneer to her voice and her implication was clear.

"I offer the young lady no insult," Silas replied, his voice firm, a little irritated that Lucia hadn't at least told the woman that he'd offered for her. "I have asked her to marry me."

She didn't look surprised, and he wondered if perhaps she had known after all and was just toying with him.

"You're not the first," she replied, her tone expressionless.

The jealousy that had burned in his chest when Lucia had mentioned the man who had let her down before returned to scald his heart.

"I knew there was someone, someone who'd hurt her."

Dharani nodded but said nothing as a maid appeared with a tea tray. Once the young woman had set the tray down, Dharani waved her away with an impatient gesture.

"Would you mind?" she asked, gesturing to the tea things with a mischievous smile. "My wrists aren't as strong as they once were."

Silas bit back a grin, knowing damn well she could have asked the maid to pour and was enjoying the fact she had a viscount waiting on her.

"You know of Anna-Marie de Feria?" she asked him as he lifted the teapot.

"Her mother," Silas replied with a nod. "Yes, I know of her."

"A beautiful but unreliable creature," Dharani said with a sigh. "Lucia's father left her money to keep Lucia in comfort, but the feckless woman ran through it in no time at all. She went off with some man, leaving us behind to cope as best we could, and I found a position with a family in Norfolk. They were good people, a respectable family, and they agreed to allow Lucia to be educated alongside their own children. Two girls, and a boy."

Silas lifted the sugar pot with an enquiring gesture, a bad feeling rising in his chest as Dharani told her tale. She shook her head and reached for the cup he offered her.

"It's an old enough story, of course, and you've seen how beautiful she is. The children grew up together, happy and as playful as puppies. I warned her," she said, giving a heavy sigh. "But she was less cautious with her heart back then. The boy became a young man and developed a passion for Lucia. He promised her they would marry."

She nodded, her eyes full of sadness, staring into a far-off place in her memories. "He promised her he'd defy his parents if they objected, and that nothing would keep them apart."

Silas sat back, his heart aching for the romantic girl she must have been, even as jealousy raged at the fool who had deserted her and given her such a mistrust of men.

"What happened?"

Dharani shrugged and took a sip of her tea. "There was no great battle of wills. His parents explained to him the truth of Lucia's birth, that she is illegitimate and could never make him a suitable wife, and he couldn't drop her fast enough. He went away to university, and Lucia never saw him again."

Silas frowned. Anna-Marie de Feria was a notorious figure. Her lovers had included some of the most powerful men in the country, and she'd never married. Even some country bumpkin fool of a boy must have known Lucia was illegitimate from the outset.

"That's not what stopped him," he said, staring at Dharani. "What aren't you telling me?"

She smiled a little and stared down at her teacup. "The rest is for her to tell you, if she chooses to. If she trusts you enough. But that boy broke her heart, Lord Cavendish. Not only that, but he made her realise that people will always set her apart. She feels she belongs nowhere, that she has no place in this world."

"She's adrift," Silas said quietly, remembering the words he'd given her at Mrs Manning's dinner party, his promise to be her anchor.

"*Haan*," Dharani said, nodding, her expression telling him how much she wanted Lucia's happiness. She sat forward then, her piercing gaze searching his face. "Yes, that is it exactly. She is adrift, and it would take a strong man to change that, but… perhaps a man who is honourable to his core and would never waver, never flinch in the face of scandal, could win her trust. Perhaps even her heart."

"I'm no fool boy with a head full of poetry and romantic dreams," he said, holding her gaze. "I've had my share of scandal, and hardship. I don't give a damn for what anyone says of me, or for what people think. I know the difference between right and wrong. I know what it is live with honour even if you're in the gutter. I would protect Miss de Feria in any way that was necessary, whether that be with my name or my life. I won't let her down. I won't let you down."

She stared at him for such a long time he had to struggle not to squirm under her scrutiny but at length she sat back, apparently satisfied.

"I like you," she said, grinning at him in a way that made her face crinkle.

Silas let out a breath, only then realising how important it had been to him to hear her say that. "Thank goodness," he said with a huff of laughter. "I was feeling like a small boy due a scolding."

She chuckled, nodding. "And don't think I couldn't do it."

"Oh, I assure you, I don't," he said in a rush, before he grew serious again. "Is there nothing else you can tell me? I know this has to do with the Earl of Ulceby. I know she plans to have some form of revenge, but for what?"

Silas hesitated, not wanting to ask more, but Dharani had been forthright from the outset, and he didn't think she'd be offended.

"Is he her father?"

He waited as she let out a breath and then shook her head. “I’m sorry. These secrets are Lucia’s to give you, not mine.”

Disappointed but not entirely surprised, Silas nodded and got to his feet. “Thank you for taking the time to speak with me, and for explaining a little.”

Dharani smiled at him and he thought he saw warmth in her eyes, and perhaps a little hope too. “*Apna dhyaan rakhna,* Lord Cavendish,” she said. “Take care of yourself, and that young woman. She needs a good man, someone strong and honourable to stand beside her. I would like to believe that man is you.”

Silas bowed and saw her smile with amusement. “No more than I, I assure you,” he said softly, and bade her a good day.

Chapter 13

My dearest friend. How I miss you. Even now after so many years, yours is the opinion I seek, the voice I long to hear. Your laughter haunts my dreams along with the promises you made me.

I remember playing hide and seek and going on treasure hunts on summer days that shine in my memory. How I wish there were more adventures for us to live together, more treasure to hunt for. I wish the future we had planned wasn't just a lovely daydream.

Where are you, Luke? Where did you go? I see your face everywhere, disappearing into the crowd, glimpses of your hair shining like copper.

I will find you again. I will. You have my word.

—Excerpt of a letter from Miss Kitty Connolly to Mr Luke Baxter… never sent.

20th July 1814. Hyde Park, London.

"Drat this heat," Matilda said, sighing and waving a pretty ivory handled fan with a desultory air. "I wish we hadn't agreed to go to Green Park. I don't think I can endure this until the first of August."

Lucia hid a smile and made sympathetic sounds in reply. She wondered how Matilda would cope with an Indian summer, glancing at her pale skin and the flush of heat at her cheeks.

Her friend was prickly and irritable, and it had forced Lucia to use all manner of inducements to get her out of the house. Matilda had only agreed to a stroll in Hyde Park if they returned via *Gunter's* and ate a quantity of flavoured ice to fortify them for the return journey.

The capital was rather lacking in company now the hot weather had arrived. The lure of the spectacle promised at Green Park was enough to keep some of the *ton* in residence, but many had conceded defeat and retreated to the relative cool of the countryside.

Despite Matilda's protests, Lucia suspected she'd not miss the opportunity to see Montagu again. Sighing a little, Lucia wished she could keep a certain viscount from her own thoughts for more than five minutes at a time. It was impossible, though, and despite knowing her admission to him that night had been foolish, she could not regret it.

She could love him, so easily. This was why she ought to be glad not to have seen him all week. He was a complication she could not afford.

Lucia had known that, for her plan to work, she would have to keep herself at a distance, not for her own sake as much as to protect those who would get burned by her revelations. What she had not known was how very hard it would be to do that.

The Peculiar Ladies had become her friends, and it broke her heart to think a day might come when they would turn their backs on her, yet she couldn't ignore the possibility. When this venture had begun, she had believed it inevitable. The more she came to know these women, though, and the way they supported each other through adversity, the more she'd hoped that….

Stop it, she scolded herself.

She had dreamed of impossible things once before and had her heart broken. This time she was older and wiser. Despite all that age and wisdom, however, the face of Lord Cavendish swam behind her eyes. His promises and declarations rang in her ears and filled her heart, and she wanted to believe in him so badly it hurt.

That was why she'd forced Matilda out of the house today, despite her protests. Another day flopping about reading books and trying to fill the endless hours while Tilda grumbled about how hot it was would have driven her to do something drastic… such as going to see Lord Cavendish and giving into the desire to put her trust in him.

Foolish girl, will you never learn?

Apparently, the answer was no. She looked away from the sparkling water of the Serpentine to the path ahead, and saw the man himself striding towards them.

Lucia's heart leapt in her chest, such a burst of joy rushing through her that she knew it was already too late.

"Well, well. Now I know why you were so eager to brave this dreadful heat," Matilda murmured, a smug note to her voice that made Lucia tsk with annoyance.

"I had no idea he would be here," she protested, huffing at Matilda's sceptical expression. "I didn't!"

They greeted him politely, and Lucia gave her irrational heart a stern talking to, but to no avail. The stupid thing was fluttering like a leaf caught in a breeze.

"I came to the house," he explained, smiling at Lucia with such warmth she thought her knees might buckle. "But your housekeeper explained you were walking to *Gunter's* via the park. It seemed like such an excellent idea I thought I would foist my company upon you, gentleman that I am," he added, winking at them and smiling that pirate smile that made her feel giddy.

"No foisting necessary, my lord," Matilda said with ease as he fell into step with them. "It is a pleasure to see you." They walked on, a tense silence falling over them until Tilda said, with obvious relief, "Oh, look, there's Kitty. Do go on ahead, I'll catch you up."

"*Matilda*!" Lucia protested, glaring at the young woman, who just grinned unrepentantly and hurried after Kitty.

"Unreliable creatures, friends," Lord Cavendish murmured, amusement in his voice.

Lucia huffed, wishing she felt more annoyed than she did. "You don't say."

"Oh, but I do. Husbands are the things to pin your hopes upon. A nice, docile, biddable husband. That's what you need."

Despite her best intentions to be polite but distant, Lucia gave an unladylike bark of laughter. "And where do you propose I find such a paragon?"

"Why, Miss de Feria," he said, placing a hand upon his heart. "You wound me. I am surely the epitome of the perfect husband?"

She couldn't help it. She stared at him and then burst out laughing, finding that the delight in his eyes at having amused her warmed her from the inside out.

"Biddable?" she repeated, once she had sufficient hold upon herself to force the word out. "*You*?"

The look he cast her made her breath catch, not helped in the least by the way he caught up her hand and placed it firmly upon his sleeve. "You could have me wrapped around your thumb in no time at all, and you damn well know it," he said, his voice as soft as his eyes were warm. "I'm already there, truth be told. Damn it, Lucia, give me some hope, at least."

Lucia tore her gaze away from his, aware that she was too close to doing just as he wanted.

Remember the plan, whispered a voice in her head. *Remember everything you mean to achieve.*

Yet the voice that had shouted and raged at her for so many years was not as fierce as it had once been. It was tempered by hopes and desires for a future she'd never dared consider.

Hopes and dreams were dangerous things, though, and she could not allow the earl to get away with what he'd done. If she did not step forward when the time came, her father's plans for her would have come to nothing. She did it to honour him, his memory. If Lord Cavendish still wanted her after that....

She swallowed and turned back to look at him.

"I would like to… to give you hope," she said, feeling ridiculous as she blushed and had to turn away from him. "But—"

"But?" he pressed, the word heavy with anticipation.

"But you will change your mind, and then—"

"I won't," he said, his hand covering hers. "*I won't.*"

Lucia stared at him, seeing the strength of purpose in his gaze, the determination.

"Why are you so determined to marry me? I have no name, no breeding, no fortune, no connections. I can only close doors to you. Why are you so single-minded? Have you fallen for my pretty face, is that it?" She hated the mocking tone of her question, yet she heard the fear behind it too, the worry that it was just lust, some superficial emotion that would fade the moment he tired of her in his bed.

"A thousand ships were launched for a face I don't believe could have been as lovely as the one I look upon now," he said, smiling a little. "But no, that isn't it."

"What, then?" she demanded, alarmed by the desperation in her voice. "Tell me why and make me believe it. I *want* to believe it."

To her shame she felt tears prick at her eyes, and she blinked to hold them back.

He paused and then glanced around to see if anyone had observed them before turning back to her. "I recognise myself in you. A raw bundle of hope and hatred, of longing and determination. I see your desire to belong, and the way you keep everyone at a distance. You think if you reject them first, they can't hurt you, but you're wrong. We are kindred spirits, you and I, and I know in my heart… in my soul, that I could be happy with you, and I'd try my damndest to make you happy too, Lucia."

Lucia blinked hard and walked on, drawing in a deep breath to keep the emotions at bay as he followed at her side.

"Let me in, love. At least give me the chance to prove myself."

She let out a sound of pain, of desperation, and then clapped a hand over her mouth, shaking her head.

"Lucia," he said, his voice so full of concern and tenderness she couldn't help the tears that spilled over. "Love, please," he begged her.

"I'm frightened," she said, staring up into eyes of such blue she saw the fields that had been so familiar to her as a child, the colour a blaze of fierce indigo beneath a fiery sun.

"I know," he said, holding her gaze. "I know what it is to be afraid and unsure who to trust. I know that you've been hurt before, but not by me. Never by me."

Lucia nodded, not knowing any longer what to do for the best. She took another deep breath and wiped her eyes with her hand, hoping no one had seen her little outburst.

"Is the Earl of Ulceby your father, Lucia?" he asked.

She let out a breath of laughter at that. "Nothing so simple as that, I'm afraid," she said, smiling at him. It didn't surprise her that he asked. It was the obvious conclusion.

He frowned and then gave her a rueful smile. "You're determined to be a mystery, aren't you?"

"No," she said, realising it was true. "Not any longer. It's just that I… I don't know what to tell you. How to begin, and—"

"And you can't be sure you can trust me."

There was no anger in his eyes when she shrugged instead of answering him.

"Can we perhaps start with something small? A little revelation that will not cost you too dearly?"

Lucia gave him a curious look, wondering if there was any part of her story that wouldn't cost her dear.

"An exchange, then," he said, as if sensing her reluctance. "Let me see…." he mused and then snapped his fingers. "The very thing."

He flashed a grin at her, and Lucia felt the ground shift beneath her feet. Damn him for that devilish smile, it did ridiculous things to her heart.

"You know, I think, that I ran away from home and lived on the streets for some time?"

She nodded, wondering where he was going with this.

"My father had berated me all my life, telling me I was stupid, that I didn't deserve to inherit his title. I wonder now if perhaps… well, if perhaps he wasn't my father. I know he tried damn hard to get another child from my mother, to no avail. So, he was stuck with me, like it or not. He didn't like it," he added with a twisted smile.

Lucia listened with her heart aching as he illustrated a life where he was at the mercy of his father's hatred and furious temper. A world where he was never good enough and made to feel worthless. The last, terrible row he'd had with his father had culminated in Lord Cavendish making his father a promise. He'd take nothing from him, not a penny ever again. He'd never claim his inheritance.

Not until his own worth was twice that of his father's.

That he'd done it made Lucia look at the man beside her with a surge of compassion and pride for everything he'd achieved. Yet, as he revealed those early days when he'd turned his back on his father and his fortune, it was clear he had survived some desperate times.

"Pride is a terrible thing, and a young man's pride the fiercest of all," he added ruefully. "I was hungry and cold and frightened, but I was damned if I'd let my old friends see me in such… well, you can imagine."

"I'm so sorry, my lord," she said, unable to keep the depth of emotion from her voice.

He paused, looking a little taken aback, a touch of colour at his cheeks that made her smile, pleased to know she could affect him as he did her. "Do you think you might call me Silas?" he asked, staring down at her.

"Silas," she repeated, liking the sound of it—and the intimacy of the moment—far more than was good for her.

"Anyway, one night I… I couldn't stand it a moment longer. I went to a house I had visited often in the past. One that belonged to the family of a boy I'd been friends with."

He broke off and Lucia looked up at him. She watched as he gathered himself and took a deep breath.

"I broke in," he admitted. "And I stole from them." Her heart squeezed in her chest as he glanced at her in trepidation. "It wasn't much," he added in a rush. "Just food mostly, though… I took some silver. Just a few small items, things I could carry easily and sell with no trouble."

He ran a hand through his hair and cleared his throat nervously.

"I'm not proud of it, and… and if that story got about…."

"No one shall hear it from me, Silas," she said, her voice hardened by the truth of her feelings. "I would *never* betray you, and anyone who could hear that story and not feel compassion… well, you do not need their good opinion."

The look in his eyes stole her breath, and she knew that if they were not in a public place, he would have taken her in his arms and kissed her. The idea made her weak with longing.

"Well, then," he said, as she fought with the desire to throw her arms about his neck and beg him to never let her go. "You are guardian of one of my darkest secrets, love. Won't you trust me with one of yours?"

Lucia bit her lip and then gave a sharp nod before she could change her mind.

"Yes," she said. "I will, only… not here. Come to the house tomorrow, where we can be private, and… and we'll talk."

She watched as he exhaled, such relief in his expression she couldn't help but smile.

"I've been a terrible trial to you, I think," she said, feeling sad to have caused him such concern, but he only shook his head.

"My fears and concerns are all for you, love," he said, keeping his voice low as the street around *Gunter's* was more crowded than the park had been. "And I regret nothing."

Chapter 14

Kitty, wherever did you get to last night? Why do you disappear like that? One moment you're there and the next you're gone!

—Excerpt of a letter from Miss Harriet Stanhope to Miss Kitty Connolly.

20th July 1814. *Gunter's*, Berkeley Square, London.

"What do you suppose they are talking about?" Kitty asked, as they walked a discreet distance behind Lucia and Lord Cavendish, who appeared deep in conversation.

"He's trying his best to win her heart," Matilda said with a dreamy sigh. "And she's a fool if she doesn't let him."

"You like him?" Kitty said, giving Matilda an enquiring glance.

"I do," Matilda replied, nodding. "The good men, the truly honourable ones, don't come along often, but he's one."

"You're right," Kitty said, a despondent note to her voice that made Matilda look back at her. "Those are the ones you hold on to with all your might, come what may."

"You speak from experience?" she asked, a little surprised. Kitty was one of the youngest women in their group, only twenty-one if Matilda had to guess.

She flushed a little and nodded. "Yes, though no doubt you'll think it foolish."

Matilda frowned in consternation. "Why on earth would you say so?"

"He was my childhood sweetheart," she said. "We grew up together. His house was near to mine and we saw each other nearly every day. We always knew we would marry when we grew up, but…."

"But?" Matilda demanded, wondering what fate had befallen them.

"But he just… disappeared."

"What do you mean?" Matilda asked. People didn't just vanish, after all.

"Simply that," Kitty said with a shrug. "I waited for him to appear in the garden so we could be off on our adventures as usual, and he never came, so I went to his house." Kitty took a deep breath and Matilda realised that this was something that had hurt Kitty deeply, a pain she still carried. "It was empty, as if he'd never been there at all."

"But surely someone must have known—"

Kitty shook her head. "He lived with his widowed mother. The family was English, and they didn't have much money, though you'd think them descended from royalty by the airs and graces she put on. She kept to herself, though, and no one seemed to know or care where they'd gone. But Luke… he wasn't like that. He loved me, and I loved him."

Matilda hesitated. "But… would he not have written to you, Kitty, or come looking for you when he was old enough?"

Kitty shook her head. "My mother died the following year, and I went to live with my aunt and uncle. His family would never have allowed it anyway. They thought I was beneath him."

She shot Matilda a sceptical look. "I suppose you think it's foolish, just a silly crush. That's what my family think, and I know we were young. He was only thirteen when he went away, and I was eleven, but it was real, Matilda. I feel it here."

She put her hand to her heart, her eyes glittering too brightly.

"Oh, Kitty," Matilda said, her own heart aching for the young woman. "No, I don't think it foolish. How could I? Love is precious, wherever and whenever it comes to us, and I'm so sorry for your pain."

Kitty let out a little huff of laughter and tried to smile. "Thank you. I haven't spoken of him for such a long time, and sometimes… sometimes I feel like I dreamt him, like I made the whole thing up, but I didn't, Tilda. *I didn't.*"

"No, of course not." Matilda's voice was soothing as she put her arm about Kitty's waist. "Have you tried to find him?"

Kitty nodded. "Yes, but I don't have contacts who could track him down, and no one seems to want me to find him. My family never liked his either, so they won't help." She let out a shaky sigh. "I'm frightened I'll never see him again, and my uncle wants me to marry soon. He's tired of supporting me. Yet how can I fall in love with someone else when I'm still in love with him? And what if I marry, and then—" She broke off, clearly distressed.

"I see him, you know," she said, looking mortified now. "Glimpses of him in the crowd, a flash of red hair that I think must be his. Sometimes I follow it, desperate to know if perhaps…." She trailed off, so utterly miserable that there was only one thing for it.

Matilda squeezed her tightly. "I'll help you," she said, smiling and feeling a surge of determination. "Nate knows everyone in London. If he's here, he'll be found, and…." She drew in a breath, wondering what it might cost her to ask the question, but knowing she couldn't let Kitty down, not when her whole future was at stake. "And there's Montagu. He's about the most powerful man in the country. If he wants someone found, I bet they turn up quick enough."

Kitty looked at her with wide eyes. "Montagu? Oh, no, Matilda. He'd never do that for me, and if he does it for you, you'll be in his debt and you know he'll be despicable about it. No. No I couldn't let you, but if you *could* ask Nate, that would be wonderful."

"Very well," Matilda said smiling. "Nate first, and we'll keep everything crossed that he can find something out."

Matilda felt a surge of pleasure at the renewed hope and cheerfulness in Kitty's eyes. It was worth almost anything, she thought, to help her friends find their happy ever after.

Kitty hugged her, almost squeezing the breath from her lungs. "You are the best, *best* friend anyone could ever have, Matilda. We are all so lucky to have you."

Flushing with the compliment, Matilda thought her heart might burst with affection, not only for Kitty, but for Lucia and Alice and Prue and all the Peculiar Ladies. Somehow, their happiness had become as important as her own. Perhaps more so, as she held out so little hope for her future.

"Now," Kitty said, a mischievous glint in her eyes. "What about Mr Burton?"

"What about Mr Burton?" Matilda replied tartly, though she was smiling, knowing exactly what Kitty was about.

"He's very handsome."

"Yes," Matilda agreed. "He is, and intelligent, witty, kind, and let's not forget… terribly rich."

"Ooooh," Kitty breathed, looking thrilled. "So, you *do* like him?"

Matilda thought about this for a moment. "I do," she agreed, nodding.

"So, what now?"

"Whatever do you mean?" Matilda said, laughing, though of course, she knew full well.

"Are you going to let him court you? Do you think you could marry him?"

Matilda took a deep breath, a little unsettled by the question, despite it being one she'd asked herself several times. "I don't know," she said, with complete honesty. "Perhaps, but it's too early to say. I shall get to know him better, though," she said, gaining a squeal of excitement from Kitty. "But I make no promises, so don't go planning a wedding just yet."

"I won't," Kitty said with a sigh. "But I do hope you marry him, Tilda. I thought he seemed lovely."

"I shall certainly give him a chance, and give it a lot of thought, Kitty. I can promise you that much."

"Lovely. Oh, here we are," Kitty exclaimed in surprise as *Gunter's* came into view. "My, what a lot of people."

Matilda looked around at the dozens of open carriages parked beneath the plane trees. More fashionable people milled about in the shade, chatting as everyone sampled *Gunter's* flavoured ices.

Berkeley Square was an interesting mix of fashionable houses and trade with a large tree-lined park at its centre. Waiters scurried back and forth at breakneck speed, carrying little cups of ice to their customers before they melted in the heat.

Kitty and Matilda followed Lucia and Lord Cavendish into the shop with murmurs of relief to be out of the sun. Matilda watched with amusement as Kitty erupted into sighs of rapture over all the lush treats so beautifully arrayed before them. The air was heady with the scent of fresh baked cakes and fruit, and all things sweet and succulent. Cakes of lavish design with decadent ingredients jostled with biscuits and sweet treats of every conceivable colour and flavour, and that was before you even looked at the list of ices.

Matilda took some time to decide on elderflower as her choice, whilst Kitty chose strawberry, Lucia decided on the cinnamon, and even Lord Cavendish indulged with a maple flavoured ice.

As the shop was crowded with ever more people coming and going and making their selections, the party followed the example of everyone else and headed to the park at the centre of the square.

"This is divine," Kitty said with a sigh of pleasure as she leant back against the trunk of a plane tree and ate her treat.

Matilda could only agree, the ice melting on her tongue in a burst of sweetness and cooling a little of the overheated irritation that had plagued her in the sweltering temperature of the city. She moved away from Kitty a little, luxuriating in the cool of the dappled shade and closed her eyes, savouring the sugary ice, and then exclaimed as she was almost knocked off her feet.

"*Oh*!"

"Oh, dear!"

Matilda looked down to see a little girl of perhaps eight years old staring up at her. Her hair was of the palest blonde, her eyes a light shade of blue, and there was something terribly familiar about her.

"I'm so sorry," the girl squeaked looking mortified as she stared at the sticky mark her equally sticky hands had left on the delicate skirts of Matilda's muslin gown. "It was an accident," she added, staring up at Matilda with wide, frightened eyes. She turned then, wringing her hands together. "I'm sorry, Uncle Monty."

Matilda's head snapped up as she realised why the girl looked so very familiar.

The marquess sighed as he looked down at the little girl, one hand resting on his silver topped cane. "I believe I requested you go to your nanny to get cleaned up, not to use this lady's dress as a napkin."

"I'm sorry," she said again, biting her lip.

"Well." Montagu looked up at Matilda then, the ghost of a smile at his lips. "I'm afraid our fate is in your hands, Miss Hunt. What would you have of us for such a heinous crime?"

Matilda laughed as the little girl looked back and forth between them with alarm.

"Oh, I don't think we need send for a magistrate," she said, crouching down to the girl. "Hello, there. I'm Miss Hunt. What's your name?"

"M-Miss Phoebe Barrington," the girl stammered.

"How lovely to meet you, Miss Barrington. Now, then, I think you had…." Matilda inspected the brown finger marks on her gown with interest. "Chocolate ice?"

Miss Barrington nodded.

"Was it delicious?"

"It was," she admitted, smiling shyly. "But it melted very fast."

"I agree," Matilda said, holding out her own little dish of ice. "This is elderflower. Should you like to try it?"

The girl's eyes lit up, but she turned first to look at the marquess. "May I, Uncle Monty?"

For the first time and to her astonishment, Matilda saw a softer look enter the man's eyes as he smiled at his niece. "Go on then, you dreadful creature. If Miss Hunt doesn't mind."

The little girl took Matilda's spoon and helped herself to a generous mouthful, then grinned at her.

"Delicious," she said with enthusiasm. "Though the chocolate was better."

"And now, go to Nanny Johnson and insist she makes you look like a young lady again, and not a street urchin," Montagu said, sounding rather stern, though the girl just flashed him an impish smile.

"Yes, Uncle," she said, and ran off once more.

Montagu sighed and shook his head. "I despair of ever teaching her manners," he said.

"Nonsense," Matilda replied, getting to her feet. "She's a delightful child, and manners are overrated."

He raised one eyebrow at her. "I beg to differ, but coming from you, that does not surprise me in the least."

Matilda wondered why the comment pleased her when it was really an insult, though she felt it hadn't been meant as such. She regarded him with a touch of irritation as she noticed he still looked unaffected by the heat. Unlike most of the men around them, his cravat and collars had not wilted, and he looked as cool and immaculate as always.

"I was right, wasn't I?" she said, her lips twitching as he returned a questioning look. "Well, this appalling heat doesn't appear to bother you, so you really must have ice in your veins."

He looked back at her, his pale eyes intent. "Only in my heart, Miss Hunt," he said, with such sincerity she felt a little unsettled by it.

Matilda turned away from him for a moment, but she couldn't resist the urge to needle him a little more.

"I believe you, and I admit I'm surprised to find you in company with a little girl. I would have thought the top-lofty Marquess of Montagu far too cold and proud to take small children for ices."

Montagu narrowed his eyes at her with a look of resentful resignation. "Even I cannot withstand the constant nagging of an eight-year-old girl once she's set her mind on a trip to *Gunter's*. At least, not that of Miss Barrington," he said with dignity. "She's remarkably single-minded."

"I wonder where she gets that from," Matilda murmured.

Montagu chuckled at that and Matilda did her utmost to suppress the shiver of pleasure the sound elicited.

"Do you see a lot of her?" she asked, before her remark could divert the conversation into dangerous waters.

"As she lives with me, I do."

"Oh?"

The marquess gave her a sceptical look. "My brother is dead, Miss Hunt. Surely you knew that?"

Matilda looked at him and coloured a little. "I didn't," she said, feeling a little guilty, though she wasn't sure why. "I'm sorry for your loss."

Montagu nodded, that cool, indifferent expression settling back over his face like a mask. "We are all that is left of our line. Imagine that," he added with a sneer. "To think I am the only person she has in the world. Now your tender heart bleeds for her, does it not?"

Matilda stared at him, a little shocked by his tone, and by the challenge in his eyes. For a moment she almost agreed with him, but then she remembered the trusting look in the girl's eyes as she'd begged her Uncle Monty's pardon, and the soft look of affection Montagu had perhaps not realised he'd revealed.

"No," she said, surprising herself. "I think she's a lucky girl. For surely no one in England protects his kin with more ruthlessness than you, Lord Montagu?"

There was a long pause, and though she could read nothing from his expression, she suspected he was surprised by her comment. At length he gave a soft laugh.

"Well, Miss Hunt, you of all people should know." He inclined his head a little, before walking away and leaving her alone.

Chapter 15

I'm sorry if I disappeared, Harriet, I thought I saw someone I knew, that's all. Sadly, I was mistaken, but never mind that. I don't understand how you can't be excited to go to the country and attend St Clair's ball? I know you've been lots of times, but even if you can't stand him (which I simply don't understand) there will be so much fun to be had.

At least you could console yourself at the idea of having my scintillating company!

—Excerpt of a letter from Miss Kitty Connolly to Miss Harriet Stanhope.

21st July 1814. South Audley Street, London.

Silas was unaccountably nervous as he rapped on the door. Lucia had promised to tell him her secrets today. He'd racked his brain and been quite unable to think of a single thing that could change his mind about her, short of murder or treason. Somehow, he didn't think her capable of either of those crimes, so why he was so filled with misgiving, he couldn't fathom.

Excitement and anticipation thrummed in his blood as the butler left him in the drawing room and went off to inform Lucia of his arrival. He didn't have long to wait.

Looking effortlessly cool and lovely, despite the fierce heat of the day, Lucia entered wearing a cream muslin gown, which floated about her like a delicate cloud. The colour highlighted her golden skin and the thick black tresses of her hair, and he caught his breath, stunned all over again.

"I'll never get used to it," he said, taking her hand and kissing her fingers with a light brush of his lips.

"What?" she asked, and he could see the nervousness in her tense stature, the slight hitch behind the word.

"How beautiful you are."

She smiled at him but still looked ill at ease.

"You must tire of hearing men say foolish things to you at every turn," he said, seeing her shrug a little in reply.

"It depends why they say it, and if they expect anything in return."

She sat down on an elegant silk upholstered settee and gestured for him to join her. Silas did so, watching the way her slim hands tangled together, one gripping the other so tightly that her knuckles whitened.

"You're afraid," he said, his voice low.

She nodded, not looking at him. Silas reached out, covering her hands with his.

"I won't change my mind, Lucia. I can't think of anything you could tell me that would change my feelings for you."

Lucia drew in a deep breath. "Well, I suppose we shall see," she said, her voice a little tart. "You asked me if the Earl of Ulceby was my father, and I told you he was not," she said, and he could see the rapid rise and fall of her chest as she forced the words out. "That is not entirely true."

Silas frowned a little, puzzled, but she hurried on.

"The present earl is not my father, but… but the previous earl… He was."

She cast a defiant glance at him before carrying on. "My father loved me despite my illegitimacy, and recognised me as his natural daughter. When he lay dying of malaria, he changed his will. Although he could do nothing about the entailed property, he left me a large sum of money which would become mine on my twenty-first birthday. He also gave my… he gave Anne-Marie enough to keep us in comfort until that time came."

She looked down at Silas's large hand encompassing hers as he squeezed a little, encouraging her.

"There's nothing here so far that makes me think less of you, love. I can't believe you could imagine it would. Not of me."

Lucia swallowed and turned to look at him. "I promised to give you a part of my story, Silas, not all of it."

"Very well," he said, smiling at her. "But have a little faith, eh?"

That, at least, drew a hesitant smile from her. "I'll try.

My father was ill for a long time and his heir, the current earl, got to hear of it. A spy must have reported to him that my father intended to change his will, to leave much of his wealth to me."

"I can imagine that news was not well received?"

Lucia gave a bitter laugh. "What, that the late Earl of Ulceby could be so lost to propriety as to settle a large sum of money on his bastard daughter? No," she said with wry distaste. "It wasn't well received."

"What happened, Lucia?" Silas prompted, warmth behind the question, gently encouraging her to continue as she'd subsided into silence.

"My father knew he was dying, and that his heir was a ruthless man who would stop at nothing to get his hands on my fortune, despite everything he was due to inherit. He feared for my life. So, he made plans for Anna-Marie to smuggle me out of India, but… the man arrived much earlier than we anticipated."

"Your father thought Ulceby capable of murdering a child?" Silas said, revulsion lancing through him at the idea.

"He thought it, and he was right," Lucia said, the words increasingly uneven as her emotions rose. "I had to run. Dharani woke me in the middle of the night and made me run and hide in the indigo fields close to our home. She told me that… that evil man ransacked the house, looking for the will, but Father had already ensured it, and several copies, were with his solicitors both there in India and in England. When he realised that destroying the will wasn't possible, he wanted me. There were other men with him, and they were brutal, terrorising the servants. None of them would betray me. He beat Dharani, demanding he tell her where I was. He hurt her so badly, Silas, but… but somehow, she had the courage to lie for me. She told him I'd left a week earlier, and she didn't know where, but it was somewhere he'd never find me."

"My God," Silas breathed, unable to take in the horror. He'd known the present earl to be a despicable man, but to kill a child…! "Lucia, my love, I'm so sorry."

Though she was rigid with misery, he gathered her in his arms, pulling her close.

"You poor child. My sweet girl." He rocked her as though she was a little girl still, murmuring endearments and stroking her hair as her composure cracked and she sobbed into his shoulder, crying her heart out until he thought his own would break at the sound.

When she was calmer, he spoke again. "When did this happen? How old were you?"

"I was six," she said, her voice thick. "I spent the night in the indigo field all alone, terrified that he'd find me, or that there were snakes in among the flowers. There had been sightings of a tiger close by days earlier too, and so that—" She gave a muffled sob and shook her head. "I was terrified. By the time Dharani came for me the next morning I couldn't speak, I was so scared."

"And so, Dharani and your mother brought you to England?"

Lucia nodded. "My father wanted me to be educated here, and he thought I'd be safest under his heir's nose. He said the man was a fool and would never think to look for me in England. Whether or not he did, I don't know, but he never found us. No one knew about Anne-Marie, you see. She was only with my father a short time and no one had ever known about the affair, so he could never connect her with me. We were supposed to live quietly until my birthday, when I would take my place in the world as he'd intended."

Silas held her in his arms, too overwhelmed to speak for a moment. He wanted to murder Ulceby with his bare hands, but he knew and understood that Lucia needed to face him, to stare down the man who had tried to kill her and take everything that was hers as she took it into her own keeping. He drew in a breath, trying to calm the desire for retribution.

"Dharani told me that your mother squandered your money and left you," he said, understanding now why Lucia found it so hard to trust anyone.

She jolted in his arms, staring at him. "You spoke to Dharani," she said, clearly outraged and struggling to get up.

Silas let her go but held her gaze, steady in the face of her anger. "I'm sorry, love. Perhaps I ought not have, but I was desperate to help you. Besides which, she refused to tell me much more than that. Though… she did say she liked me, for what that's worth."

Lucia stared at him a moment longer as anger and bewilderment shone in her eyes, but then she seemed to give in. She laughed. "Somehow, that doesn't surprise me. She's always had a soft spot for a rough diamond."

"That's me," he said, grinning at her. "Am I forgiven?"

He watched as she frowned at him, considering, and then nodded.

"Come here, then," he said, holding out his hand to her.

Lucia clutched her arms about her waist, looking shy all over again. "I shouldn't," she murmured, blushing a little. "It's scandalous."

"The most enjoyable things usually are," Silas replied, winking at her.

With a sigh and a roll of her eyes, Lucia returned to him and Silas drew her down, settling her on his lap with her head on his shoulder.

"Better?" he asked softly.

Lucia nodded, though she didn't answer.

He just held her like that for a long time, thinking this was as close to heaven as a man like him had any right to get.

"He killed my father."

"What?" Silas said, stunned even though from what she'd told him so far, it ought not surprise him.

Lucia turned her face into his coat for a moment, and he could feel the effort she took to remain calm so she could speak again. "My father was terribly ill from the malaria, and very weak. We knew he didn't have long, but he wasn't about to die that night… but he did. When that vile man entered his room, he was alive and when he left it, he was the new Earl of Ulceby, and my father was dead."

***

Lucia closed her eyes, enjoying the quiet strength of Silas's arms, the thud of his heart beneath her ear as she snuggled closer.

Despite her fears, she felt happier for having told him. She knew she could trust him with this much, though she hadn't given him the last of it. There was still one secret left to her, the one which Ulceby would use against her, to deny her right to her inheritance and prove her father's will to be worthless.

"Thank you for telling me, for trusting me. I know how much courage it took, Lucia, and I'm honoured by your faith in me"

He kissed the top of her head and Lucia sighed, feeling weary but far more peaceful than she might have believed, as though the burden of her past and her future had lightened a little.

"I know that's not all," he added, making her smile at his 'dog with a bone' attitude. He'd never give up until he knew all her secrets. "But I can wait. You'll tell me, when you're ready. Won't you?"

Lucia nodded, knowing she would. It was the only way. If she wanted to be with him—and there was little point in protesting anything other than that was true anymore—she owed him all of it.

"Lucia," he said, and she could hear the note of trepidation in his voice. "When is your birthday, love?"

She let out a breath, looking up at him "The second of August."

"Ah," he said quietly.

"That's why I came out of hiding this year," she said, smoothing her hand over his chest. "Dharani had a jewel, you see. A ruby, something she was given when she married. She's kept it hidden all these years. She said she always knew it had a special purpose, and she'd know what it was when it happened. We sold it last autumn, and I came to London. We spent it on accommodation, and on outfitting me as a fine lady. Dharani said if I just appeared on my birthday, I would be a nobody and the earl would find a way to be rid of me. She said, I had to make a name for myself, to make sure I was noticed, and then… then he'd not be able to hide what he'd done."

"A wise woman," Silas said, and she was taken by the catch in his voice and looked up.

His eyes were too bright, soft with sadness and love and Lucia felt her heart give a leap in her chest. Other than Dharani, no one had ever really cared for her, but… but *he* did. Didn't he?

"I will be at your side when you face him, Lucia. You're not alone in this any longer and I won't let him hurt or frighten or abuse you. I want to make it better," he said, his voice fierce. "I want you to have everything, love, just as your father intended for you. I want you to be my wife. Let me love you, Lucia. You'll never be alone or scared or unhappy again, I swear it. We'll bring Dharani too, if it pleases you and she wishes it."

Lucia reached out and touched a reverent hand to his face. It was a harsh face, uncompromising rather than handsome, but it had become so dear to her. She wanted to believe he meant it, that he wouldn't let her down like George had. The idea he could look at her the way George had after he'd discovered the truth made her heart thunder with terror.

Was she being a fool for even considering he could be trusted?

"Ask me again, after my birthday. Please, Silas. Then… when you've learned everything, if you're sure it's what you want. I… I would like very much to marry you, but I shan't hold you to it until then."

He gave a startled sound of pleasure, and before she could say another word, he'd pressed his lips to hers.

Lucia melted into him, allowing herself to dream for the first time in a long time. What might life be like with Silas as her husband? As his mouth searched hers with deep, tender strokes of his tongue, she could not help but believe it would be rather wonderful.

"Lucia." He breathed the word against her lips, and she wanted to give him everything, her true name and the last of what she'd hidden from him, but then his mouth was on hers again, and she simply couldn't think.

She tangled her arms about his neck, her hands in his hair as he pressed kisses down her neck, nipping and tracing patterns with his tongue as his hands explored her soft curves.

"I love you," he said, the words desperate against her skin as her heart soared. "My God, Lucia, I'm out of my mind for loving you."

Lucia laughed a little, astonished and delighted and dizzy with desire.

One large hand swept up her side and cupped her breast, and pleasure rippled through her.

"I want to kiss you everywhere," he said, frantic now as his mouth returned to hers and his hand squeezed and caressed.

Lucia jolted with both shock and desire as he gave her nipple a light pinch through the thin fabric of her gown.

"May I kiss you here?" he asked, making her blush like fury at the question even as she quivered with anticipation.

Quite unable to form a reply, she simply nodded and held her breath as he made short work of tugging the little puff sleeve of her gown down her arm and pulling at the neckline until the small, dark circle of her nipple was exposed.

Silas stared down at her, breathing hard now. "Exquisite," he murmured, sounding awed and overwhelmed. He lowered his mouth, circling the tight little bud with his tongue as Lucia gasped and clutched at him and when he drew her into his mouth, she was helpless. She arched in his arms as the sensation rocked through her making her heart pound and the tender place between her thighs throb with need.

"Silas," she whispered, quite undone as he suckled at her breast and then returned to kiss her mouth, slow and tender.

"I want you so much, Lucia," he said, his eyes dark with the evidence of his desire. "I want you beside me always. I want to share all my secrets with you, and for you to allow me the honour of yours. I want you in my bed, to wake with you every morning, and to have the chance to show you what it is to be loved. I won't let you down. I will *never* let you down."

"Yes," Lucia cried, feeling tears prick at her eyes again, though these tears were different, born of hope and happiness. "Yes, I want that too."

Silas took a deep, shuddering breath and pulled her sleeve back up, putting her gown back to rights with obvious regret. Lucia decided she regretted it too as he leaned in to kiss her again.

"I should go," he said, sounding as if it was the last thing in the world he wanted.

Lucia smiled. "I suppose you should," she replied, sounding no more enthusiastic about the idea.

"I *am* going to court you now." There was a rather ferocious look in his eyes, and she could not help but smile, knowing no amount of warnings would stop him. Though she still couldn't be certain, she simply prayed he wouldn't ever come to regret it, and she nodded.

"Very well, Silas," she said, and was thoroughly kissed for her troubles.

Chapter 16

Lucia is spending a deal of time with Lord Cavendish. The whisper is that he's courting her. Oh, Prue, do tell me it's true!

—Excerpt of a letter from Mrs Alice Hunt to Her Grace, Prunella Adolphus, Duchess of Bedwin.

28th July 1814. Mr and Mrs Digby-Jones' ball, London.

Lucia closed her eyes. Dancing with Silas was the nearest thing to flying she could imagine. Oh, he was far from the best dancer she'd ever taken to the floor with, it was true, but being in his arms was her place of safety, and he made her heart soar.

Of course, everyone believed Lucia had chosen her protector, but she didn't much care. Silas did his best to counter the gossip by clarifying he was courting her and that there was nothing the least scandalous going on. That bothered her more, tying him ever closer to her and the very real scandal that would erupt soon enough. She had warned him, but he would not listen, so she had given up trying. Despite her best intentions to keep him and the world at arm's length, she trusted him.

Lucia had not meant to allow anyone close ever again, and yet here she was, madly in love with a man who didn't even know her real name, and with a cluster of young women who had become dear friends urging her on and excited for her happiness. She'd broken every rule she'd ever made to protect her own heart and yet, tonight, dancing in Silas's arms, she couldn't bring herself to regret it. There would be time enough for her heart to break if things went badly, but for the first time since her first love affair had ended, she promised herself she would not be afraid.

George Norton. She had not thought of him for so long. He had been three years older than her and seemed so worldly, so wise. He had two sisters, Hannah and Jane, and she had loved all of them. Their mother and father had been strict, god-fearing people who were rather distant parents, content to leave their upbringing in the hands of Dharani and a variety of tutors.

She had gone to live with them when she was ten, after moving about a fair bit in the wake of Anne-Marie and her various lovers. It had been the first home she'd ever had since leaving India, and she'd been happy, safe.

George had begun courting her in secret at sixteen, holding her hand and stealing the odd kiss under the stairs when he could. Lucia had loved him with all her heart, and dreamed of a day when they would marry and have a home of their own. But when he'd finally faced his parents, a few months before her eighteenth birthday, the dreams she had constructed proved to have been built on sand.

When he'd discovered everything, he'd returned to face her. He'd been cold and distant and so removed from the way she'd known him she could not understand the change he'd undergone. At first, she believed it was his parents manipulating him, but she'd soon realised that wasn't the case.

Lucia had seen the disgust in his eyes when he accused her of lying to him, of trapping him in her web of deceit. If she'd not been so desperately hurt, she might have laughed at that. She'd been so very innocent. Yet, everything had been her fault, everything they had been to each other now seemed viewed in a different light, tainted simply by the blood in her veins.

It had very nearly destroyed her. It might have, if not for Dharani. They moved away, and Dharani tried to find another position. In the meantime, they'd lived on the savings the old woman had put aside and the occasional gift from Anne-Marie, when her conscience pricked her enough to send money. It wasn't often, but they managed and, little by little, Dharani helped Lucia pick herself up and face the world again.

Dharani had made her see that it was George who was weak and stupid, and that it was his heart that would never have been true. She taught Lucia to have pride in herself, and in everything she was. No matter her illegitimacy, one day she would find her place in the world, and Dharani would be there to crow with delight when she did. So, Lucia did it for her, for *Nani maa,* who had always protected her and lifted her up when the world seemed a terrifying place to be, and the future too hard to face. She did it for the memory of her father who had loved her, and had wanted her safe, happy, and loved.

She had promised herself she would be strong and fearless when she faced the *ton* and their cruel scrutiny, but she'd thought that had meant doing it alone. For the first time, she allowed herself to hope she'd been wrong.

"Lucia!"

She turned, a little breathless and still laughing as Silas escorted her from the dance floor.

"Prue!" she exclaimed, moving to embrace the young woman. "Oh, and Alice, too. How lovely," she said, delighted to see the two young women. Both had married recently and the fact they'd chosen their husbands well shone in their eyes.

Prue had stunned everyone by marrying the Duke of Bedwin, a rather dark and frightening figure who'd been dubbed *The Damned Duke* by the *ton*. Prue assured everyone it was absolute rubbish, and he was a pussycat in reality. Her lofty title had not changed her down-to-earth attitude in the least, and Lucia would have put money on the fact her fingers were ink-stained beneath her lovely silk gloves.

Alice had also married a man no one would have paired her with. She had tamed Nathanial Hunt, libertine and amiable scoundrel, and proprietor of the exclusive gambling club, *Hunter's*.

He looked excessively happy about it, too.

"It's been too long," Alice said, beaming at her. "And we've been missing all the gossip."

They waited as Silas gave Lucia a sly wink and removed himself on the pretext of fetching her a drink.

"Is it true?" the two women chorused at once, almost bouncing on their toes. "Is he courting you?"

Lucia laughed, charmed by their obvious delight. "It is," she admitted, flushing a little.

They then subjected her to a barrage of questions about Lord Cavendish, and Lucia realised why the man had hurried away as fast as he could. Her fiancé-to-be was no fool.

As they chatted merrily, the other members of their peculiar group gathered around them. Kitty and Harriet arrived arm–in-arm, bickering about something in the good-natured manner of fast friends. Ruth arrived next and took Lucia's arm, quietly congratulating her on her good fortune.

"He's a fine man," she said, nodding with approval. "I insist you introduce me, however. Just so I can be certain, you understand," she added, her eyes dancing with laughter. She adopted an expression of studied nonchalance before asking, "Does he have any friends?"

Lucia grinned at her. "I'll see what I can do," she promised.

"It's so romantic, Lucia! You are lucky," Minerva said, joining their little clan with Bonnie in tow. "Though Mama would have murdered me for marrying a man with his reputation, title or no."

Bonnie gave an unladylike snort of laughter at Minerva's rather blunt comment, but Minerva just gave her a defiant glare and carried on.

"But *I* shouldn't have cared a jot if he loved me like Lord Cavendish loves you. It's so obvious he's besotted with you, and what's the point of having a title or a spotless reputation if the man is a fool, or cruel, or you're not in love with him?"

"You're very wise." Lucia nodded, hiding a smile and pleased to hear such words from Minerva. She'd been so intent on catching herself a title at the beginning of the season and had been quite ruthless about it, endearing herself to no one.

Prue had since confided that it was Minerva's mother who was full of ambition, and had pushed her daughter to ingratiate herself wherever possible. Minerva had recently made a vow to marry for love, however, no matter where she found it.

Noticing dancers taking the floor for the next set, she saw Matilda being led forward on the arm of Mr Burton. He'd been paying her some very marked attention over the past weeks, and the house had been besieged by daily deliveries of exotic hothouse flowers. The colourful arrangements decorated all corners of their house, their heady scents becoming somewhat cloying en masse.

Lucia also knew that there had been another delivery, one that Matilda had not told her about but that their maid, Sarah, had let slip.

It was the only one she kept in her room.

With a little persuasion, Sarah had gone into raptures over it, declaring it the loveliest thing she'd ever seen in her life. *It* was a rare blue–and-white orchid. Lucia herself had never seen an orchid before, except in botanical prints, and had been tempted into peeking around the door to see the lovely thing in all its glory.

Sarah had said her mistress was now terrified of killing it and had been desperately seeking advice on how to care for it.

Lucia had been little surprised to discover who'd sent such a difficult and staggeringly valuable gift.

She looked about the room, finding the man himself, cool and aloof as ever. He too watched Matilda take to the floor, watched her laughing as Mr Burton made some amusing comment.

Montagu's expression did not change, but Lucia shivered nonetheless. The marquess did not like Mr Burton's attentions, of that she was certain.

He didn't like it one bit.

***

29th July 1814. Friday Street, Cheapside, London.

"*Nani maa*!" Lucia called out as she headed to the parlour. "I come bearing gifts," she added, pushing the door open and getting hit in the face by a wave of heat. "Goodness, it's stifling in here."

Dharani looked up from the book she was engrossed in and scowled as Lucia dropped the parcel she was carrying. She hurried to the window, sliding it open as far as it would go.

"Close that down, do you want me to catch my death?" Dharani grumbled.

Lucia turned to stare at her, hands on hips. "*Nani maa*, it's boiling outside, and you have a fire lit? Are you trying to roast yourself? It's as hot as Calcutta before the *kal baisakhi* in here."

"My old bones don't hold the heat like they used to," the old woman complained, setting aside her book and spectacles so she could wag an arthritic finger at Lucia. "And you should have more respect for the comfort of your elders."

"Nonsense," Lucia said briskly, casting aside her hat and spencer. "Now stop complaining or I shan't give you the present Lord Cavendish has sent for you."

To her amusement Dharani perked up at once, her eyes alight with interest. “Give it to me,” she said, holding out her hands and making grabbing motions.

Lucia snorted and shook her head. “You’re a spoilt old magpie, that’s what you are,” she said, though she knew the affection in her voice was clear enough. “Here you go, *Nani maa.* I don’t know what you said to him, but he seems very taken with you.”

Dharani preened, clearly delighted by that. “Well, naturally. The boy has taste.”

“Hardly a boy,” Lucia murmured, blushing as Dharani proved her hearing was not as terrible as she sometimes made out.

“True,” she said, nodding. “He’s a fine-looking man. I might be tempted myself if I were twenty years younger.”

“Oh, ho!” Lucia exclaimed, laughing. “Only twenty?”

Dharani smoothed down her thick, white hair. “I’m very well preserved, *bhanvaraa.* I remember a few tricks.”

Lucia held out a hand and grimaced. “Stop right there,” she pleaded. “Just open your present.”

Dharani sent her a wicked grin and tore into the brown paper and then gasped as she drew out the vibrant yellow silk sari. She touched it with reverent fingers, her eyes so soft and bright Lucia felt her throat tighten. It was embroidered all over with blue butterflies. Lucia thought it the loveliest thing she’d ever seen. She’d been touched and a little overwhelmed when Silas had asked for advice for a present for Dharani, though he’d made light of it.

“Well, of course, love. I’m not a fool,” Silas had said, grinning. “If I want to marry you, I need her onside or she’ll make my life hell.”

But she recognised his desire to be well thought of, to befriend someone he knew was very important to Lucia, and that had meant more to her than she could express.

"It's beautiful," Dharani said, looking overwhelmed by the gift.

"Yes. He buys and sells goods from all over the world, *Nani maa*. Spices and fabrics, and… oh, all sorts of things. So he could find something really lovely for you."

"A good man," Dharani said again, nodding and tracing a delicate butterfly with one finger.

Lucia got up and sank to her knees beside the old lady, taking her hand. "Do you really think so?" she asked, staring up at the woman who had always protected her, no matter the cost. She'd given everything up to come to a foreign land and start again among strangers, all for Lucia. "Do you think I can trust him?"

Dharani reached out a hand and stroked Lucia's cheek. Her hand was rough from years of work, work she'd done to keep them fed and clothed, to keep Lucia safe.

"I think you already know the answer to that, *bhanvaraa*," she said, smiling. "But if you want my opinion… I will never trust my judgement again if that man lets you down."

Lucia let out a sob of relief, not realising until that moment how much she'd needed Dharani's blessing.

Dharani pinched Lucia's chin, raising her head up. "You must tell him, Lucia. Tell him everything. All of it."

"Yes," Lucia managed, nodding as the tears rolled down her face. "I will. I will tell him."

"Now, now, no waterworks," the old lady said, chuckling. "You've already let a north wind blow through my parlour. Don't go soaking me to the bone, too."

Lucia made a choked sound somewhere between laughter and tears, and wiped her face.

"All better," she said, sniffing a little as she looked up again.

Dharani nodded in approval and stared at her, giving Lucia the strange but all too familiar sensation that she could see right through her. "You love him."

"I do," Lucia said, the words a little uneven as she realised she'd not even admitted as much to herself until that moment.

Dharani sighed with contentment and sat back in her chair. "I can die happy now," she said, regarding Lucia with a beneficent smile and looking pleased with herself.

"Oh," Lucia said, laughing and getting to her feet. "Don't give me that. You're too stubborn to die. Besides, you always said you'd die in India, not some foreign land."

Dharani shrugged. "Maybe I will, maybe I won't," she said, a trifle petulantly. "It's not so foreign now, after all. You're here, where you belong."

Lucia stilled, looking down at the old lady. "Do I?" she said, feeling breathless suddenly.

"Come here," Dharani said, gesturing for her to bend down.

She did, and Dharani placed her hand flat over Lucia's heart. "This tells you where you belong, Aashini. Only this. Follow it, and you'll find your home."

All at once, Lucia was blinking back tears again and she leaned in closer, kissing Dharani's wrinkled cheek.

"I love you, *Nani maa*. You are the wisest person I know."

Dharani beamed and then sat up straighter, making *give me* motions with her hands again. "Now then," she demanded, all business. "You said *gifts*, not gift. Where's the other one?"

Lucia laughed at the outrageous old woman and shook her head before reaching for the books she'd bought.

Chapter 17

Dearest Nate,

I'm sorry I shan't see you and Alice at Green Park, but I don't blame you for escaping this shocking heat and retreating to the country. I do hope Alice feels better soon and hope to see you both at St Clair's house party.

I have a favour to ask (don't roll your eyes at me, and yes, I know you are doing just that). You remember Miss Kitty Connolly? If not, I know Alice will remind you. Well, she is looking for an old friend....

—Excerpt of a letter from Miss Matilda Hunt to Mr Nathaniel Hunt.

30th July 1814. South Audley Street, London.

"Darling girl!"

Lucia hurried forward, throwing her arms about Silas's waist and holding him tight. She had long since given up any pretence she was indifferent to him, and since talking to Dharani the day before, she'd taken her courage in hand. She loved him, and he deserved to know it… and everything else.

"Well, this is new," he said, laughing with pleasure at her exuberant greeting. "Though I'm not complaining, you understand."

He closed his arms about her and bent his head, kissing her tenderly. Lucia sighed, melting into the embrace.

"I missed you so much," she said, finding her eyes blurring with a mixture of happiness and trepidation.

Silas framed her face in his hands, frowning a little. "Now then, what's this? What's happened?"

Lucia laughed and shook her head. "Nothing," she said, feeling giddy and overwhelmed as the words jostled in her chest, bursting to get out. "Only… only I love you, Silas."

He stilled, staring down at her, his own eyes glittering now. He made a sound low in this throat and pulled her into his embrace, holding her so tight she could hardly breathe.

"Lucia," he murmured. "Oh, Lucia. Thank you, thank God, thank Kali too, if that is who I owe this to."

Lucia laughed, pushing away from him a little to stare up at him to find him grinning at her. "You're happy?" she asked, reaching up to stroke his face.

He captured her hand, turning into it and kissing her palm. "I am the happiest man in the world, Lucia. Surely you can't doubt it."

Lucia swallowed, knowing she must be brave now, that if she loved him, she must trust him and allow him to prove his sincerity.

His face fell.

"What it is, darling? Why do I keep seeing those clouds in your eyes? Are you frightened, with your birthday so close? You know you won't face him alone, love. You'll never be alone again."

She hugged him tight, pressing her face into his chest and breathing in his scent: clean linen, soap, and healthy male. It was a heady perfume.

"Talk to me, Lucia."

Lucia took a deep breath and looked up. "I… I want to tell you the rest, Silas."

He stared down at her, smiling, such a gentle expression in his eyes as he leaned in and pressed a soft kiss to her mouth. "Thank you," he said. "For trusting me."

Silas took her hand and led her to the sofa where they sat down, side by side. Lucia twisted her fingers together. No matter how much she told herself she trusted this man, she was terrified. She had been rejected before when her heritage had been revealed, and if Silas did the same….

She didn't think she could recover from that.

His large hand reached out and enclosed hers, unknotting her fingers and drawing one hand to his chest, where he held it close.

"I'm not going anywhere, Lucia. If you're not ready—"

She shook her head, determined now.

"No. I want to tell you." Her heart was racing, her chest too tight, making it hard to breathe. Sweat prickled down her spine and she closed her eyes, drawing as much air into her constricted lungs as she could manage. "I'm just afraid you—"

"I'll not change my mind," he said fiercely. "I love you."

Lucia drew in a sharp breath, torn between laughter and tears as his words sank in.

Trust him, Aashini.

"My name is not Lucia de Feria," she said, struggling to get the words out. She turned to face him then, needing to see the look in his eyes when she told him, and praying she would not see disgust or resentment replace the warmth and love that resided there now.

"Anne-Marie de Feria is not my mother. My real mother died not long after my birth, and Anne-Marie was only my father's lover for the last six months of his life. I think she did love him," she said, smiling a little. "She was devastated when he became ill. That's why she promised him she'd look after me and pass me off as her own daughter when she returned to England."

Silas still held her hand tight, but he reached out and stroked her cheek. "That was good of her, but I suppose it explains why she abandoned you so easily, too."

Lucia nodded. "Anne-Marie was never cut out for motherhood," she said, feeling no bitterness over the fact. "She is everything that is fun and vivacity. She is ridiculous and lively, and the most spendthrift woman you will ever meet in your life. I've known her to be generous to a fault, and quite spectacularly selfish, but without her I'd have not made it to England. I'll never forget that."

"So, you've lived as Señorita de Feria, daughter of a Portuguese courtesan?"

"Yes," she said, feeling the pounding of her heart in her chest like the drumroll before the fall of a guillotine blade. "Not because I am ashamed of the truth," she added, her voice severe. "Only because if Lord Ulceby had heard the slightest rumour, he would have come for me. He wants me dead, Silas. If I'm dead, the money set in trust will be his."

Silas's face darkened with a murderous glint, his jaw tightening, but he refrained from saying anything further than, "I understand." His hand was warm and reassuring as it clasped hers, giving her the strength to continue.

"He's tried to have me declared dead before, but *Nani maa* paid someone in India to write to the lawyers with updates about me, assuring them I would come on my twenty-first birthday to claim my inheritance."

"She's a wise woman."

Lucia smiled and nodded. *Just tell him*, said the voice in her head, but the next words caught in her throat, George's expression of disgust vivid in her memory. She couldn't bear the thought Silas could ever—

"Dharani is your grandmother, isn't she?"

She gasped in shock, her eyes flying to his to find nothing but warmth and love, and perhaps a little reproach.

"H-How…?" she stammered, not knowing what to ask, what to feel. "How do you know that?"

Silas smiled at her. "I didn't, not until this moment, but once you admitted you were not Portuguese, it wasn't so very hard to work out."

Lucia gave a broken sob and Silas lost no time in hauling her into his lap. His strong arms closed about her and held her tight as he stroked her hair. "It's all right, love. You've told me, and the world didn't end. It changes nothing. I love you."

"You d-do?" she managed through a storm of very unattractive sobs.

He pulled out a handkerchief and put it in her hands. "Of course," he said, sounding a little impatient, though he was smiling at her fondly. "I can't believe you'd think otherwise of me."

"Why wouldn't I?" she countered, holding his gaze.

Silas stared at her and nodded. "You're right. You had every reason to be afraid, but I mean to take that fear from you, Lucia. You can rely on me, I promise you that. I won't let you down, not ever."

"You never have," she said, wiping her eyes and staring up at him as her heart calmed its frantic thudding. "So, I will have to start believing you, won't I?"

He leaned in and pressed a kiss to her forehead.

"Tell me about your mother."

Lucia smiled and settled back into his arms, her head on his chest. He always knew exactly the right thing to say, the right question to ask.

"She was beautiful."

"Well, that much is obvious." Silas chuckled, kissing the top of her head.

"*Nani maa*—my grandmother, Dharani, has always been a resilient woman. Her husband was a worthless layabout who drank their money away. Happily, she had a strong and loving family, and her father helped her get enough money together to start again. So, she took my mother when she was a child and left her husband. She moved from the north to Bengal and found work in my father's household in Calcutta. As soon as she was old enough, Sharmila—my mother—found work there too."

"A remarkable woman, your grandmother," Silas said, smiling at her.

Lucia nodded, her pride in Dharani stronger than ever. "When my father's wife died giving birth, Sharmila became ayah to his son, Alexander. My half-brother, I suppose," she said, wondering what her life might have been like if the boy had lived. "My mother had him in her care from almost a new-born babe and Dharani said she loved him dearly, but he wasn't a strong child."

Silas took her hand again, tangling their fingers together as Lucia spoke.

"Alex fell ill when he was three years old, a dreadful fever. He died two days later. Dharani said both my father and Sharmila were beside themselves. They'd both adored him, and in their grief…" Lucia shrugged, feeling a well of pity for her father, who had lost so many of the people he'd loved and died far too young himself. "And I'm the result," she said with a wry smile.

"What a lot I owe them," Silas murmured, looking down at her with such love in his eyes that her throat grew tight. He traced the line of her jaw, touching her as though she were precious, as though he couldn't believe his good fortune.

"I like to believe they're together now," she admitted, "that they're watching over me."

Silas let out a breath that wasn't altogether even. "They'd be so proud, love. My God, everything you've endured, everything life has thrown at you and the courage with which you've faced everything. It's astonishing. *You* are astonishing, and I'm so proud of you too."

Lucia blinked back tears, overwhelmed by his words and loving him so fiercely that she wondered at the power of her own feelings. The sudden desire to protect him was overwhelming.

"The *ton* will ridicule you, for marrying me when I'm… I'm… *Kutcha butcha*," she spat the words out, but she needed to be explicit. He'd only just learnt the truth, after all. He'd not had time to consider. "It means half-baked bread, neither Indian nor British. I belong nowhere, Silas."

She watched as his jaw tightened, his eyes growing dark and furious. "I need neither permission nor approbation in deciding who it is I love. I'm the head of my family and I turned my back on the blasted *ton* when I was a boy. Frankly, I don't give a… a snap of my fingers for their opinion." He took a deep breath, struggling to get his temper under control. "I'd put it in more accurate terms, but I try to moderate my language in front of ladies," he added, sounding so mutinous she couldn't help but smile at him.

"All the same," she said gently, reaching out and putting her hand to his cheek. "Perhaps… perhaps you should take a little time to consider… *oh*!"

There was a flash of some dark emotion in his eyes and he moved before she could finish her sentence. He swept her up, removing her from his lap and putting her down again, none too gently. Taking a moment to tug at his waistcoat and adjust his sleeves, she watched in astonishment as he got to one knee before her.

Her breath caught as she realised his intent, and then she smiled as he opened his mouth to speak and shut it again.

“I don’t know your real name,” he said in surprise as she gave a startled little laugh.

It was the one part of her history she’d still not shared with him.

“Aashini,” she said, feeling suddenly shy, which seemed ridiculous but was true.

“Aashini,” he repeated, her name spoken with such reverence she blushed a little. “How beautiful.”

“It means ‘a lightning bolt,’” she said smiling. “Which you may live to regret.”

Her heart swelled as she looked at the man she loved on bended knee before her. Whatever came next, whatever they faced together, she would always remember this moment, and never regret it.

“Never,” he said, taking her hand in his. “You’ve struck to the heart of me, and there you shall remain, Aashini.”

“It will take some getting used to,” she admitted. “I’ve been Lucia for such a long time.”

“For both of us,” he said, nodding. “But whether you are Lucia or Aashini, you will have me at your side. Which leads me to my next question.” He grew serious, raising her hand to his lips and kissing her fingers. “Aashini, will you marry me? *Please*, darling?”

She laughed then a choked sound that caught in her throat as his face blurred with tears.

“Yes,” she said, opening her arms to him. “Yes! Yes, please.”

***

Matilda paced her bedroom, wondering how much longer she ought to wait.

It was the height of impropriety to allow Lord Cavendish to be alone with Lucia, but she trusted him. He was a man of honour, she was certain. Lucia was also not a woman who would give her favours away lightly. Good Lord, she'd had some staggering offers for the privilege of bedding her, the kind of sums that would have seen her wealthy for the rest of her days. Yet she had turned aside every single one with disdain.

There was a proposal coming today too, Matilda felt certain of it, but this one was the kind with a marriage, children, and security.

"Oh, say yes, Lucia," she muttered, feeling breathless with anticipation.

Why she felt so certain it would be today, she wasn't sure, only… the looks she'd seen between them the last time they were together had been eloquent. Her heart ached, wondering what it must feel like to be so loved, and to love so completely. Would she ever know that?

An unwelcome surge of jealousy filled her heart and she shook herself, forcing it away. Lucia and all her friends deserved their happiness, and she took joy in it. Matilda would never, *could* never, reproach them for their happiness. Only she wished to experience it too.

Yet she was increasingly aware that the greatest barrier to her own happiness was herself.

She had once told her brother, Nate, she just wanted a good man, an honest one.

"*I want someone who will be kind. Someone warm and loving and loyal. Is that too much to ask*?"

It had seemed so simple a request, and there was Mr Burton, wanting to court her. He was that someone, warm and kind and loyal, and no doubt loving, should she give him the slightest encouragement.

She hadn't.

Oh, they were very good friends, and she enjoyed his company, but….

But.

She felt nothing for him. He was everything she'd hoped for, and yet….

Nothing.

It wasn't the fact he was a Cit, either. She wasn't a snob in the least. In fact, she admired him. Any man who could overcome the circumstances of his birth and make such an astonishing success of himself deserved accolades and acknowledgment. The ranks of the *ton* ought to welcome him with open arms, and their disdain made her furious. No. It wasn't that.

Her eyes drifted to the orchid sitting on her dressing room table. The dratted thing was impossible. No one seemed to know what to do to care for it and she felt certain she'd end up killing it. It was so damned perfect, she thought with a sudden burst of fury. If it died, she'd be mortified. She ought to have sent it back the moment it had arrived. She'd meant to, only… only she'd seen nothing so beautiful in her life before and she'd wanted it for herself.

She could ask Montagu, of course, except that she'd rather bite her own tongue off.

Why did he do this to her?

There was Mr Burton, the perfect gentleman, doing everything right, and there was Montagu.

He was rude, insulting, arrogant, and—not to forget—the reason no gentleman of status could contemplate marrying her.

Mr Burton was offering her marriage.

Montagu was offering to ruin her completely.

Yet his inconsiderate gift of a stunningly expensive plant that was doomed to die in her care had affected her far more than any of Mr Burton's far more practical and plentiful bouquets.

She put her head in her hands and groaned.

"You're such a fool, Matilda Hunt."

A knock at the door jolted her out of her dark musings and she hurried to answer it.

Lucia was there, flushed and a little dishevelled, her face alight with happiness.

"Oh!" Matilda squealed, clapping her hands together.

"He proposed," Lucia said, sounding a little stunned.

"And?" Matilda demanded, hardly daring to breathe.

"And… I said yes."

Chapter 18

St Clair,

I wonder if I might trouble you to attend me Monday afternoon. You see, I am to be married and find myself in need of a best man …

—Excerpt of a letter from Rt. Hon. Silas Anson, Viscount Cavendish, to Rt. Hon. Jasper Cadogan, Earl of St Clair.

1st August 1814. Cavendish House, The Strand, London

Silas tutted as he watched Fred preparing to shave him. The fellow hadn't been able to stop grinning since Silas had confided his news on Saturday.

"Good heavens, man. You've had a day and a half to get used to the idea, must you keep smirking like that?"

"Reckon so, my lord," the fellow said, chuckling as he mixed up a nice thick lather. "I mean, I don't like to say I told you so, but—"

"Oh, you can laugh," Silas said, letting out a breath and tilting his head back to allow Fred to slather the foam over his face and neck. "Honestly, I'm too happy to care." He paused for just a beat before adding, "Besides which, rumour has it you and Mrs Winston are walking out together. Reckon you'll be following in my footsteps with my housekeeper in a matter of weeks, don't you?"

To his delight, Fred went a quite remarkable shade of red before flipping open the razor with a little more flourish than was necessary.

"Never a good idea to aggravate a man with a blade in his hand, my lord," his indignant valet muttered, while Silas chuckled with delight.

He sat still and docile after that, though. The man had a knife, after all. "What's our new mistress like, then?" Fred asked, and the question caused a spike of anxiety to prick at Silas's heart. He well understood Lucia… no, *Aashini's* concerns. Her illegitimacy would be hurdle enough to overcome when marrying a peer, but how would his household receive the news she was of mixed race? He wasn't fool enough to believe there wouldn't be those who would cut them, that there wouldn't be gossip and prejudice against them. Whilst he'd long since grown a thick skin, that Aashini might be hurt was a pain he found unbearable.

"That bad, eh?" Fred quipped, grinning as the silence stretched on. His valet must have seen the concern in his eyes though as he paused, frowning. "What is it?"

"You've heard rumours, no doubt?" Silas said, hardly daring to ask.

Fred snorted, glowering a little. "What do you take me for? Some sneaksby who lives for the next scandal? I ain't got no time for tittle tattle. You'll tell me what's what if I need to know, that's good enough for me."

Though he was touched by his sincerity, with Aashini's safety in the balance, Silas needed to be sure. "Swear you'll hold your tongue until I say otherwise?"

With a curse, Fred paused in his work. "Bleedin' hell, we're back to that, are we? I told you. Your secrets are my secrets. I'll take them to my grave."

Silas relaxed, knowing it was true. He ought not to doubt Fred, of all people. "She's illegitimate."

Fred rolled his eyes. "Along with half the *ton,* if the truth were told. That it?" he asked, watching Silas intently. "No, didn't reckon it was."

"Her father was the late Earl of Ulceby; her mother one of his Indian servants."

"Ah," Fred said, that one word soft and full of understanding. "Well, ain't no one going to hear a word from me."

"No." Silas shook his head. "Everyone will know soon enough, Fred. There will be the devil of a scandal when it comes out. You see, she's due to inherit a fortune on her birthday, but to get it, the truth will have to come out." He stared at his valet, wondering what he was thinking. The pride of the Cavendish family was something Fred seemed to care about more than Silas ever had. "How many of my staff will jump ship?"

Fred scowled. "None, if they know what's good for 'em," he muttered and then let out a breath as Silas continued to stare at him. "I don't know. Not the ones who came with you, but some of your father's staff…." He shrugged. "You're a fair master and you pay well. They'd be touched in the head to think they'd be better off elsewhere."

"Well, I suppose we shall just have to wait and see."

Silas looked up, surprised as Fred laid a fatherly hand on his shoulder. "Don't you go letting no naysayers spoil your happiness, my lord. You've earned the right to it, and I for one am right glad for you. I'll raise a toast to you and the new Lady Cavendish with Mrs Winston later, and we'll be proud to welcome her into the household."

To his chagrin, Silas felt his throat tighten at that. It took a moment for him answer. "Thank you, Fred. That means a lot to me."

***

"Oh, Lucia, you do look lovely. I don't think there has ever been such a beautiful bride. Poor Lord Cavendish won't be able to take his eyes off you."

Aashini stared into the looking glass, seeing the sincerity shining in Matilda's eyes as she fastened a simple single strand of pearls about her neck.

"You may keep those," Matilda added, smiling at her and resting her hands on Aashini's shoulders. "Consider them a wedding present."

"Oh, Tilda, no, I couldn't." She turned to look into the eyes of a woman who had become her closest friend and wondered if her luck could possibly last any longer. "It's too much."

"Nonsense," Matilda said, laughing. "I want you to have them." Suddenly her eyes were too bright, and she batted away a tear. "Goodness, the ceremony hasn't even begun, and I've already turned into a watering pot. A new low even for me." Matilda laughed and snatched up a handkerchief, dabbing at her eyes.

Aashini got up and crossed the room, taking Matilda's hands in hers. "I've never had a friend like you before," she said, smiling as Matilda gave a little sob. "I'll miss living with you."

"Don't be silly. With your new husband to keep you busy?" Matilda said, struggling not to cry. "Oh, I shall miss you too, Lucia."

She flung her arms about her and Aashini hugged her back, caring nothing for creasing her gown, or anything else, but that her friend was crying.

"Matilda," she said, once they'd both calmed themselves a little. "There is something I need to tell you."

"What, dear?"

Aashini took a deep breath. Her birthday was tomorrow, and from this afternoon she had Silas at her side. She was no longer alone, and Matilda had earned the right to the truth.

"Come," she said, taking Matilda's hand and pulling her to sit beside her on the bed. "I think it's time I told you the truth about who I am."

She kept the story brief this time, only giving Matilda the salient points. There would be time enough for discussions, should Matilda still wish to continue her friendship.

Once her story was done, she sat and stared at the floor for a moment, before gathering her courage and meeting Matilda's eyes.

"I… I always knew you were full of secrets," Matilda murmured, obviously taken aback by the story. "But I never imagined…."

She stopped, and Aashini could not read her expression as a variety of emotions seemed to chase over her lovely features. Finally, however, there was one she recognised well enough.

Anger.

Aashini held her breath, feeling her heart ache at what must be to come.

"That… that *bastard*!"

She widened her eyes. Matilda rarely cursed, and never with such… such *venom.*

"My word, Lucia… no, I beg your pardon, *Aashini*—goodness, I shall have trouble remembering that—but really. He deserves to hang. Terrorising a little girl and… and if he'd found you? *Oh*! Oh, my dear."

To her astonishment, Aashini was hauled into a fierce hug as Matilda clung to her.

"Don't you worry, though. Now Lord Cavendish will protect you, as will the Peculiar Ladies. We'll all support you, Luc—*Aashini,* you know we will. Oh, just wait until Nate hears about this…! But… but why are you crying?"

In fact, Aashini wasn't certain if she was crying or laughing, but either way the tears wouldn't stop. The relief of it was too immense, too overwhelming. She knew that Matilda could not speak for all the young women in their group, but that she assumed they would feel as she did, gave Aashini hope. On top of that… Matilda knew, and she was still her friend.

"Oh, now stop that," Matilda said, appalled. "You can't get married all red-eyed and puffy. Stop it, I say. At once!"

At her obvious panic and indignation, tears turned to laughter and it took some time before either of them was calm enough to hold a sensible conversation.

Once sanity had been resumed, Matilda guided her back to the dressing table and set about repairing the damage they'd done with their hugging and crying.

"There, good as new," she said, with a contented smile as Aashini looked back at Matilda for the first time with no secrets between them.

"I'm afraid you're stuck with me," Matilda said with a wry smile. "Friends who can put up with me are scarce. I'm not letting go of you now. Besides, I have you down for two months in the autumn when I'm a batty old maid. I figure if I visit you all on rotation, you'll not get too sick of me."

"What are you wittering about?" Aashini said, laughing and shaking her head and feeling so happy she might just burst from it. "You have Mr Burton dancing attendance on you for one thing. He'd propose if you so much as lifted a finger to encourage him. I hardly think you'll end an old maid."

She watched as Matilda smiled at her, and found she was not entirely convinced by it.

"True," Matilda said, suddenly in motion and heading for the door. "Now, I must finish getting ready. The carriage will be here soon."

Aashini watched her friend go, feeling concerned for her and knowing she wasn't the only one who'd been keeping secrets, or at least… not telling the complete truth.

***

"Well, I can see where my wife has inherited her beauty from," Silas said, grinning with mischief as he handed Dharani down from the carriage. "And such a lovely sari, too."

Naturally it was the one he'd given her as a gift, and he took it as an excellent sign that she was wearing it.

The old woman huffed, concentrating on getting to solid ground before glaring up at him. "I knew you were trouble the moment I set eyes on you," she grumbled, though Silas wasn't fooled, there was no hiding her delight and—he suspected—her enjoyment at having someone new to bicker with.

"Oh, I don't doubt it," Silas said easily. "That's why you liked me so much."

"Hmph," she said, breathless as he supported her up the steps to his home. "I can't deny it though. I always had a soft spot for a troublemaker."

Silas chuckled. "Oh, I think we shall get along famously."

"So long as you always agree with me and do as I say, things should go smoothly enough," Dharani allowed, giving him a wicked grin.

"So long as you understand I *will* agree… and then I'll do whatever the devil I like, yes, I should think so," Silas countered.

The old woman paused, narrowing her eyes at him.

"Jackanape," she said.

"Harridan," Silas retorted.

The two of them stared at each other until Dharani gave a bark of laughter.

"You'll do," she said, shaking her head. "Now get me somewhere to sit down, and mind it's nowhere draughty. My old bones don't hold the heat like they used to."

Once Dharani was installed and further buttered up with a gift of a heavy silk shawl to keep the chill off—on a scorching day that was already making Silas fear his collars would wilt—he went to greet St Clair.

"Thanks for doing this," he said, shaking the earl's hand.

"Pleasure," St Clair said with the kind of lazy smile that sent any unwed woman in a twenty-yard radius into a swoon. "I do love to be in on a scandal before it breaks."

Silas let out a breath and gave him a hard look, but St Clair beat him to it, holding up one hand.

"If anyone so much as breathes a word against the future Lady Cavendish, you may rest assured I shall break their nose," St Clair assured him. "Though I suppose I must think of an alternative punishment for the ladies," he added with a frown.

"Good man," Silas replied gruffly. For all St Clair's charm and devil may care attitude, there was a sincere and good-hearted fellow beneath the veneer.

"Now then, where is the beautiful bride? Doesn't the best man get a kiss on the wedding day?"

"Not if he wants to make it out the house with his own nose intact, no," Silas replied, only half joking as his butler moved to inform him that his wife to be had just arrived.

"Right then, away with you, scoundrel," St Clair said, taking charge and giving Silas a little push. "Go and take your place. Oh, who's giving her away, though?"

Silas froze, a sudden panicky feeling rising in his chest.

St Clair rolled his eyes. "Oh, good heavens, man. Must I think of everything?"

"I only proposed yesterday afternoon," Silas said, a touch indignant, yet relieved he'd had the forethought to arrange the licence days earlier. "It's been a bit of a rush. Oh… wait…." He grinned and hurried down the stairs to where Fred was getting under Mrs Winston's feet.

"Fred!" he called, as the fellow turned around in surprise. "Stop harassing my housekeeper, she has a wedding breakfast to organise, and I have a job for you."

Fred looked a little surprised but followed Silas back up the stairs.

"St Clair," Silas said, drawing Fred nearer. "My valet, Mr Frederick Davis."

The earl looked between Silas and his valet, a little surprised but he nodded. "Mr Davis."

"My Lord St Clair," Fred said, utterly perplexed.

"Jasper," Silas said, wondering if he was about to insult one of his few friends.

"Oh, Lord," St Clair said, appalled. "Jasper, is it? I am in the basket."

Silas laughed. "No, but I shall be if there's no one to give my wife away. Please, would you do the honours for me? I'd be eternally grateful."

"Of course," the earl said, brightening at once, until he asked. "But who'll be best man?"

Silas cleared his throat and turned to Fred who blinked up at him. "Did you want me to run and fetch someone?" his valet asked, still looking mystified about what was going on.

"No, you daft beggar," Silas said, shaking his head. "I'd like you to be best man, if you don't mind?"

Fred gaped at him, his colour rising dramatically before his face turned a stark white.

"B-But I c-couldn't, my lord," he stammered. "You're a viscount and I… I—"

"You've been a good friend, Fred," Silas said, his voice low. "And this wedding will cause scandal enough whether or not my valet stands as best man, and I for one don't give a tinker's cuss. Are you in?"

Silas watched as Fred squared his shoulders and stood tall, his eyes suspiciously shiny.

"It would be a great honour, my lord."

Silas beamed and let out a breath of relief. "Right, then. Come along, what are we all waiting for? I have a beautiful woman who wants to marry me, and I want it done before she comes to her senses."

"It's a fair point," St Clair said, hurrying away to greet the ladies before Silas could retaliate.

Chapter 19

Kitty!

The most extraordinary thing has happened. Lucia is marrying Lord Cavendish by special licence at his home this afternoon!

Naturally, in the circumstances, I think the two of them will be unwilling to go to Green Park for the fireworks tonight. I depend on you in that case to bolster my courage enough to face Montagu.

Oh, how I wish we'd found a way to get out of it!

Come to stay with me for a few days, there's a dear. The house will be dreadfully quiet without Lucia.

—Excerpt of a letter from Miss Matilda Hunt to Miss Kitty Connolly.

1st August 1814. Cavendish House, The Strand, London

"Here."

Matilda looked around to see St Clair holding out a handkerchief. Just as well, as the one she'd brought was sodden.

"Thank you," she murmured, hoping she didn't look too much of a fright. "I always cry at weddings," she added, sniffing.

"So does my mother," St Clair said, with the weighty sigh of a man well used to carrying extra handkerchiefs for such occasions.

Matilda turned her attention back to the couple at the front of the room and sighed. The way they were staring at each other made a lump rise in her throat. It was rather wonderful, and yet somehow too intimate. She didn't doubt Lord Cavendish would have the house cleared bare moments after they'd served the wedding breakfast. He looked like a man eager to be alone with his wife.

Not that she could blame him. Aashini looked stunning. Dressed in a vibrant green dress, she was young and fresh and lovely, her golden skin glowing with health and vibrancy. There was a pretty flush at her cheeks and a sparkle in her dark eyes that Matilda had never seen before. She looked happy. Radiantly happy.

As did her grandmother.

Matilda had not yet been introduced to the old lady who was sitting and watching proceedings with as much emotion as her, but she was eager to be. She was fascinated by her, by the glorious colour of her yellow gown, which seemed to be one lengthy swathe of fabric, and by the red mark painted on her forehead. Questions crowded her mind as she realised how ignorant she was about the country of Aashini's birth, and she hoped she'd be able to answer some of them after the ceremony.

She turned her attention back to the happy couple as the minister spoke the final lines of the service.

"For, as much as Silas and Aashini have consented together in holy wedlock, and have witnessed the same before God and this company, and thereto have given and pledged their troth either to other, and have declared the same by giving and receiving of a ring, and by joining of hands; I pronounce that they be man and wife together. In the name of the Father, and of the Son, and of the Holy Ghost. Amen."

Matilda found need of St Clair's handkerchief once again and was relieved that the minister carried on through another prayer and a sermon before bringing the ceremony to a close, so she could get herself under control.

***

The wedding breakfast was an intimate affair, for which Aashini was grateful. She was feeling thoroughly overwhelmed.

Just Matilda, St Clair, Dharani, and Mr Davis were in attendance, though Silas's valet insisted he ought not be eating with the *quality*.

"Stop objecting and sit down," Dharani scolded the man, making Aashini bite her lip, wondering if the fellow would take offence. "What?" her grandmother demanded, catching her anxious look. "I'm hungry, if no one else is. Aren't you hungry?" she demanded of Mr Davis, who looked at the impressive spread in front of him and shrugged.

"I could eat," he admitted.

"Excellent," Dharani said, waving at him to sit down at the place beside her. "You sit there," she instructed, as Mr Davis looked as though he dare not do anything less. "Now, I understand valets know everything about their masters, is that true?"

"Well, of course," Mr Davis replied, looking very much on his dignity.

Dharani grinned and leaned into the man, making very sure to look Silas in the eyes as she stage-whispered, "Tell me *everything*."

Aashini turned to her new husband and held up her hand, pointing to the ring finger. "You can't change your mind," she said. "Before God and everyone."

Silas snorted and took her hand in his, bringing it to his lips. "I couldn't be happier, and don't worry; I have your grandmother's measure," he said with a wink, before adding with a rueful smile. "The only trouble is, I think she has mine too."

Aashini laughed, feeling her heart expand as Matilda bent her head to listen to her grandmother, her expression eager as Dharani held her new audience captive.

"Are you happy, love?"

She turned then, beaming up at Silas and wondering how he could possibly ask such a ridiculous question.

"I feel like I'm dreaming," she admitted, staring at him in wonder. Goodness, but he was handsome. Not like St Clair, it was true. He wasn't refined—his features and manners were too harsh, and his way of speaking too direct—but that was what she loved about him. Silas Anson was a good man who knew what it was to face adversity and overcome it. Her husband was a man who would always respect her wishes, and never bully her or make her feel less than his equal. That was a rare thing. She knew it, and she would never, ever take it for granted.

"When can we make them leave?" he murmured in her ear, making her blush and a strange, coiling heat unravel in the pit of her stomach.

"Not yet," she replied, scandalised and delighted all at once.

"Are you sure?" he grumbled, even though he knew the answer very well.

"Perfectly sure."

She laughed, delighted by his mutinous expression and couldn't resist leaning into him and allowing him to steal a kiss. "Until later," she murmured.

It did seem an interminable time before the party broke up but, thankfully, Matilda and St Clair both needed to prepare to attend the fireworks at Green Park.

"I'm sorry I can't accompany you tonight," Aashini said to Matilda, who just snorted.

"Liar," she said, laughing and making Aashini blush.

"Well, yes," Aashini admitted. "But I'm leaving you with Montagu."

"No, no," Matilda replied, with an airy wave of her hand. "I have my companion: Mrs Bradford for propriety, and Kitty for moral support. The marquess holds no terror for me, I assure you."

Aashini sighed, privately wondering whether she'd be less concerned if Matilda *was* terrified.

"You will take care, won't you, Tilda," she said, taking her friend's hands and holding them tight. Matilda rolled her eyes.

"Of course!" she exclaimed. "Stop worrying." Moving closer, she whispered in Aashini's ear. "You're the one with a wedding night ahead of her not me."

"Oh, hush!" Aashini protested, and then waved her friend off.

St Clair had departed a few minutes earlier and she looked up to see Mr Davis escorting Dharani up the stairs to her room, deep in conversation with her charismatic grandmother.

"Don't worry, it's a big house," Silas murmured as he slid his arms around her waist and pulled her back against his chest. "And her maid is awaiting her in her room."

"You've thought of everything, Lord Cavendish," Aashini said, turning in his arms and feeling suddenly rather shy.

"Indeed, I have, Lady Cavendish," he said, making her breath hitch.

"Oh," she said. "That's the first time I've heard it said. Lady Cavendish."

"It suits you very well, love," Silas said with a smile, his eyes warm.

"Yes," Aashini said, grinning despite the fact her nerves were all on end. "It does rather."

Silas looked as though he would kiss her, but there was the bustle of activity as his staff cleared away the wedding breakfast, so he held out his arm instead.

"Come with me," he said, a wicked glint in his eyes that made her stomach do the most peculiar flip. "I have something to show you."

He guided her to the stairs and Aashini laughed, raising one eyebrow. "You have something to show me upstairs?" she teased as she put her foot on the first tread. "You do realise we're married? There's no need to resort to subterfuge."

Silas gave a huff of laughter. "Give me a little credit, love," he said, looking reproachful. "I have a present for you."

"Oh!" Aashini beamed at him. "I like presents."

"So do I," Silas replied, holding her gaze. "And I can't wait to unwrap mine."

Aashini felt her cheeks heat at that comment, and couldn't hold his gaze as he chuckled and led her to his bedroom.

She took a deep breath as she looked around, inhaling the masculine aroma of his room. Starched linen and the faint scent of bay rum cologne lingered; it seemed to slide over her skin, sending illicit thrills of excitement through her blood.

Silas left her to investigate his private sanctuary for a moment as he went through an adjoining door, and Aashini trailed her hands over heavy wood furniture and luxurious fabrics in shades of dark green and blue.

She turned as he came back, bearing a large, flat leather box and looking nervous but rather pleased with himself.

"Here," he said, placing the box in her hands. "I took Dharani's advice, but it was a hard thing to find at short notice."

Curious, Aashini opened the box and gasped. Inside was a piece of traditional Indian jewellery: a *maang tikka,* which was worn over the forehead and into the hair. It was a large circle of jewels, surrounded by pearls that moved when she lifted the piece in her hands. In the centre was a large emerald, in the shape of a teardrop, surrounded by diamonds. From the large jewelled disc came fine gold strands, studded with pearls, that would lie in drapes over her hair.

Aashini's throat grew tight as she moved her hands this way and that, watching the light catch the jewels and sparkle like a night sky.

"I…." she began, too overwhelmed to know what to say.

"We can change it," Silas said, his voice urgent. "If it's not right. Get something more to your taste. I'll have it made for you. Hell, I have a dozen made if it would please you."

Aashini shook her head, torn between laughter and tears, not for the first time that day.

"N-No," she stammered. "It's beautiful, glorious…. Oh, Silas, it's *perfect*."

She heard him exhale and looked up, his face blurred by the tears in her eyes.

"You really like it?"

"I really do," she said. Just to reassure him she moved to stand before the full length looking glass in the corner of his room and held it up, showing him just how it ought to be worn.

Silas caught his breath as he stared over her shoulder at her.

"Astonishing," he said, sounding awed and breathless. "My God, Aashini, what the devil did I do to deserve you?"

Aashini put the lovely gift back into its silk-lined box and closed the lid with care, setting it on the bedside table before turning to him and wrapping her arms about his waist.

"You were there when I needed you. When no one else was, when no one else troubled to look further than what they thought they saw, you did. You saw *me*, Silas, like no one has ever done before, and I couldn't help but fall in love with you."

She saw his throat working, and the emotion in his eyes as he lowered his head, pressing his forehead to hers.

"I love you," he said, the words so sincere that her heart swelled.

"I know."

She lifted her mouth to his, and he needed no further invitation. Aashini sank into his embrace, relishing the strength of him, the heat and the tenderness that lay in the big hands that caressed her back. He deepened the kiss, and she felt she could have purred like a happy cat as his touch eased away any nerves she might have had.

Dharani had never left her in ignorance, unlike many of the young ladies who had become her friends. *Nani maa* had always been of the opinion that one could not stop a scoundrel ruining you, if you didn't know what tricks were up his sleeve, or anywhere else for that matter. Still, it was one thing understanding the mechanics in theory, and quite another to be facing your wedding night… but now, in her husband's arms, she couldn't think of a single thing to worry about.

He would take care of her, he would rather die than hurt her, and—if the pleasure simmering in her blood already was anything to go on—she was unlikely to leave this room in any way dissatisfied with her marriage.

"Aashini," he whispered, and the sound of the name that had been lost to her for so long, whispered with such love, made her smile up at him. "I love this colour on you," he murmured, tracing a finger over the neckline and making her shiver. "It reminds me of spring and sunshine, when everything is fresh and new and vibrant." He paused and then gave her a wry smile. "Having said that… I can't wait to get it off you."

She laughed and turned around so he could do just that.

"Dressmakers are the least romantic people in the world, did you know that?" he muttered, on being confronted with a rather large number of tiny buttons. "A lesser man would rip the bloody thing in half."

"Less complaining, more unbuttoning," Aashini instructed, trying not to giggle.

"Yes, wife," he said, obediently returning his attention to the job at hand.

At last, the dress fell, sliding down her body in a rustle of satin as she heard his breath quicken. She helped him with the petticoats and stays, amused to discover his hands fumbling in his eagerness to unwrap his prize. Finally, only her shift and stockings remained, and Aashini could not suppress the shiver that ran over her as the weight of his gaze took her in.

He looked up, noting her tremor, his dark brows pulling together. "You're not afraid? Of me, or—"

She silenced him, putting a finger to his lips and shaking her head. "Not of anything, not anymore. Not with you." With a devilish smile, she looked up at him from under her lashes. "And Dharani made certain I was well informed, I promise."

To her amusement, Silas looked somewhat daunted by that. "Why does that make me uneasy?"

Aashini shrugged and tugged at his coat. "You're still dressed," she said, sounding rather bereft.

"But I've not finished," he said, grinning and reaching for the hem of her shift. "May I?"

Her heart was hammering in her chest now, anticipation thrumming in her veins and making her feel lightheaded. "You may."

In one swift motion the shift was gone, and she watched as Silas caught his breath, his eyes so dark the vibrant indigo blue she loved was almost drowned in the depths of his desire.

His eyes met hers and she knew he couldn't speak, but that was better than any pretty words he might have spoken. Knowing that this meant so much to him that it had stolen his ability to speak made her heart sing.

He kissed her then, drawing her close, his hands exploring tenderly as he caressed her.

"Come here," he said, sounding breathless as he took her hand and led her to the bed. "Lay down."

She did as he asked, feeling a little exposed, laid out before him as his hungry gaze roved over her, but the smile on his face was so utterly dazed with happiness that it didn't last long.

"Still too many clothes," she reminded him, snapping him out of his reverie.

"Oh, yes," he said, laughing a little.

She watched in amusement as he flung his clothes to the floor as fast as he could, leaving everything in a heap. Her amusement faded to avid interest once his chest was bare and only his small clothes remained. Suddenly, her throat felt dry.

The final items hit the floor and he stepped towards the bed, grinning and looking outrageously smug as Aashini stared at him with wide eyes.

"This is the point where you say, *oh my*."

"Oh," Aashini said, her eyes riveted to the dark patch of hair and the very male part of him she simply could not look away from. "Oh *m-my*?"

"Yes, just like that," he said, chuckling and climbing into bed beside her.

He pulled her into his arms, and Aashini gasped in shock at the sensation. His skin seemed to burn against hers, so much hotter and yet soft too, except where the rough hair covered him on his chest, and his legs and… there. Her hands roamed over him as he watched her, allowing her time to get used to him.

She looked up, caught for a moment in the warmth of his smile, before returning to her exploration. His chest was heavily muscled beneath her hand, and the dark hair was coarse and wiry. Aashini ran her fingertips through it before moving to touch his nipple, intrigued at how the skin grew taut as she circled it.

Silas sucked in a breath and she looked up, a little startled.

"Don't stop," he urged, smiling at her. "I'm all yours."

"And there's such a lot of you to have," she murmured, biting her lip and looking up again as he shook, to discover he was laughing. "Well, there is," she protested, blushing a little.

"I wasn't complaining, love," he chuckled. He shifted onto his side so they were face to face. "Don't stop," he urged again. "Touch me."

Emboldened by the desire in his eyes, Aashini traced the path that led between his ribs and down his stomach until her hand met skin so fine that she gasped with wonder. She caressed him with slow, careful movements, until she realised he was breathing hard.

"Like this?" she asked, curious as to how to please him. He nodded, and then covered her hand with his own, showing her how he liked to be touched. Aashini copied him, delighted by the sensation of power as he groaned and closed his eyes. "You like that," she murmured, grinning as he made a helpless sound somewhere between a laugh and a sigh.

She moved closer, pressing her lips to his, and it appeared her explorations were at an end for the moment as he tumbled her onto her back. He kissed her for long, delicious moments as she revelled in the feel of him, the weight and heat that might have overpowered her and made her nervous. Yet that was impossible with Silas, with his smiles and his soft eyes, and his murmurs of sweet words and encouragement.

His mouth left hers, trailing down her neck and over her skin. She arched up as he kissed her the way he had that day when she'd agreed to marry him—if he asked her again, after her birthday. That day was tomorrow, but she didn't much care now. Thoughts of revenge and retaliation seemed a long way away, and of much less importance than they ever had before.

Only the present and the future mattered now.

The past wasn't going anywhere.

"You're so sweet," he murmured, against her skin. "I've tasted nothing so decadent and lovely in all my life."

"Not even cake?" she asked, feeling like laughing as happiness bubbled up inside her.

"Not even close," he said, kissing his way down her stomach and making her eyes widen as he nuzzled the tender skin at the apex of her thighs.

"Ices at *Gunter's*?" she said, so breathless now it was hard to speak.

"Never," he said, his voice firm. "There is nothing else in the world as sweet as you, especially here."

Aashini gasped as his tongue found her most private flesh, and she couldn't think of a single thing to say, which was probably for the best. She didn't want him to have to stop and answer her.

The pleasure was so intense that she squirmed beneath him, uncertain of how to endure it, but his large hands held her in place as the feeling crested and coalesced. Aashini held her breath, aware she was lingering on a precipice, before tumbling over the edge. She grasped at the sheets, feeling as though she might fly away if she didn't hold on tight, but Silas was there, steadying her, easing her through the waves that gentled now. He kissed and nuzzled her, ensuring he'd coaxed every last delicious jolt from her body before his mouth moved on.

She lay dazed, her eyelids as heavy as her limbs as he kissed his way back up her body, painting soft patterns over her stomach and breasts with his clever tongue.

As he nuzzled into her neck, she sighed and somehow found the strength to raise her arms and put them around him, one hand stroking his hair.

"So lovely," he murmured, making her gasp as he pressed his arousal against the still sensitive place between her thighs.

She arched in surprise as he slid against her slick heat, and the pleasure he'd conjured sparked to life once more, even stronger than before.

Instinctively, she opened her legs to him, raising her hips, needing him in a way she'd never experienced before. Something inside her clamoured for him, ached for him to fill the emptiness that she only now recognised for what it was.

"Yes," she whispered, her hands caressing his powerful back.

"I don't want to hurt you," he said, concern in his eyes as he positioned himself and nudged gently forward.

"You won't," she said, smiling up at him. "I trust you."

"Tell me if—"

She pulled him down for a kiss and he moaned as he slid deeper inside.

In truth it did hurt, but Dharani had promised her that if she relaxed and trusted her husband, all would be well, so she did. She closed her eyes and breathed deeply, concentrating on the feel of his large body surrounding her, the pleasure of being close to him, and little by little the pain faded.

Silas made an incoherent sound of pleasure so raw that a visceral shock of desire surged through her. Goodness, she wanted him to make that sound again, so primitive and desperate. She moved with him and got her wish, gratified as her own pleasure intensified and she moaned herself, a little startled to have made such a wanton sound.

She looked up as Silas stared down at her, his eyes dark with need, and she realised the sound of her pleasure affected him too.

"Aashini," he murmured, his voice rough as their bodies moved in concert, the momentum gathering further with each passing moment.

Silas reached down, hooking his arm beneath her knee and opening her further. All at once, the angle was just right and the pleasure grew so intense that she couldn't breathe. As before she waited, knowing what was to come now, trembling with anticipation of the moment as she clung to him, knowing he was there too.

Silas gave a fierce cry and bucked in her arms, tipping her into the dazzling light that sparked and glittered behind her eyes and in her blood as she arched beneath the weight of him, glorying in the moment, in him and the joy he'd brought her.

He stilled, breathing hard, his skin damp with exertion as they came back to the world by increments. She blinked up at him, still hazy with desire as he gave a startled laugh.

"My word," he murmured, staring down at her and then grinning like a boy who'd just discovered a full bag of sweets. "My word," he said again and then laughed as he rolled onto his back, taking her with him.

He shifted a little, so her head rested on his arm and he could look at her. "Are you all right?"

Aashini nodded, fairly certain words were too much of an effort for the moment.

"I didn't hurt you?"

She shook her head this time, unable to stop the idiotic grin that stretched out over her mouth. Silas reached out and traced the line of her jaw.

"Thank you," he said, his heart in his eyes for her to see. "For trusting me, for loving me. I still can't quite believe it, but… thank you."

Aashini didn't have words for that either, but she hoped the tears in her own eyes and the ridiculous smile… and the kiss, would make her feelings plain.

Chapter 20

Harriet, she's done it! Lucia has married Lord Cavendish! That's one in the eye for the old tabbies!

—Excerpt of a letter from Miss Kitty Connolly to Miss Harriet Stanhope.

2nd August 1814. The Earl of Ulceby's residence, Hyde Park, London.

"There's nothing to be afraid of."

Aashini looked at her husband, finding his expression grave, but his voice so full of warmth and reassurance that she could not doubt him.

They sat in his carriage, outside the Earl of Ulceby's home, while Aashini and Dharani gathered their courage. His valet, Mr Davis, was with them too. Why, she wasn't certain, but he and Dharani seemed to have become fast friends, and he was a cheerful soul and a rather heartening presence, so she didn't mind.

"We've come this far, *bhanvaraa*," Dharani said, reaching out and clasping her hand, holding on tight.

She turned to her grandmother, seeing the beloved features of a woman who had faced so much and not only endured, but triumphed. It was *Nani maa* who had brought Aashini here, her guidance that had kept her strong. Suddenly, what she must do now was less about revenge and more about doing this for her grandmother, for her father, for the people that had loved her and wanted her to have a good and happy life.

Aashini took a deep breath.

"I'm ready," she said.

Silas smiled at her, a smile that promised her he'd never let her down and that made her heart lift.

He helped both her and Dharani out of the carriage, taking her arm as Mr Davis escorted Dharani. Her grandmother looked fierce today, dressed in a bright red sari, a look of defiant determination blazing in her dark eyes.

The butler looked startled as he opened the door to them.

"I'm afraid Lord Ulceby—" The man began, but Silas cut him off, pushing past him.

"Where is he?"

"In his study, my lord, but you cannot—"

"Oh, I think you'll find I can," Silas said, glowering so fiercely that the butler quailed and offered no further objection. They both knew where the study was, of course, as Aashini had visited it before, and Silas had spied on her doing so.

Aashini's heart was hammering, but it was impossible to be afraid with her husband at her side. She glanced back at Dharani, who flashed her a wicked grin, and Aashini's breath caught. It would be all right. No matter what happened, she wasn't alone.

Silas flung the study door open and strode in as Aashini put her chin up, searching the room until her gaze rested on the Earl of Ulceby.

He was a lot less frightening than he'd ever been in her imagination, or the few times she'd seen him before, somehow. Sitting behind the massive oak desk where she had smoked a cigar—what seemed a lifetime ago—he looked shrunken, somehow diminished, his face as grey as his hair. She realised then that he'd feared this moment. He'd lived in fear just as she had. Somehow, that made her feel better.

It gave her courage.

"What is the meaning of this?"

Aashini looked at the short, stocky man who had made this indignant statement. He had the air of a lawyer, and she didn't doubt she'd guessed correctly.

Ulceby said nothing. He didn't need to ask. He knew.

She watched as his eyes drifted to Dharani, and then to her.

He gave a snort of disgust. "It's her," he said to the short man who stood at his back. "The late earl's mixed breed bastard."

Aashini felt the jolt of fury surge through Silas and gripped his hand tighter.

"Shut your damned mouth or I'll do the job for you," he said, staring at Ulceby with undisguised loathing. "You're not fit to look upon her, let alone speak of her."

Ulceby laughed, a low mocking sound that made unease slide beneath her skin. "I see she's leading you around by your prick, same as she has the rest of the male members of the *ton*."

The earl sneered. Silas let go of her hand and surged forward, smacking both hands down on the man's desk with such rage that everyone jumped.

"Insult my wife again, and I will forget my promise to her to do no violence today."

"Your *wife*?" There was a flash of anger, and something that might have been concern in the man's eyes at that.

A claim from an illegitimate, half-breed Indian girl was no doubt something he'd believed he could overcome. The wife of a viscount, however….

"Yes, my wife," Silas growled, and Aashini could feel the power of his anger, the desire in him to hurt the man who had caused her such pain. "And you'd best keep a civil tongue in your head or, so help me, I'll eviscerate you."

The earl stared back at Silas, apparently unmoved, but Aashini had seen him flinch, and seen what little colour he had bleed from his face. He was afraid.

Nonetheless, the earl was a powerful man, and one motivated by greed.

"I tell you what, Cavendish," he said, his eyes settling on her husband with stark hatred. "Leave now, and I'll not tell the world about her heritage. Everyone can go on believing she's simply a Spanish whore, at least that won't close quite so many doors to you as the truth."

"Silas!"

His name rang out in the bare second before he lunged across the desk, but he stilled, turning to her.

"Please," she said, shaking her head at him.

She saw the effort it took to control himself, but he did so because she asked it of him. He took a step back, and Aashini moved forward to stand before the earl, meeting his gaze.

"How strange," she said, as much to herself as she looked him over. "My whole life you have been such a huge presence, like a terrifying monster waiting in the dark. Yet, you aren't a monster at all, are you? You're just a man, a weak and greedy man who would stoop to murdering a child to get what you want."

She was gratified as he flinched a little, and the stuffy little lawyer gave a gasp of shock.

"I can destroy you," he said, the disgust in his eyes as he stared at her blatant. "I will, if you're so foolish as to try to claim—"

"Claim what's mine?" Aashini interrupted him, realising she truly wasn't afraid. Not any longer. "Yes, I shall claim what is mine, what my father always intended should be mine, and no, you won't destroy me. That is not in your power."

"Oh, but it is, I shall tell the *ton* just what you are, and they shall revile you for it."

Aashini gave a soft huff of laughter. "And you think that can destroy me?" She shook her head and turned to look up at her husband, who was staring at her with such adoration that she felt any hatred she had for the bitter man before her fizzle away. She didn't have room in her life for such destructive emotions, not any longer.

She turned back to the earl. "*I* will tell the *ton* who I am. I haven't the least intention of hiding it. I only did so to hide from you until I was strong enough to face you. I am strong enough, and there is nothing you can do to hurt me. I pity you," she added, realising she meant it. She could see the strain of living in his eyes, the weight of too many years of hatred and loathing poisoning his soul.

"So you should, Aashini."

She turned then, seeing a dangerous look glittering in Dharani's eyes as her grandmother stepped closer to the earl, with Mr Davis supporting her.

"Kali comes for you," she said, giving him a smile that even unnerved Aashini. "You who have defiled your body and soul with your love for gold, a love so great you would have slaughtered one of her children to line your pockets. Such arrogance, such attachment to earthly pleasures…oh, she is displeased, and she hears my prayers, my lord."

Aashini turned back to Ulceby to see him staring at Dharani, his face ashen.

"Superstitious heathen nonsense," he scoffed, but there was no one in the room that believed him unmoved. He would dream of Kali with her garland of severed heads, sword in hand, coming for him.

Silas moved back to the desk, staring at Ulceby with loathing as Fred joined him and put a sheaf of papers into his hands. Silas threw them down on the desk.

"Just so things are abundantly clear," he said. "Those are details of every debt you have outstanding from everyone in the country. Every gambling club, every merchant, every private debt, they're all there."

"What of it?" Ulceby sneered, striving to look unconcerned, though Aashini could see he was sweating now, and breathing hard.

"I bought them," Silas said, smiling and holding the man's gaze as his meaning became clear.

Ulceby's gasp of shock echoed Aashini's. She hadn't known that, hadn't known that Silas had been working to ensure she was safe for… *for how long*? How long must it have taken to gather all that information and…?

Her throat grew tight.

"I own you," Silas said, his voice hard and cold. "I need only call in these debts and your house of cards comes toppling down." He put his hands on the desk once more and leaned over it. "Give me a reason," he said, his voice low and threatening.

The Earl of Ulceby swallowed.

"We will be paying a visit to the late earl's lawyers later this afternoon," Silas carried on. "I expect there will be some papers to sign, but otherwise I don't imagine there will be any impediment to my wife's inheritance. *Will there*, my lord?"

Ulceby didn't look at Silas, didn't speak. Aashini wasn't sure he could. He looked ill, but he shook his head.

"Excellent," Silas replied, looking almost jovial now as he held his arm out to Aashini. "Come along, my lady. Unless you had anything further to add?"

Aashini turned back to look at the man who had destroyed so much of her life. He was grey and sweating, and she wondered who would mourn him when he was gone.

"No, my lord," she said, looking now at Silas, smiling up at the man who had helped her find her place in the world, who had helped her find her home. "Nothing further."

Silas escorted her back to their waiting carriage and, even after everyone was settled and the carriage in motion, it was several minutes before anyone spoke.

Naturally it was Dharani.

"I thought that went well."

Mischief glittered in her eyes, and Aashini burst out laughing alongside everyone else, all of them grateful to her for breaking the tension.

"Aashini," Silas said, taking her hand and raising it to his lips. "I was never so proud in my whole life. The way you faced him. You leave me breathless, love."

"He's right," Dharani said, nodding with approval, her eyes so full of love that Aashini had to blink back tears. "I have always been proud of you, *bhanvaraa,* but never more so than today. Such dignity, and such strength of character. Kali was with you, as proud of you as I am."

Aashini gave a shaky laugh, trying hard not to cry. She was grateful to Mr Davis, who leaned across the carriage and offered her his handkerchief.

"Thank you," she mumbled, drying her eyes. "I can't believe it's over. It *is* over?" She looked to Silas, who nodded.

"He's all but bankrupt. Even if I don't call in those debts, he will have to sell everything that's not entailed if he wants to survive."

"But, Silas," she said, staring at him in wonder. "How, when?"

Silas grinned and shook his head. "It's Fred here who deserves your thanks. I set him to investigate the earl, not realising I'd released a bloodhound. He sniffed out every debt from here to Land's End."

Fred flushed scarlet as Aashini turned to look at him. "Only because his lordship asked me to," he said, rubbing the back of his neck and shrugging.

"When?" Aashini asked. "How long did this take?"

"It was after the Countess St Clair's garden party," Fred said, frowning a little. "I remember, 'cause his lordship showed me up by arriving looking like he'd slept in a ditch."

Aashini gave a startled laugh and turned to Silas, who just shrugged.

"But that was weeks ago," she said, smiling at him. "All this time, you've been working on my behalf?"

Silas shook his head, humour glinting in his eyes. "On my own behalf, I assure you," he said, squeezing her hand a little tighter.

Aashini beamed at him and stared about the carriage, at her husband, at Dharani, and even Fred, whom she barely knew, but who seemed to have accepted her and her grandmother as part of his household without so much as a blink.

There would be those who jeered and tried to hurt her, and those she cared for. That was the world they lived in, and there was no denying it. Yet, she felt it no longer had the power to hurt her in quite the same way it might once have done. She was loved and respected, she had a home, a place where she belonged, and that was an armour of sorts, one she would wear with pride.

"Should you like to return to India one day?" Silas asked her, surprising her with the question.

"I-I don't know," she said, smiling as she realised she could. She could go back and revisit the place she'd been born.

"Your father left you the property there, *bhanvaraa*. It's yours. You ought to go back, pay your respects to your parents, explore the past now there are no ghosts to haunt you."

Aashini nodded, realising Dharani was right. She turned back to Silas.

"But would you like to go?" she asked, realising he might not want to travel so far.

"Would I like to go on an adventure with you?" he said, laughing. "What a ridiculous question. Just tell me when."

She grinned, sitting back against the plush seats of the carriage. "Well, not for a while. There are plenty of adventures to have here, for the time being, I think." She looked up at Silas from under her eyelashes, intrigued and pleased by the way his eyes darkened.

"As you like, love," he murmured, raising her hand to press a kiss to her fingers. He turned back to Dharani, still clasping Aashini's hand.

"And you, Dharani. Will you come with us when we go?"

"Me?" Her grandmother pulled a face and shuddered. "No. The journey nearly killed me the first time, I'll not go again. Besides, this is home now." Dharani looked out of the window at a fine English summer's day, and a blue sky dotted with white clouds before turning back and shivering. "It's too cold, too grey, and too…*drizzly*— why can't it rain properly? —but, anyway," she said with a sniff, "I'm used to it now."

"Just as well," Silas remarked. "I'll need someone to keep an eye on the staff in my absence."

Dharani chuckled as Fred huffed and looked a little indignant.

"What are you sulking about?" Silas demanded. "I can hardly go to India without you, can I?"

Mollified, Fred grinned and then looked anxious. "'Ere, aren't there snakes in India?"

Aashini sighed as she watched a look of pure devilment pass across her grandmother's face, and settled in to listen to a lecture about all the dangerous and deadly things poor Fred was likely to encounter, from man-eating tigers and stampeding elephants, to scorpions and crocodiles. She knew full well that Dharani had likely not seen half of the things she listed in her lifetime, but *Nani maa* was having so much fun that she kept her mouth shut.

She could always reassure Fred later.

Chapter 21

Your presence is required for an urgent meeting of the Peculiar Ladies!

Lucia needs us.

—Excerpt of a letter from Miss Matilda Hunt to all the Peculiar Ladies.

4th August 1814. Meeting of the Peculiar Ladies, Upper Walpole Street, London.

"She's here!" Bonnie exclaimed from her position at the window.

"All right, dear, there's no need to shriek," Matilda said, laughing as Bonnie bounded back to where Ruth was inspecting a table groaning under the weight of cake and cream buns.

"Now, where are the macaroons?" Ruth muttered. "I know Cook made some."

"More to the point, where would you *put* macaroons?" Bonnie asked, gesturing to the overcrowded table top.

Ruth returned a look of bewilderment. "Oh, I can always find a space for macaroons," she said, with perfect sincerity.

"Shh! She's coming," hissed Kitty, who'd been standing with her ear to the door.

They'd gathered all of the Ladies today except for Alice, who had gone to the country early to escape the heat. Poor Alice would be so disappointed she was missing out again, but she'd been out of sorts, and Nate had decided getting out of the city would do her good. Privately, Matilda couldn't help but wonder if there was another reason for her friend's indisposition, but she kept such thoughts to herself.

The ladies all stood arm-in-arm and smothering their laughter, until Aashini walked through the door.

"*Good afternoon, Lady Cavendish*!" they all chorused, like a gaggle of unruly children, before exclaiming and squealing, and running to shower the new arrival with rice and congratulations.

"Don't fall over this time," Ruth called out to Bonnie, who'd almost broken her neck—not to mention her behind—the last time rice had been scattered about Ruth's opulent home.

Too late, Bonnie shrieked, and it was only Harriet's fast reactions that kept her upright, though only momentarily. Matilda covered her mouth with her hand as the two young women sank slowly and inelegantly to the floor.

"Oh, dear," she murmured with a sigh, trying hard not to laugh.

It was an effort she abandoned as she caught Aashini's eye.

Matilda held her arms out to her and Aashini ran forward, hugging her tightly.

"Oh, how good it is to see you," Matilda said, beaming at her friend. "And how wonderful you look! My, but you are glowing. Married life agrees with you, I think?"

"It does," Aashini replied, grinning and blushing. "Silas is…." She blushed harder and then laughed. "He's rather wonderful, actually."

"Lucky girl," Matilda said with a sigh, before looking around. Shrieks of laughter could be heard as Harriet and Bonnie tried to get up, only to go over again as the combination of polished wood floor and rice conspired against them. "I think perhaps a grown up is required."

"Do you know where we can find one?" Aashini asked, smirking a little.

"No idea."

Once order had been restored and the ladies settled with tea and cakes, Matilda tapped her teaspoon on the side of her cup. She glanced over at Aashini, recognising the anxiety in her eyes and returning a reassuring smile. Matilda knew these women, knew and loved them as though they were her own sisters. They would not let them down.

***

Aashini swallowed, setting down her cup as it rattled in the saucer. The sound of Matilda's teaspoon chiming against the fine porcelain made her heart leap, but she would not back down now. These women had been her friends for the past months, she had to trust them.

"Ladies," Matilda said, smiling at the gathering. "We are here, in part, to congratulate our dear friend on her recent marriage."

Aashini flushed a little as everyone turned and grinned at her. Prue, who had recently become the Duchess of Bedwin, sent her a saucy wink before reaching for another cake.

"That, however, is not the only reason. Our dear Lucia has a remarkable story to tell you." She turned and smiled, and Aashini licked her lips, knowing that was her cue.

"Good afternoon, ladies," she said, before amending. "My friends. I think I ought to begin by telling you… my name is not Lucia de Feria."

***

12th August 1814. Cavendish House, The Strand, London

"What if no one comes? The season is over. Everyone who's anyone has gone to the country."

Dharani sighed and looked up, levelling a look at Aashini that suggested she stop wittering. "With the amount of gossip flying about this past week, Fred tells me the place will burst at the seams as everyone comes to gawp at the new Lady Cavendish."

Aashini frowned as her stomach tied itself in a knot. "I'm not sure that's making me feel better."

When the Peculiar Ladies had suggested it, a ball had seemed the very thing. A grand celebration of her marriage to Silas, a belated twenty-first birthday ball, and the first time the *ton* would see Aashini, not Lucia de Feria, take her place among them as her father had intended.

Aashini smiled as she remembered the appalled silence that had filled the room when she'd finished her tale, right up until Bonnie had thrown her arms around her and kissed her cheek.

"Can I meet your grandmother?" she'd demanded in the next breath. "She sounds like someone I need to know."

Aashini had quailed a little at that. She didn't think Bonnie needed the least encouragement towards plain speaking, but was touched all the same. After that, everyone was talking at once. There hadn't been one of them who had looked at her askance or made her feel she no longer belonged. It made sense, of course, now she thought about it. That had been the purpose of the Peculiar Ladies, after all: a safe place for all of those who didn't have the perfect combination of beauty, wealth, breeding, and flawless reputation. They all had experiences or circumstances which set them apart, and which brought them together, too.

Matilda had grinned at her then as the cacophony only grew, a smug *I told you so* expression in her eyes that Aashini didn't begrudge her one bit.

"Keep still."

Aashini was brought back to the present by Dharani's admonishment. She looked up to see her grandmother holding a small dish of vermillion powder called *sindoor* which she was applying to the parting in her hair. Once done, Dharani set the powder aside and reached for the *alta*. This was a red paint also made from vermillion, used to cover the tips of her fingers and soles of her feet, and her toes. Aashini bit her lip, trying not to squirm as Dharani applied the paint with a soft brush. It was cold and it tickled. It was the Bengali tradition for a bride to apply paint in this manner during the days of celebration following her wedding, and Aashini was embracing her traditions today.

The *ton* had come to see Aashini, and see her they would.

Dharani applied the *bindi* next, the small red dot position close between her eyebrows. The bindi denoted *ajna* or the sixth chakra, the seat of concealed wisdom, and Aashini had never worn it before. The sense of connection, of belonging, became stronger as Dharani's eyes met hers and her grandmother smiled, understanding.

Once done to Dharani's satisfaction and the paint dry, her grandmother reached for the box containing the *maang tikka* Silas had given her. She opened the lid and smiled down at the glittering jewels with approval.

"A good man, your husband," she said, grinning at Aashini. "Rich, too. This is always helpful."

Aashini snorted and shook her head.

"Keep still or you'll be wearing it on your nose," Dharani scolded, settling the heavy disc in place upon her forehead and then arranging the fine gold chains, studded with pearls, so they rested in pleasing drapes over her forehead and hair.

"Ah, so lovely." Dharani clapped her hands together, looking gleeful. "Mary, bring me the sari," she commanded as her maid scurried to bring the carefully folded swathe of glorious material. It was a bright scarlet red *banarasi* silk sari, trimmed with a wide gold band, and Aashini felt her heart skip with a combination of excitement and fear. Red was the traditional colour for Bengali brides, but most of the *ton* would never have seen an outfit like this before, and she could only imagine what they would make of it.

"Like this, *Nani maa*?" she asked as she wound it about her hips and tucked the edge of the sari into the petticoat beneath.

Dharani nodded and watched, adjusting here and there as Mary held the material out to keep it taut as she worked. On her upper body, Aashini wore a fitted blouse in the same red-and-gold as the sari. It had short sleeves and was cropped beneath her bust, leaving her stomach exposed. It took some time to fold and pin the lush fabric of the sari, pulling a layer out to cover Aashini's stomach and drawing it around her side. Finally the heavy pleat went up and over her left shoulder, where it was neatly folded to a point on her back, before it returned to drape over her right shoulder.

Aashini tried not to fidget as Dharani tweaked and fussed, examining each gather with a critical eye until she was satisfied. She looked up then, a glint of approval and excitement in her eyes before she turned back to her maid.

"Mary, bring that box I showed you this morning."

The maid flashed a grin and squealed with excitement, hurrying off at once.

"What box?" Aashini asked, looking at her grandmother with surprise.

Dharani shrugged. "Something I kept for you."

A moment later Mary reappeared, carrying a heavy wooden box that Aashini could not recall having seen before. The girl placed it on the bed with care and then stepped back, looking as if she might burst with excitement as Dharani gestured for Aashini to come forward.

"I have saved these items for you, Aashini. They were given to your mother by your father, and he added to them in the years after her death. He always intended that you should embrace your heritage." She smiled, smoothing her hand over the box. "He was not perfect your father, but he loved you, *bhanvaraa*."

Aashini's throat tightened as she stared at the box.

"Open it," Dharani said, gesturing for her to hurry as both she and Mary were clearly dying for her to see the contents.

Swallowing hard, Aashini lifted the lid, and had to blink as the astonishing blaze of gold and jewels dazzled her.

"*Oh*!"

She didn't know what else to say. There were dozens and dozens of bangles, necklaces, earrings and rings and… *Good heavens.*

She turned to stare at Dharani.

"You've had all this since we left India? All these years you've worked and scrimped and saved to keep us fed and clothed, and all the time—"

"These things are yours, Aashini," Dharani said, her voice adamant, her expression fierce with pride. "I would rather have starved than sold them."

Aashini stared at the old woman, at the ferocious will contained in such a small frame. Dharani had never allowed circumstances to break that will to survive, to see her granddaughter safe and in possession of what was rightfully hers. That the woman's blood ran in her veins gave Aashini a sense of immense pride and such love that she feared she might cry.

"Don't you dare cry," Dharani scolded, though her own voice was thick now, her eyes too bright.

"*Nani maa*," Aashini managed, before throwing her arms about the woman and hugging her tight.

"You'll crease the sari!" the old woman protested, but she was laughing and hugging Aashini too, obviously as full of joy and emotion as her granddaughter. "That's enough," she said a moment later, before giving Aashini a look that reminded her of a small child choosing sweets. "It will take a while to put this lot on, so we'd best make a start."

It was true enough, and it was some time later when Aashini was finally allowed her first glimpse of herself in the looking glass.

"Oh, my lady," Mary said, her hands pressed to her heart as she stared at Aashini with awe. "I never saw nothing so beautiful. Not ever in my life."

Aashini laughed, hardly recognising the woman staring back at her, but finding she liked her. She liked her very much. She looked happy, and at peace with herself, and… yes, she looked beautiful.

Her eyes appeared massive, rimmed in black kajal, and everywhere she glinted, from the glorious red–and-gold silk sari to the dozens of bangles on each arm. Most were gold, but there were also a pair made from conch shells, called *shakha* and *pola,* one red, one white, and both delicately carved.

Rings adorned most of her fingers, from which fine gold chains fell and wrapped about her wrists. Jewels glinted at her throat, the *navaratna* so eye-catching that she could hardly bare to look away from it. Its nine stones were thought to bring the wearer power and luck. Each colourful stone was set in diamonds, and enormous pearls hung in tiers below them. A ruby was set in the centre, representing the sun, as all the stones had meaning, an emerald for Mercury, a yellow sapphire for Jupiter, a diamond for Venus, and so on.

In India, it was believed that flawless pearls prevented misfortune, and Aashini was so covered in them she felt nothing bad could ever happen again. She laughed, her heavy earrings glittering and swaying as she turned her head.

"I feel like I've fallen into a jewellery box," she said, overwhelmed and bubbling with happiness. She couldn't wait for Silas to see her.

"Oh, Aashini, your mother would be so proud of you." Dharani's voice cracked a little and Aashini turned to see her wipe her eyes.

"Of you too, *Nani maa*," she said gently. "I would not be here if not for you. I shall never forget that."

Dharani took a deep breath and exhaled, slowly. "Well then, *bhanvaraa*. You are ready. It is time to show your husband, and the world, just who you are."

Aashini nodded and crossed the room, pausing to press a kiss to her grandmother's forehead.

"*Main tumse pyaar karti hoon, Nani maa,*" she whispered. "I love you."

Mary ran forward, eager to open the door for her.

"He's been pacing the hallway this last twenty minutes or more." The maid giggled, making Aashini smile as she stepped outside her room.

True enough, Silas was awaiting her at the top of the stairs. His back was to her, as he stared down to where the sounds of music and the chatter of guests could be heard. All of them awaiting Aashini's grand entrance.

"At last," he said, sounding amused as he turned around. "I was beginning to think...."

The words died on his lips as his gaze fell upon her and she heard his breathing hitch. Aashini gave him a shy smile, a little anxious now as the moment stretched on and he did nothing but stare at her, mouth open.

"Silas?" she prompted, feeling a little anxious.

He wasn't used to seeing women dressed in such a manner. Had she been foolish to believe he would like it?

"Aashini," he said, his voice rough. "I've never… I… I don't…."

"Tell her she's beautiful, you great oaf," Dharani called from around the door frame.

This, at least, seemed to snap him out of his reverie.

"Beautiful isn't the word for it," he said, shaking his head as he took her in. "My word, Aashini, you… you look like a goddess."

Aashini let out a breath she hadn't realised she'd been holding, and laughed. "Thank you."

He walked closer, staring down at her, his blue eyes alight with love, pride, and wonder. "My beautiful wife," he said, such a smile at his lips that Aashini knew she would never forget this moment. His expression would be engraved on her heart as long as she lived. "How proud I am. I love you, Aashini. So much."

Aashini blinked up at him, a smile at her lips she doubted she'd be able to lose for days to come. "And I you, husband."

"Come," he said, holding out his arm for her. "Let us go and show your friends, and all those who are dying of curiosity, just what a remarkable woman I married."

***

"Where is she?" Bonnie complained to Matilda as they moved back into the entrance hall with the rest of the Peculiar Ladies, all of them anxious for their first glimpse of Aashini.

"She wants to make an entrance," Matilda replied, not for the first time. Though in truth she was dying of impatience too. Aashini had confided in her that she would be wearing the traditional costume of her country and the description of it had intrigued her. She was beside herself with excitement now.

"Oh, there's Lord Cavendish," Kitty said, waving at him as he looked down over the banisters.

His lordship grinned and waved back and then, a moment later, moved away.

"Can you see anything?" Harriet asked, craning her neck.

"Not a thing," Bonnie complained.

"Here you all are." Everyone looked around as the Duke of Bedwin moved into the hall, in search of his wife. Prue hurried up to him and took his arm.

"Isn't it exciting," she said, bouncing on her toes. "I've had to promise Alice to write down every detail about tonight. She's so disappointed not to be here."

"Yes, it's a shame," Matilda replied, smiling a little. "But she's still feeling under the weather."

Prue met her eyes and the two women grinned. They both suspected it wouldn't be too long before there was an announcement in that quarter. Matilda felt a burst of happiness for Nate. It was everything her brother had always wanted, marriage and family. A house bursting with noise and bustle and the madness that a large family inevitably brought with it.

"I'm so looking forward to St Clair's house party. You are still going, aren't you, Matilda?" Kitty asked, taking hold of Matilda's arm. "I have to complete my dare, remember."

"Of course! How could I forget?" she said, smiling at Kitty. "I am all agog to see this impressive bear dressed as a gentleman, not to mention St Clair's face when he discovers it. I wouldn't miss it for the world."

"Wouldn't miss what?" Ruth asked, appearing arm in arm with Minerva who was looking very glamorous tonight in a gown of bright yellow satin.

"St Clair's house party," Harriet murmured, looking like she wanted to roll her eyes.

"I can't believe I'm going to dress his bear up," Kitty added, snorting with laughter and shaking her head.

"You won't spoil it by being a stick in the mud, will you, Harriet?" Bonnie demanded, scowling at her. "I don't know why you dislike St Clair so, but the rest of us don't and we are going to enjoy ourselves."

Harriet blushed. "Of course not," she exclaimed, looking affronted by the idea. "My family goes every year. Not that I have any choice, but I can be polite if it's necessary," she assured them. "Even if it kills me," she muttered under her breath.

Bonnie sighed, glimpsing the man himself as he passed the open doorway. "Well, I'd marry him," she said dreamily before her expression darkened. "Though I'd marry that footman over there if I thought he'd save me from Gordon Anderson," she added with a glower.

Matilda raised her eyebrows at the rather short, dumpy and balding footman who was hurrying past with a tray of drinks. "Oh, come now, Bonnie. I can't believe he's that awful. When was the last time you saw him?"

Bonnie shrugged. "Two years ago."

"Well, there you are, then. That's a long time for a young man. He may have changed," Matilda said, trying to soothe her. "It may be he's not as bad as you remember."

"I thought that the last time I was due to see him," Bonnie admitted, pursing her lips. "I thought he couldn't possibly be as bad as I remembered as it had been over a year that time."

"And?" Matilda said, smiling hopefully.

"He was worse."

Matilda gave up and turned her attention back to the stairs where she'd caught a flash of red from the corner of her eye. "She's coming!" she exclaimed.

Everyone turned, gazing up to the top of the stairs. A collective intake of breath preceded a hush of absolute quiet as Aashini appeared on her husband's arm.

Lord Cavendish looked as if he was about to burst with pride, which Matilda thought quite appropriate as she took in the vision descending the staircase.

"I think I might cry," Prue said, reaching to take Matilda's hand and squeezing tight.

"I beat you to it," Matilda said, laughing and wiping her eyes, though she couldn't look away from her friend as she walked towards them.

She was a vision in red silk, every inch of her bedecked in gold and jewels that sparkled and glinted as she moved.

"She looks like a princess from a fairy story," Minerva said, wide-eyed with astonishment.

"Well, then," Ruth said, sounding wistful, "this must be her happy ever after."

"Hello, ladies," Aashini said, on reaching the hallway.

She was beaming, her eyes so alight with happiness that Matilda couldn't help but return the expression. "Oh, Aashini, I'm sure your husband must have told you already, but… how lovely you are."

All the women agreed, each of them pushing forward, eager to add their comments and welcome husband and wife to the party that celebrated their union.

"Well, Lady Cavendish?" Silas said, grinning from ear to ear. "I think we had better begin the celebrations, don't you?"

"Yes, my lord, I think we should," Aashini replied, staring at him with such adoration that Matilda's throat tightened again.

She remembered how vehement the young woman had been in her hatred of men, in her determination to never marry, but Lord Cavendish had set out to prove himself worthy of her, and Matilda could only agree that he truly had. She suspected their lives would be full of adventure and romance, and was privileged to be allowed a place in it as Aashini's friend.

Word must have reached the rest of the guests, for they all moved forward, everyone desperate for their first glimpse of the new Lady Cavendish. Murmurs of shock and approval, exclamations of wonder and scandalised gasps, all echoed about Cavendish House.

Moving closer, the Peculiar Ladies—with the Duke and Duchess of Bedwin at their head—gathered about their friend and escorted Lord and Lady Cavendish into the grand ballroom, where the celebrations could truly begin.

***

"My feet hurt," Kitty complained, many hours later, as she settled into the carriage next to Matilda.

"Mine too, dear," Matilda admitted. "But what a wonderful night it was."

Kitty nodded, hugging her arms around herself. "Lucky, lucky, Aashini. Did you see the way Lord Cavendish looked at her? Like the sun shone for her and no other reason."

Matilda laughed and nodded, knowing just what she meant. "You're a romantic, Kitty."

"I suppose so. Aren't you?" Kitty looked over at her, frowning, and Matilda shrugged, not entirely sure how to answer that.

"I was once, but now…. Oh, I don't know, Kitty. So much has happened I find it hard to believe in fairy stories now."

"What? Even after everything you've witnessed this season? Three of us married, Matilda. *Three*! How can you not believe?" Kitty shook her head in astonishment. "And it isn't fairy stories, it's us."

Matilda frowned, turning to look at Kitty more closely. "What do you mean, it's *us*?"

"It's the Peculiar Ladies," Kitty said, rolling her eyes as if she was speaking to a particularly dim child. "Ever since our group came together, things have happened. We were all alone before that, all adrift in our own little worlds, but now… now we have each other. We have friends and confidantes, and people who would drop everything and come to us if the need ever arose. It's changed us, Matilda, all of us. It's like…." Kitty paused, searching for inspiration, her brow puckered. "It's like our friendship has given us some kind of power, like we've made magic."

Matilda laughed and gave her a sceptical look. "The power to attract a husband?"

"No!" Kitty exclaimed impatiently. "The power to be ourselves, to *believe* in ourselves. The men are incidental, really.

Those three just happened to be intelligent enough to notice what was happening."

"So, you're saying we've begun attracting husbands because we're growing in confidence, because there are people who support us?"

"Yes, exactly," Kitty said, nodding.

Matilda stared at the young woman, surprised and impressed. "How astute you are, Kitty. I should never have considered it that way, but yes, I believe you might be right."

"Of course I'm right," Kitty said with a snort, making Matilda laugh. There was silence for a little while until Kitty spoke again. "Did you hear from your brother yet?" she asked, sounding casual, though Matilda could hear the desperate desire for information all the same.

"I did," she said. "I'm afraid he doesn't know of a Luke Baxter, but he's promised me he will make enquiries. Matilda gave her a sympathetic smile as Kitty sighed with disappointment. "We'll find him, Kitty."

"Oh, I know we will," she replied, surprising Matilda with the certainty in her voice. "I feel it in my heart. I know we shall be together again, it's meant to be. It's our fate. I just wish fate would hurry up and get a move on." She moved closer and laid her head on Matilda's shoulder. "I miss him. So much."

Matilda put her arm about Kitty and hugged her, and fervently hoped that Luke Baxter felt the same way. According to Kitty they'd been children when the boy had disappeared, and there was no guarantee he hadn't forgotten all about Kitty. He could already be married with a family of his own.

Please no, Matilda prayed, desperately hoping that everything turned out just as Kitty wanted.

It could happen.

Childhood sweethearts did reunite and live happily ever after.

Didn't they?

Kitty yawned. "I'm so tired," she said with a sigh.

"We'll be home soon," Matilda said, feeling more like a mother hen than ever, the thought making her smile.

Well, three little chicks had left the nest so far, and she couldn't be happier for them. Why shouldn't Kitty and all the others follow suit?

Perhaps she'd even get her turn?

Matilda swallowed, remembering the night at Green Park and the sincerity of Mr Burton's words. He'd said he wanted to court her in earnest, and she knew she ought to allow it. Yet something was holding her back.

Unbidden, an image of the Marquess of Montagu filled her mind, his cold silver eyes reflecting the dazzling display of the fireworks above them. Matilda closed her own eyes and forced the image away. That path led to nothing but misery and ruination. An affair with him would blaze as bright as the fireworks had, a dazzling display that would light up the night, and then leave her cold and alone.

"No," she said.

"What?"

Kitty jolted, startling Matilda, who'd not realised she'd spoken aloud.

"Oh, sorry, dear. I was just wool gathering," she said, smiling at a sleepy Kitty, who just sighed, smiled, and settled back on her shoulder again.

"How many days until St Clair's party?"

Matilda chuckled. "Eight days, dear."

"Wonderful," Kitty murmured. "There's bound to be lots of eligible men for you there, Matilda. Though Mr Burton is lovely," she added, before subsiding once more and snoring gently.

"Yes," Matilda said with a wistful sigh. "Mr Burton *is* lovely." And she would have to try a good deal harder to fall for him.

What's next for the members of The Peculiar Ladies Book Club?

To Follow her Heart

Girls Who Dare, Book 4

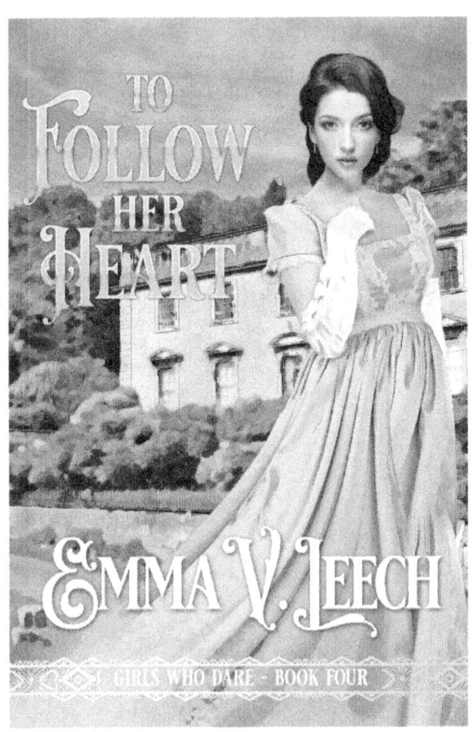

A lost love …

Kitty Connolly has spent the whole of the last season assuring her uncle she's been trying to find a husband, but there's a problem he is unaware of.

She already has one.

Admittedly, she was only eleven when the ceremony took place in the presence of her family's dog, and her betrothed was only thirteen. Yet, vows were exchanged and as far as Kitty is concerned, a promise is a promise. Luke Baxter promised to love her till death do him part and he's not getting out of it.

The problems don't stop there, however, as Luke disappeared from her life just weeks after their secret wedding, and Kitty never saw him again.

Until now.

Hope reignited …

When Luke appears out of the blue at the Earl of St Clair's summer house party and announces his betrothal to lovely heiress, Lady Francis Grantham, Kitty is stunned …

… and honour bound to point out the problem.

One determined heart …

All hell breaks loose when Kitty threatens to sue for breach of promise and she has a matter of days to convince Luke that his childhood sweetheart is worth more than Miss Grantham's fortune.

But this Luke is not the carefree boy of her childhood, and reminding him what it means to live for love might mean risking more than just her heart.

Prologue

London. 28th July 1814.

I perceive, at last, that I must be a very selfish kind of man. Fate has intervened and given me a position in life I neither expected nor feel worthy of. Soon – if I do as Trevick expects and wishes – I will add great wealth to my good fortune. Any other man of my position must look upon such a change in circumstances as the hand of a beneficent god.

Why, then, do I feel so cheated?

—Excerpt of a letter from Mr Luke Baxter to an unknown correspondent. Never sent.

1st July 1800. Ballyhill House, Armoy, County Antrim, Northern Ireland.

Luke ran as fast as he could. He ran away from the large house, with its empty, echoing rooms, away from his weeping mother and his father's fury. Why Father was so cross, Luke couldn't fathom. It was all his fault. They'd lost everything, not that there had been much to lose, but Father had frittered away the only thing left with any value: his honour.

It was a dreadful scandal. What exactly the scandal was about Luke wasn't certain, except *that woman* had been a part of it. He was only nine, so his thoughts and feelings counted for nothing. All he had gleaned through a few snatches of overheard conversation was that his father had disgraced the family. The head of their illustrious line, the Earl of Trevick, was displeased, and so had dispatched his youngest brother, Mr Derby, to deal with Luke's father.

They had been banished within a matter of days, threatened with being cut off from the family and snubbed if they did not leave until the horrid affair died down. Mr Derby said it might take years.

Decades, even.

Years stuck in this faraway place, far from his school and his friends, from anything at all. Those years stretched out before Luke, a vast expanse of nothingness and uncertainty.

The house in which they would live out their exile was dirty and smelled of decay, though it had been grand once. There were mice scuttling in the walls and cobwebs everywhere. They couldn't afford enough staff to right it and run it as it should be run, but those they'd brought had set to trying to find some order in the chaos. The dust still clung to the back of his throat and prickled his nose. Luke didn't like upsets and chaos, or disorder, or change.

He'd liked his life, his school, his pals. He'd liked the predictability of knowing what would come each day, just the same as the one before it.

Scrubbing his sleeve over his face, he scolded himself for crying. He wasn't a stupid baby. He hated his father and couldn't bear his mother's tears, and he'd lost everything, but he wouldn't cry about it. It wouldn't change a thing; that was a lesson he'd learned long ago. His father ignored him whether he cried or shouted, or behaved impeccably. His mother was too busy crying herself, forever at the mercy of her nerves. Luke had a healthy terror of his mother's nerves. Anyway, there was no point in fighting fate; it only fought back harder.

"What's the matter?"

Luke jolted, having believed he'd run into the middle of acres of nothingness and was all alone, a state he must endure for years to come. The soft voice—gentle, with a lilting accent—startled him half to death. He spun around, confronted at once with a girl.

She was slender, with a cloud of thick black curls that surrounded the sweetest face, as delicate as a fairy's. Her eyes were enormous, almost as dark as her hair, and thickly lashed. There was the faintest touch of pink at her cheeks, and her delicate lips were just a shade darker. He thought perhaps she was a year younger than he was; two at most.

He'd seen nothing as beautiful as her in all his life and, for a second, he wondered if she was real. There was a local woman working at the house who'd told him stories of the Sidhe, the good folk who could bless or curse you on a whim. She'd said they were beautiful beyond belief and that, once you'd seen them, your life would never be the same again.

In that moment, Luke believed it.

He would love her and follow her anywhere she led if she asked him.

His heart made an odd little thump in his chest and he hated himself for thinking anything so thoroughly nauseating. She was only a girl, not a tricksy fae, not a beautiful Sidhe princess. His friends would have pounded him if they'd known.

"Why are you crying?" she asked, her accent so unfamiliar and impenetrable it took him a while to comprehend.

"I'm not crying," he retorted, indignant at the accusation, no matter how accurate.

"My, don't you talk funny," she said, her dark eyes bright with interest.

"Not as funny as you," he retorted, stung by the observation.

She watched him for a long minute, as though studying a foreign entity, something she'd never seen before and wanted to understand. Her pretty head tilted to one side.

"Your hair is so red, red as garnets when the sun's on it." Her gaze was full of admiration as she added, "I like your freckles too. You'll be a handsome fellow one day."

Luke blinked as a flush burned over his cheeks. He'd spend a goodly amount of his school life pounding bullies for teasing his red hair and freckles. *Ginger, carrot-top, poison-pated, bran-faced....*

She *liked* them.

He'd hardly begun to get to grips with this strange phenomenon, and the stranger feelings that her reactions provoked, before she returned to her original question.

"So, why were you crying?"

Luke, who was still reeling from discovering he *liked a girl*, and that she thought he'd be a handsome man one day, was appalled to think she'd believe him a crybaby.

"I wasn't," hc bit out, clenching his fists.

She gave him a pitying look and moved closer. To his astonishment she took his hand, unfurling his fingers like the sun opening a bloom, and raised it to her cheek, which was every bit as soft as he'd imagined. Luke's breath caught in his throat as he was torn between gratitude and outrage.

"Sure ye were," she said, the words chiding him, though gently. "But it's none o' my business, I suppose. Though if ye tell me, I shall take it to my grave, swear on it."

Her elfin face was so earnest that he blinked in surprise. Perhaps she was fae after all, there was something in her eyes, those dark, dark eyes, something he knew he could trust in. He gave a hopeless sigh and startled himself by replying with the truth.

"We've been banished here, and I've lost everything. We've no money, and I've no friends. I hate it here and... I'm all alone."

"No, you're not," she said, giving him a smile that made him feel a little dazed. "Because I've found you, and you've found me, and so… we shall be together, and never alone again."

***

Four years later

12th September 1804.

Kitty clung to the branch which swayed in a rather alarming fashion.

"Just admit it, Kitten. You're stuck."

She glared down to where Luke was staring up at her, looking so damned smug she reached up and snatched an apple—the reason she'd gone up in the first place—and lobbed it at his head. She missed, and it rolled towards her dog, Khan, a massive brindle mastiff. He sniffed the apple, gave her a long-suffering look and laid his head back on his paws.

"I'm not stuck," she said, stubborn to the last. "I… I just can't see which is the best way down… yet," she added. "But I shall."

Luke folded his arms and said nothing. Khan gave a sigh.

Kitty swallowed as the wind gusted again, large clouds scudding across a sky which had been blue only half an hour earlier. The sharp breeze made the boughs—already heavy with fruit—sway in a manner that made her heart skitter in her chest. She'd climbed a deal higher than she'd intended, but that was typical of her. She rarely thought before she acted, just threw herself headfirst into whatever it was. Luke admired her for that, though he said she frightened him half to death, too. For her part, she wished she had an ounce of his unshakeable calm. If ever you were in a fix, Luke would get you out of it, and Kitty was always in a fix. Like now, for example.

The tree swayed again, harder still. She gave a little shriek, and then saw that Luke was climbing up to her.

"Stubborn little Kitten," he said with a sigh as he drew level with her. "I told you you'd never be able to climb in those heavy skirts, but you just had to prove me wrong."

Kitty felt a strange, rather breathless sensation fill her chest as he got closer. At thirteen, Luke had become a very handsome fellow, just as she'd predicted. His hair shone a coppery red, and she adored the scattering of freckles over his nose. His eyes were blue, bluer than any sky she'd ever seen. Sometimes it hurt to look at him.

She adored him *and* his freckles.

"I know," she said, huffing with frustration. "And I don't see why I must wear the dratted things. They're impossible."

"*You're* impossible," he said, grinning at her. "And you know why. It's so you can be a proper young lady and not a hoyden. Your father wants you to have every advantage, now he can afford to dress you properly."

"I don't want to be a young lady," Kitty replied, a stab of anxiety hurting her heart. Her father wanted to send her away soon, to live with her aunt and uncle in London where she would learn to be a proper lady and grow up to marry some impoverished nobleman who needed her dowry. She'd have to leave Luke and Khan behind. She'd rather die. "I don't want to grow up. I want us to stay here, just like we are, forever."

His face softened and the breathless sensation increased. "But if you don't grow up, I shan't be able to marry you."

Kitty felt her breath catch and hold this time, and she could do nothing but stare at him.

He blushed, the colour vivid on his pale skin. "Unless… you don't want to—"

"Of course I want to!" Kitty exclaimed and threw her arms about his neck, then felt a blush rise to rival his. "You know I do," she added, a little chagrined for her outburst as he was looking smug again.

Of course he knew. She'd never hidden it from him, not from the very first day when she'd found him all alone and miserable. They'd been inseparable ever since. It was her and Luke against the world, it always had been and it was just how they liked it.

"Come along," he said, helping her untangle her skirts and find a suitable foothold. "We can't discuss the future with you stuck up a tree."

"I wasn't stuck," Kitty said, dogged as ever.

"No," Luke said, his tone soothing. "I know. You were just resting."

Kitty held her tongue, too in charity with him to argue the point, and allowed him to help her down. As she jumped the final distance, however, she stumbled, and Luke caught her, steadying her. He was always doing that. Kitty was reckless and pig-headed, and obstinate, with a temper that led her into trouble without fail. Luke was calm, patient, and understanding, and never complained—or at least rarely—when he too ended up in trouble. He was steadfast and loyal, the best friend she'd ever had, and she loved him with all her heart.

He was looking at her a little oddly now though, and Kitty stilled, wondering if she had dirt on her nose. She was about to ask him when he leaned in and pressed his mouth to hers.

It only lasted for the briefest moment, and then he was staring at her again, scarlet-faced and unsure of himself.

"Do you mind?" he asked, breathing hard.

Kitty felt a ridiculous smile curve over her mouth, and she shook her head, her black curls dancing in disarray about her face.

Luke let out a breath and kissed her again, for a fraction longer this time. Kitty closed her eyes and clung to him and knew this was the happiest moment of her entire life.

"Will you really marry me?" he asked, his blue eyes as serious as she had ever seen them.

"Yes," she said, the one word breathed on what little air remained in her lungs, for he'd stolen it with the kisses he'd taken. "Yes, please, Luke."

They sat together, hands clasped, leaning back against the gnarled trunk of the apple tree, making plans to run away as soon as they were old enough to marry. Khan lumbered over and heaved his bulk down beside them, placing his heavy head on her skirts and pinning her in place.

"You know your parents won't allow it," Luke said after a blissful few moments of sitting with her head on his shoulder. "Not now you've got money. So, we shall have to elope," he said, looking troubled by the idea. "I'm sorry for it, as there will be a scandal. My family has scandal enough, so that's of no matter, but yours…."

She watched him shrug and knew how badly his father's disgrace rankled.

"Your family has become wealthy since your father built his mill, and since my father died without making the least effort to…." He shrugged again and her heart ached for him.

As far as Kitty could see, Luke's mother was a miserable woman who spent a deal of energy lamenting their impoverished position and berating his dead sire, but never lifted a finger to do anything useful. Her only purpose in life seemed to be to make Luke as wretched as she was by reminding him daily of everything they'd lost, everything that ought to be theirs.

"I've nothing, Kitten, nothing to offer you, but I won't be like my father. I shall work hard and earn my fortune, like your father has done. My tutor at school seemed to think I've a brain in my head and I won't let you down, I promise I won't."

"I know that," she said, staring up at him and feeling like her heart would burst from happiness and pride. "And I don't care how much money we have, so long as we're together."

"I care," he admitted, the words a little taut. He reached out and tugged at a dark curl, winding it around his finger. "I want you to have everything. Pretty dresses, and carriages, and—"

Kitty snorted and shook her head. "Much I care for such things," she said, giving him an indulgent look.

"You should," he said, frowning again. "If Father hadn't ruined everything, I'd at least still have a name worth a damn, instead of his reputation as an adulterer and a murderer hanging about my neck."

Kitty winced to hear him curse. He rarely did so, but he'd never forgiven his father, and his anger was still palpable. She'd heard the tale, prised out of him a little at a time, once he'd discovered the truth of it. Even out here the rumours had followed them. His father had fallen madly in love with an opera singer, as had another—also married—man. They'd fought a duel and his opponent had died. It had been hushed up, naturally. The Earl of Trevick had seen to that, but they had shipped Mr Baxter, his hysterical wife, and their son off to an abandoned family estate in Ireland before the story could hurt the earl by association. They could return when the scandal had quieted, the earl had said. Except Luke's father had died three years ago, and Trevick seemed to have forgotten they even existed.

"I love you, Luke," she said, gazing up at him and knowing he'd be a fine man one day.

Even now, young as they were, she saw this in him, recognised the strength of his heart and purpose. He always seemed far older than she, far wiser too, and she depended on that—on him—to keep her from falling into folly with her wild spirit and impetuous temper.

"I shall love you always, Kitten," he said, just as solemn.

She knew they ought not say such things, let alone think them, but her parents had let her run amok until recent months, and Luke's mother cared for nothing but her own comfort. They'd been left too much alone and had clung together until the idea of one without the other was too fantastic to contemplate. There had barely been a day since Luke had arrived that they had not spent together.

The words, once exchanged, seemed to alter something between them, the quality of the air about them somehow different.

"I don't want to wait," Luke said, and the vehemence of the words startled Kitty. "I wish we could marry now and go away, far away from all of them. Especially my mother."

"I wish that too," Kitty said, a little cautiously. She was unused to being the voice of reason. "But we're not old enough, Luke. They'd only find us and bring us back, and this isn't so bad for now, is it?"

She looked up at him and Luke smiled, slipping his arm about her shoulders and kissing her nose.

"No," he said, though he sounded uncertain. He was quiet for a long moment. "But… but what if we could marry now?" he asked, suddenly breathless, his eyes bright with excitement.

"Whatever do you mean?" she asked, laughing at his enthusiasm.

"I mean, what if I got a bible, and a ring and we said the words? I know it wouldn't be legal, not really, but… *we'd* know in our hearts it was real, that it was done."

Kitty caught her breath. "Truly?" she said, hearing the tremor in her voice.

Luke squeezed her hands and nodded. "Truly. Right now, today."

He shifted beside her, going down on one knee and looking to her like the most chivalrous knight of old as his blue eyes met hers. "Kitty Connolly, my own Kitten, will you marry me?"

"I will," she said, her throat growing tight. "I already told you so."

He beamed and got to his feet. "Then don't move from this spot," he said, laughing.

"But where are you going?" she asked, laughing too, for his delight was infectious.

"Why, to get a bible and a ring, of course!" he exclaimed, and ran away, back through the orchard and out of sight.

Chapter 1

Ten years later.

My dearest friend,

Tonight is the firework display at Green Park. I am so looking forward to it, especially as I am going with Matilda. I think she is lonely now Aashini is married, so she has invited me to stay with her until we go to St Clair's house party. That too I am excited for. There is much to enjoy in life if one is inclined to look for it, and it is not in my nature to mope as you well know.

I have found some lovely friends during this last season, yet beneath all this excitement and happiness my spirit is torn asunder. Everything is coloured by your absence and I don't know how to mend the tear in my soul.

My heart is still yours, you see, and always shall be, just as we promised that lovely day in September. The ring you gave me is too small now, but I have it still along with the vows we made each other. Please come back to me, dear Luke. I feel my heart grows a little emptier each day that we are apart.

—Excerpt of a letter from Miss Kitty Connolly to Mr Luke Baxter… never sent.

1st August 1814, South Audley Street, London.

Kitty smoothed her gown, feeling unaccountably nervous. The Marquess of Montagu was escorting both her and Matilda to the fireworks at Green Park tonight and the man scared her half to death. She was bound to do or say something outrageous—she always did when nerves got the better of her—and then he would despise her even more than he already did. Why he'd invited her at all, she couldn't fathom, except she suspected it had more to do with Matilda than her. That too was a worry.

At least Mr Burton would also be there. He was a handsome, sensible sort of fellow, a self-made man, which meant the *ton* despised him despite his great wealth.
What nonsense. Matilda would do well to marry a man like that, one who'd made his fortune through his own cleverness and industry, rather than having been born to it.

Kitty's own family was an illustrious one, though her Irish heritage meant she may as well have been born in a bog and raised by wolves as far as the *ton* were concerned. Their fortunes had floundered for a while until the linen trade had flourished, and the family's wealth with it. Her father owned hundreds of acres of flax and three mills now, and he had plans for another.

Her parents, eager for her to snare a titled husband, had sent her to stay with her aunt and uncle. Aunt Clara Henshaw had wed an English gentleman and had become so thoroughly English herself most people had forgiven or even forgotten her Irish heritage. Her aunt had tried hard to erase her accent but Kitty refused to lose it, though she was aware it had lessened over the past years with her aunt and uncle forever correcting her. Still, she clung to it, as stubborn as ever. What did it matter? She had no intention of catching herself an English husband. She already had one.

She'd just… temporarily misplaced him.

The thought made her heart ache, and she pushed it away. She would not allow herself to sink into the dismals. For the first time in a long time, she had hopes of finding him. Matilda's brother had promised to ask about, and Nate Hunter knew everyone.

"Are you ready, dear?"

Kitty looked up as Matilda called out to her and then poked her head around the door.

"Oh, you do look lovely, Kitty," she said, smiling and looking Kitty over. "That shade of blue is very becoming."

Kitty smiled and thanked her, not mentioning that she'd chosen it as it was the exact shade of Luke's eyes. She noted then that Matilda wore a beautiful soft silver-grey gown and fought back a surge of misgiving.

"I understand the Earl of St Clair will be with the marquess this evening?" Kitty said, trying to quell her nerves.

Matilda at least looked as cool and composed as ever, so hopefully the event would go without a hitch.

"Yes, thank heavens," Matilda said with a conspiratorial grin. "So, we need not sit in terror of the marquess' disdain, with St Clair's charm and address to diffuse the tension."

"That is a comfort," Kitty said with a sigh. "Though I suppose it will put Harriet in a pelter. Do you have any idea why she hates him so?"

"No, I don't," Matilda said, looking thoughtful now. "But I don't believe the feeling is mutual."

"Oh?" Kitty replied, delighted with this information. "Whatever do you mean?"

Matilda shrugged and gave her an enigmatic smile. "Just watch St Clair this evening, when Harriet is around. You'll see."

With this intriguing nugget of information, Kitty had to be satisfied, and she followed Matilda downstairs to await the carriage.

***

Jasper Cadogan, Earl of St Clair, cast a curious glance across the carriage towards the Marquess of Montagu. They were not exactly friends, barely acquaintances, yet when the marquess had invited him to attend as his guest this evening, Jasper had been too curious to refuse. The marquess was a mystery, a solitary man who guarded his privacy like a dog with a bone. Jasper suspected no one knew him at all, which naturally made everyone ravenously curious.

"I'm holding a party at Holbrooke House, from the twentieth of the month. Should you like to attend?"

The marquess looked around, his habitually bored gaze settling on St Clair.

"Kind of you," Montagu replied, before returning his attention back to the window. "But I am obliged to return to Kent. I have neglected my affairs for too long and they won't wait any longer."

"Of course," Jasper said with ease, before some urge to play devil's advocate provoked him to speak when he'd do better to hold his tongue. "Mr Burton will be there."

A glint of amusement flickered in Montagu's cold silver eyes as he studied Jasper. "You mean to imply that I risk losing my quarry," he said mildly.

Jasper stared at him, wondering if he was truly as bloodless as he appeared, before giving a nonchalant shrug. "I believe he intends to court Miss Hunt."

The faintest glimmer of a smile played around Montagu's hard mouth. He lifted his hand and snapped his fingers, the sound echoing in the dark of the carriage. "For Mr Burton," he said, and returned his attention to the window.

By God, what an arrogant bastard, Jasper thought, wondering what life must be like when viewed with such absolute certainty. For his own part, Jasper liked Mr Burton and thought Miss Hunt a fool if she turned up her nose at him, though most of the other guests would likely regard him as a mushroom, one of the encroaching newly rich who tried to buy or marry their way into the *ton*. From what he'd seen, Mr Burton could hold his own, though, and he deserved a proper chance to secure Miss Hunt's attentions without the marquess muddying the waters. Jasper could only wish him luck.

The carriage rocked to a stop outside of the smart house on South Audley Street and soon the ladies were ensconced within. Jasper smiled at them both, complimented their dresses and enquired as to their health, whilst the marquess continued to look out of the window. He was a strange fellow to be sure. It was a matter of minutes before they arrived at their destination.

The impressive facade of a fortress dominated their first glimpse of the park in the fading light. Though a temporary structure erected solely for the evening's entertainment, the ramparts were one hundred feet square. A round tower in the centre rose a further fifty feet from the ramparts, and what looked increasingly to be thousands of people were gathering around it. All had come to view the evening's spectacle, from London's hoi polloi to the upper echelons of the *ton*. The masses stood, whilst seating had been arranged for the quality, but all looked on in amazement at the scale of the structure.

"We must hope it doesn't burn down this time," Montagu mused, smiling a little as Jasper laughed.

"This time?" Miss Connolly enquired, eyes wide.

"I believe Montagu refers to the last such event, some sixty years ago. As I understand it, the first fireworks caught the structure alight and all the remaining fireworks went off at once. Some tens of thousands of them," he said as Miss Connolly looked somewhat alarmed.

"I'm sure it's all under control this year," he said, with a soothing smile which fell as the rest of the guests joined them… including his nemesis, Miss Harriet Stanhope.

"What ho, Jasper."

Jasper nodded as his best friend and the nemesis' brother, Henry Stanhope, hailed him with his usual jaunty grin.

"There's a devilish lot of people here," Henry said as he drew closer, before becoming all stiff and formal to greet Montagu.

The marquess had that effect on people.

Soon, everyone was gathered. Mr Burton had made a beeline for Miss Hunt, Jasper noted, an event which the marquess had not yet deigned to notice, though Jasper felt certain he was perfectly aware of it. Countess Culpepper looked bored and resigned to behaving herself, as her husband was accompanying her. Mrs Manning, a rather fine-looking widow who'd made unmistakable overtures to him at their last meeting had no such restraints on her, and cast him a flirtatious smile to which Jasper politely inclined his head.

"You lucky devil."

Jasper looked around to discover his younger brother, Jerome, and sighed. "What are you doing here?"

"I was invited," Jerome replied, grinning broadly as he knew this would irritate Jasper. Jerome's life work was irritating Jasper. "Now, do me a favour and introduce me to Mrs Manning."

"Damned if I will," Jasper said with a bark of laughter. "She eats little boys for breakfast."

Jerome glowered at him. "I'm only three years younger than you."

Jasper returned a quelling look, one he'd spent years perfecting.

Jerome narrowed his eyes.

"Fine," he said, and stalked off, no doubt to find another method of ruining Jasper's evening other than flirting wildly with Mrs Manning and making a spectacle of them both.

Jasper watched his brother's progress, and the smile which lit Harriet's face as she greeted him. He suppressed a vicious stab of jealousy which he knew was beneath him. Harriet then introduced Jerome to her friend, Miss Bonnie Campbell. The young Scottish woman was a curvaceous bundle of trouble if ever Jasper had seen one, and he recognised the gleam of interest in Jerome's eye all too well.

Jasper suppressed a sigh and wondered when he'd become so ruddy old. At that moment, Harriet looked up and his heart stuttered in his chest as her cool, bespectacled gaze met his. Wide brown eyes that were even larger behind the glass of her spectacles settled on him for a second, during which time all the warmth and laughter chilled to arctic temperatures before she looked away again.

"Would it kill you to smile at me, Harry?" he murmured, before pasting a smile to his own face and attending to his friends.

***

Kitty stared at the skies until her neck ached, amazed and delighted by the spectacle above them. The festivity, intended to celebrate the centenary of the House of Brunswick and the peace with France, had been done on a scale Kitty had never experienced. The faux fortress was like nothing she'd seen in her life. Rockets thundered from the battlements, at once impressive and beautiful and yet giving the crowd a tiny taste of the power and horror of everything the men involved in the conflict must have faced. Smoke and noise, flashes and fire as explosions rocked through the spectators, drew startled gasps of wonder from even the most jaded onlookers.

For a moment, she allowed her attention to drift away from the sparkling skies as flurries of golden stars fell to earth, and focused instead on those below. Hundreds and thousands of people. As she always did, she searched their faces, though it was impossible to see in the crush, and beneath the light that changed in a moment from brilliance into darkness and back again. Was Luke here somewhere? If he was here, why hadn't he come for her, or at least sent word? Had he forgotten her, had he found another? Perhaps he was married now.

Had the words he'd spoken with such gravity meant nothing to him?

She knew it was foolish, or at least that anyone else would believe it so. She'd attended a real wedding earlier that day, when Viscount Cavendish had married Aashini. It had been an informal affair and yet with all the attendant solemnity and intent it ought to when two peoples' futures joined together—till death them do part.

She and Luke had been children: innocent, silly children with no notion of real life and responsibilities. Yet it *had* meant something to her, and to him. Kitty knew in her heart he'd felt the weight of his promise to her, and he'd meant the words. So why hadn't he come to her? Why hadn't she been able to find him? How could a boy who'd told her he loved her with such devotion disappear, and never so much as send her a note of explanation?

A barrage of sound drew her attention back to the fortress amid a violent display of flame and smoke and the thunder of artillery. The giant edifice was slowly transformed by the removal of giant screens to expose the Temple of Concord beneath the layers of the fortress. The rockets continued to fire overhead, and the temple was revealed like a butterfly from a chrysalis. Each rocket contained a multitude of smaller rockets that burst and burst again, brighter than any star, illuminating the scene beneath. An ethereal blue light was cast over the world around them, everyone from the lowliest to the grandest dipped in silver and, for one transient moment, appearing equally magnificent.

At last the skies subsided, and the land grew quiet again, until the crowd erupted with cheers and laughter, clapping and exclaiming about all that they'd seen.

Kitty stared still at the heavens, at the billows of smoke that drifted over the clear night sky. The stars began to appear, one by one, shining tentatively now the gaudy display was done. Though it was foolish, Kitty searched for and found the north star as she'd done with Luke when they were children, usually with one or other of them wishing for nonsense—a pony or a puppy, or that Papa shouldn't discover who'd broken the vase in the dining room.

"Let me find him," she begged, focusing on the tiny light and feeling the ache in her heart with as much sorrow as she'd done the day she'd discovered him gone. "Please. *Please* let me find him."

Chapter 2

Dear Bonnie,

We are leaving tomorrow for St Clair's House Party!

I'm so excited. Aren't we lucky to have found such generous friends, for surely neither you nor I would have a hope of attending such an event without them? You would be destined for Gordon Anderson for certain, and my father would be haranguing me for not having found a husband, but now we have a chance to live a little longer and hope for better things.

We must grab the chance and hold on tight!

—Excerpt of a letter from Miss Kitty Connolly to Miss Bonnie Campbell.

19th August 1814, South Audley Street, London.

"It's so good of you to take me with you," Matilda said, embracing Harriet as the young woman's eyes widened at the number of valises and hat boxes assembled in the hallway. "Oh dear," Matilda added, seeing Harriet's alarm. "I've packed far too much, haven't I? You don't have space?"

Harriet laughed and shook her head. "No, indeed. We have plenty of space, only… you've brought three times as much as I have, and now I feel anxious I didn't pack enough."

"Well, I'm sure you barely have a trunk full, once you discount the two you filled with books," her brother Henry remarked as he oversaw the servants trooping back and forth. "I never knew a girl less interested in clothes," he added, shaking his head. "You're an oddity, Harry, no getting away from it."

Poor Harriet blushed scarlet and Matilda took her arm.

"Don't listen to him, you're certain to have just the exact right amount of everything. You're always so organised. I'm afraid I'm horribly vain and can't make a decision to save my life. Packing is torture so I just cram in everything I can and hope for the best."

Harriet smiled though she didn't look entirely reassured, but at that moment Kitty came thundering down the stairs.

"Harriet!" she exclaimed, throwing her arms about the young woman's neck.

Matilda hid a grin; Harriet was clearly overawed by Kitty's boisterous nature. It was a little like living with a puppy, she reflected, having spent the past two weeks and more in her company. Kitty bored easily and was constantly looking for diversion. Once occupied, she was tranquil, happy, and easily pleased, but heaven help you if she took it into her head to entertain herself.

"Come along, come along," Henry said, now all the baggage had been safely stowed. "Let's be having you."

Obediently, they all hurried outside, where a smart coach awaited them.

"I'm afraid we'll be a little snug," Harriet said, pitching her voice low. "Aunt Nell insisted we must be chaperoned on the journey."

"Well, that's your own fault," Henry said tartly. "You would tell her I couldn't chaperone a sponge cake, so… hoist by your own petard, Miss."

Harriet laughed at her brother's indignation and they were soon settled inside.

They made a merry party. Henry was always a cheerful soul and he and Harriet, or Harry as he called her, seemed on very good terms. Kitty was in good spirits, too, and looking very fetching in a new bonnet crowned with cherries. Her dark hair framed her face with glossy ringlets and her eyes sparkled. Matilda prayed she'd be able to find her some news about her childhood sweetheart soon, though, for she knew Kitty was optimistic of hearing results and knew too how quickly optimism could fade when no news was forthcoming.

She worried that it was a hopeless case though. If Mr Baxter had wanted to write to Kitty, had wanted her to know of his whereabouts, he could have written a hundred times and more over the past years.

They made a brief mid-morning stop to change horses, and arrived at Holbrooke House in the early afternoon. It was an impressive sight.

"Good heavens," Matilda exclaimed.

Despite having been warned of its scale and opulence, the Elizabethan prodigy house was more than a little intimidating.

"Interesting, isn't it?" Harriet said, looking at the building with a smile. "It was influenced by the Classical style of building popular in France and Flanders during the sixteenth century. Especially by Hans Vredeman de Vries." She pointed out the window, warming to her theme. "It was damaged in the Civil War when Cromwell's forces bombarded it, so the 6th earl inserted those arched windows to enclose the gallery. The 10th earl employed Capability Brown to modernise the gardens and parkland. He also built the stables, which are rather magnificent, and an orangery, as well as a Gothic summerhouse."

"Our house is about five miles in that direction," Henry said, gesturing into the distance. "We used to spend all our time here, though. We played in that grand Gothic summerhouse as children," he added with a wistful smile.

Harriet, who had become quite animated whilst speaking of the building, fell quiet.

"What fun we had," her brother chuckled, apparently oblivious to her change in demeanour.

They were greeted by the Dowager Countess St Clair and the earl himself, as well as his younger brother Jerome Cadogan. She'd met Jerome at the fireworks and had liked him at once. There was a mischievous glint in his eyes she appreciated, though she knew he was the bane of his older brother's existence. He was a handsome fellow, like his brother, though a broken nose gave him a rakish, disreputable air.

The young man had a reputation for falling violently in love with quite unsuitable women and making something of a spectacle of himself. As the St Clair family's wealth was staggering, the earl lived in daily terror of finding his young sibling married to a fortune hunter. Rumour had it he'd already had to buy off a courtesan and placate a married lady threatening to tell all to the scandal sheets.

"How lovely to see you here, Miss Hunt," the Countess St Clair said, greeting her warmly. "I was so pleased to hear you were coming, and Miss Connolly, you are most welcome."

The countess was a glamourous woman, and it was clear where her sons had inherited their looks from. Dressed in a pale green gown trimmed with delicate lace, she looked far too young to be St Clair's mama. Her golden hair had faded a little, but it did nothing to diminish her beauty. Her vivid blue eyes were bright and full of intelligence. Jerome had the same intense blue colouring, Matilda noticed, whereas St Clair's were an unusual shade, almost aquamarine.

"I always forget how handsome the earl is," Kitty whispered to Matilda as they followed their hosts into a breathtaking entrance hall.

The sheer scale of the building was meant to impress upon its guests the wealth and power of the family who owned it. Matilda thought it was doing a wonderful job.

"He is a beautiful man," Matilda said with a smile, as Harriet rolled her eyes.

"Do you not agree, Harry?" she asked, too curious not to ask.

Harriet looked from Kitty to Matilda and put up her chin, a stubborn glint to her eyes. "He has arms and legs in all the correct places, all his own teeth and a head of hair. Add that to his title, and I should think any young lady would think him the epitome of male beauty."

Kitty frowned at her. "But I have no interest in marrying him and gaining his title, or all this," she added, gesturing around her as they followed the family up one side of an impressive double staircase. "So that has no bearing on *my* decision. But for you, Harry dear—objectively, as if regarding an artwork—do you not think him a thing of beauty?"

Harriet paused and Matilda bit her lip, aware St Clair and the others had gotten some distance ahead.

"If I regard him as an artwork, a Grecian urn, for example," Harriet said, an impatient tone to her voice, "then yes, I should say he is as lovely an example of the art as ever existed. Close to perfection, if I must be truthful. Unfortunately, he is not a Grecian urn, though his mind bears a close resemblance to the contents."

With this rather unvarnished assessment, Harriet turned and hurried up the stairs.

"Gosh," Kitty said, wide-eyed.

"Quite," Matilda agreed with a sigh. "We can only hope she doesn't kill him before this party is over."

***

Luke Baxter regarded Mr Derby on the opposite side of the carriage. As stern and severe as always, he was a handsome man, tall and broad despite the years weighing heavier on him now, and a heart condition that his doctor had warned him to manage with care. His hair was iron grey, but there was plenty of it, and his eyes contained the energy and strength of will of a man twenty years his junior.

Luke had hated the man for most of his life, but hatred was an emotion that took a great deal of energy and Luke was too good-natured to allow it to embitter him. So, hatred had faded, though not expired. Instead, it was overlaid by the knowledge that he must do his duty and that Mr Derby was a fount of knowledge about how this ought to be achieved. There were many people who relied upon Luke, and upon what his future held.

That Mr Derby didn't give a tinker's cuss whether or not Luke had wanted the position thrust upon him was something he had no choice but to set aside. He had endured too many arguments, too many bitter quarrels, all of them ending the same way—with his capitulation.

What choice did he have?

The Earl of Trevick was an unlucky man. In fact, it was said the men of the family were cursed to die young. The earl and his youngest brother, Mr Derby, had made a mockery of this old wives' tale as the earl had reached his three score and ten, and Mr Derby seven and sixty. The rest of the family had lived up to it admirably, however, with every son, grandson, nephew and cousin succumbing to war, disease, carriage accidents and—on one notorious occasion—a jealous lover.

Mr Derby himself was the father of six daughters. Having discovered his first wife was barren, he lost no time in marrying again, within mere weeks of her demise. This later union had, much to his disgust, produced six females. Indeed, the Trevick family was littered with female progeny, but not a single male survived. As his youngest surviving brother was not far behind him in years, this was a problem the earl could not ignore if the family was to endure.

Sensing impending doom, Trevick had acted when his last but one remaining heir had succumbed to a fever of the lungs. That action had been to pluck his last chance—Luke—from obscurity and wrap him up in cotton wool.

His mother had been in transports; finally the recognition and position in society she'd always craved was hers. What did she care that her son was miserable as sin? He'd be the next Earl of Trevick in one day, a circumstance any young man in their right mind ought to rejoice over. Everyone seemed well pleased with the arrangement… except for Luke.

He'd fought it, to begin with, desperate to return to Kitty and the life he'd planned for them both. He'd run away, bribed staff to write letters, and generally made himself ill with frustration and anger but, in the end, it had been for naught. What else could a boy do against the wishes of a family as old and powerful as Trevick? The staff were loyal to a fault, the grand estate so vast it would have taken him days to leave its grounds, even if he'd remained undiscovered. Besides, his mother's fury and reproaches—combined with the cold disdain of the earl himself—had been more than a very young man could endure.

Still, he'd known that Kitty would wait for him. One day he'd be a man and his chance would come to escape, and he'd take it.

Mr Derby had guessed his intent, however, and issued an ultimatum. If Luke failed to do his duty, the earl would ruin Kitty's family, destroying their fortunes and the prospects of their only daughter. Trevick had many interests in Ireland, Mr Derby reminded him, especially in the rapidly growing flax business. If that wasn't threat enough, Mr Derby made another that he promised to keep if Luke even considered fighting his fate….

He'd ruin Kitty.

It could be done easily enough, Luke knew. A woman's reputation was a fragile thing. You only need breathe a word in the right—or wrong—ear and a rumour would begin. It wouldn't matter whether or not there was any foundation, or proof… a girl like Kitty would not survive it.

It wasn't blackmail, Mr Derby said with a smile. Only a warning. He knew Luke would not forget himself, or what he owed the title, for what should happen to the women of the family. He'd often gesture to sweet little Sybil at this moment as if Luke's actions would see her out on the street. She was Luke's favourite cousin and had the misfortune to accompany them on this journey, as if her presence could guarantee Luke's capitulation. There seemed to be dozens like her in the family, her sisters and nieces and cousins, all of them dependent on the head of the family.

From then on, Luke had cared for nothing. He'd stopped fighting the future and making plans, he stopped caring about anything at all. His feelings were buried, smothered, forced away to a small corner of his being where they could no longer trouble him. Luke had few acquaintances and no one he regarded as a friend, but was regarded by all who knew him as a placid, level-headed man who did his duty uncomplainingly. He was charming—if rather dull—and handsome, too, though he lacked a certain something… whatever it was that made a man stand out from the crowd.

He knew what it was. He was dead inside. His heart still beat in his chest, but his life had ended the day Kitty had been taken from him.

By the earl's decree, Luke had been educated by tutors and sheltered from life's vicissitudes until the age of nineteen. Then he'd been sent off on a grand tour and had gone without a murmur. He'd wanted to be far away from the girl he couldn't have without ruining her and everything she loved, far enough that he could try to pretend she'd been nothing more than a childish dream.

Now he had returned after four years abroad, ready for the final stage of the earl's plan.

He was to marry.

A suitable bride had been selected, naturally. Nothing left to chance. It would be the match of the decade. Lady Frances Grantham, a duke's daughter no less, an heiress with an impeccable blood line and an older sister who had already birthed three sons. Her fertility was all but guaranteed, and her blue blood would purify anything lacking in Luke's, as he was merely a distant branch of the original Trevick line. They'd gone back three generations for his line.

The earl was beside himself with glee.

Luke wanted to put a gun to his head, or possibly the earl's.

Either would do.

Lady Frances was beautiful, accomplished, and popular. Well, of course she was, she was beautiful, accomplished, and the daughter of a duke with a dowry large enough to sink the English fleet. Popularity had been handed her on a plate.

Luke didn't like her.

To be fair, he'd only met her three times to date, so it was unkind of him to have made up his mind already. He knew he must try harder, not that he had a choice.

Yet she was all wrong. Her eyes were blue, her hair blonde, and she was always utterly composed. She never did or said anything she ought not, never laughed so loud he thought his eardrums might burst, never snorted or got stuck in trees or….

Stop it.

The fleeting image of a pair of sparkling dark eyes flickered somewhere in the depths of his soul and he slammed the door on it. *Damnation.* He hadn't thought of her in months, had banished the memories and the ache in his heart. He'd thought he'd cured himself.

Sybil caught his eye and sent him a sympathetic smile, full of understanding. Sometimes he wished he didn't like her or her sisters—that he could hate her, hate all the family—but she was just as much a victim of her father and uncle's tyranny as he was. They all were.

Luke took a deep breath and studied the landscape beyond the carriage window. He was going into English society at last; that was something to be grateful for. Luke had become adept at counting his blessings. Though he'd not met St Clair or anyone else who would be there before, having been kept away from English society, he'd read the scandal sheets. The earl sounded an interesting character, at least. A man who'd seen life, rather than being coddled like an egg.

Going abroad had offered Luke a little more freedom than he'd experienced since the man opposite had snatched him from his idyllic life in Ireland, which was something. That the bastard had exiled him there in the first place, damning his father and the rest of them by default to obscurity was ironic, but it *had* been an idyllic life.

Don't think of it.

He forced the memory away. He would not allow himself to remember the pretty orchard in spring with the scent of newness in the air, the taste of green, everywhere bursting, budding, full of life and hope and….

For Heaven's sake!

"What's that?"

Luke jolted as Mr Derby addressed him, a suspicious scowl in his eyes.

"N-Nothing, sir," he said, appalled that he'd spoken aloud. God, he hadn't slipped like that in years.

"Hmph." Mr Derby folded his arms and looked away from him. Sybil stared at him in alarm before returning her attention to the scenery once more.

Luke let out a slow breath and told himself to get a grip. No more memories, no more wishful thinking or what-ifs or daydreams. Kitty was gone, his love for her nothing more than maudlin sentimentality. He'd banished such thoughts many years ago when he'd realised nothing but madness and misery would come from them.

He was resigned. He had been for years. He was duty bound, and would do his duty. Marriage to Lady Frances first, beget an heir and a spare second, and then….

Then he would run.

Available to read for free on Kindle Unlimited

To Follow her Heart

Want more Emma?

If you enjoyed this book, please support this indie author and take a moment to leave a few words in a review. *Thank you!*

To be kept informed of special offers and free deals (which I do regularly) follow me on *https://www.bookbub.com/authors/emma-v-leech*

To find out more and to get news and sneak peeks of the first chapter of upcoming works, go to my website and sign up for the newsletter.
http://www.emmavleech.com/

Come and join the fans in my Facebook group for news, info and exciting discussion...

Emmas Book Club

Or Follow me here......

http://viewauthor.at/EmmaVLeechAmazon
Emma's Twitter page

About Me!

I started this incredible journey way back in 2010 with The Key to Erebus but didn't summon the courage to hit publish until October 2012. For anyone who's done it, you'll know publishing your first title is a terribly scary thing! I still get butterflies on the morning a new title releases but the terror has subsided at least. Now I just live in dread of the day my daughters are old enough to read them.

The horror! (On both sides I suspect.)

2017 marked the year that I made my first foray into Historical Romance and the world of the Regency Romance, and my word what a year! I was delighted by the response to this series and can't wait to add more titles. Paranormal Romance readers need not despair however as there is much more to come there too. Writing has become an addiction and as soon as one book is over I'm hugely excited to start the next so you can expect plenty more in the future.

As many of my works reflect I am greatly influenced by the beautiful French countryside in which I live. I've been here in the

South West for the past twenty years though I was born and raised in England. My three gorgeous girls are all bilingual and the youngest who is only six, is showing signs of following in my footsteps after producing *The Lonely Princess* all by herself.

I'm told book two is coming soon ...

She's keeping me on my toes, so I'd better get cracking!

KEEP READING TO DISCOVER MY OTHER BOOKS!

Other Works by Emma V. Leech

(For those of you who have read The French Fae Legend series, please remember that chronologically The Heart of Arima precedes The Dark Prince)

Girls Who Dare

To Dare a Duke

To Steal A Kiss

To Break the Rules

To Follow her Heart

To Wager with Love (November 15, 2019)

To Dance with a Devil (December 20, 2019)

Rogues & Gentlemen

The Rogue

The Earl's Temptation

Scandal's Daughter

The Devil May Care

Nearly Ruining Mr. Russell

One Wicked Winter

To Tame a Savage Heart

Persuading Patience

The Last Man in London

Flaming June

Charity and the Devil

A Slight Indiscretion

The Corinthian Duke

The Blackest of Hearts

Duke and Duplicity

The Scent of Scandal

The Rogue and The Earl's Temptation Box set

Melting Miss Wynter

The Regency Romance Mysteries

Dying for a Duke

A Dog in a Doublet

The Rum and the Fox

The French Vampire Legend

The Key to Erebus

The Heart of Arima

The Fires of Tartarus

The Boxset (The Key to Erebus, The Heart of Arima)

The Son of Darkness (October 31, 2020)

The French Fae Legend

The Dark Prince

The Dark Heart

The Dark Deceit

The Darkest Night

Short Stories: A Dark Collection.

Stand Alone

The Book Lover (a paranormal novella)

Audio Books!

Don't have time to read but still need your romance fix? The wait is over…

By popular demand, get your favourite Emma V Leech Regency Romance books on audio at Audible as performed by the incomparable Philip Battley and Gerard Marzilli. Several titles available and more added each month!

Click the links to choose your favourite and start listening now.

Rogues & Gentlemen

The Rogue

The Earl's Tempation

Scandal's Daughter

The Devil May Care

Nearly Ruining Mr Russell

One Wicked Winter

To Tame a Savage Heart

Persuading Patience

The Last Man in London

Flaming June

The Winter Bride, a novella (coming soon)

Girls Who Dare

To Dare a Duke

To Steal A Kiss

To Break the Rules (coming soon)

The Regency Romance Mysteries

Dying for a Duke

A Dog in a Doublet (coming soon)

Also check out Emma's regency romance series, Rogues & Gentlemen. Available now!

The Rogue

Rogues & Gentlemen Book 1

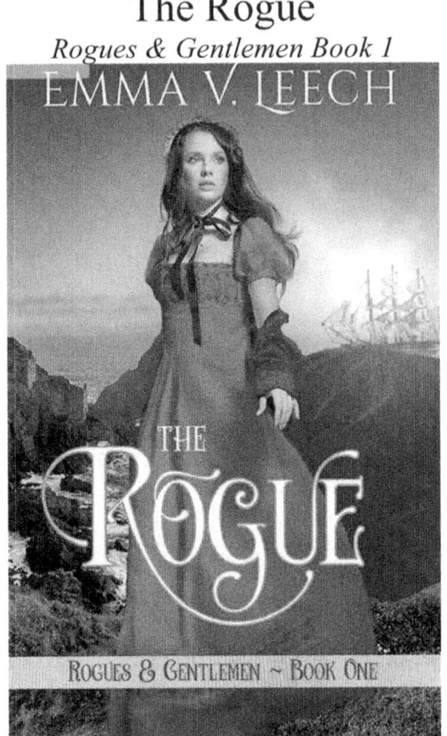

1815

Along the wild and untamed coast of Cornwall, smuggling is not only a way of life, but a means of survival.

Henrietta Morton knows well to look the other way when the free trading 'gentlemen' are at work. Yet when a notorious pirate, known as The Rogue, bursts in on her in the village shop, she takes things one step further.

Bewitched by a pair of wicked blue eyes, in a moment of insanity she hides the handsome fugitive from the local Militia. Her reward is a kiss that she just cannot forget. But in his haste to escape with his life, her pirate drops a letter, inadvertently giving

Henri incriminating information about the man she just helped free.

When her father gives her hand in marriage to a wealthy and villainous nobleman in return for the payment of his debts, Henri becomes desperate.

Blackmailing a pirate may be her only hope for freedom.

Read for free on Kindle Unlimited

The Rogue

Interested in a Regency Romance with a twist?

Dying for a Duke

The Regency Romance Mysteries Book 1

Straight-laced, imperious and morally rigid, Benedict Rutland - the darkly handsome Earl of Rothay - gained his title too young. Responsible for a large family of younger siblings that his frivolous parents have brought to bankruptcy, his youth was spent clawing back the family fortunes.

Now a man in his prime and financially secure he is betrothed to a strict, sensible and cool-headed woman who will never upset the balance of his life or disturb his emotions ...

But then Miss Skeffington-Fox arrives.

Brought up solely by her rake of a step-father, Benedict is scandalised by everything about the dashing Miss.

But as family members in line for the dukedom begin to die at an alarming rate, all fingers point at Benedict, and Miss Skeffington-Fox may be the only one who can save him.

FREE to read on Amazon Kindle Unlimited.. Dying for a Duke

Lose yourself in Emma's paranormal world with The French Vampire Legend series…

The Key to Erebus

The French Vampire Legend Book 1

The truth can kill you.

Taken away as a small child, from a life where vampires, the Fae, and other mythical creatures are real and treacherous, the beautiful young witch, Jéhenne Corbeaux is totally unprepared when she returns to rural France to live with her eccentric Grandmother.

Thrown headlong into a world she knows nothing about she seeks to learn the truth about herself, uncovering secrets more shocking than anything she could ever have imagined and finding that she is by no means powerless to protect the ones she loves.

Despite her Gran's dire warnings, she is inexorably drawn to the dark and terrifying figure of Corvus, an ancient vampire and master of the vast Albinus family.

Jéhenne is about to find her answers and discover that, not only is Corvus far more dangerous than she could ever imagine, but that he holds much more than the key to her heart …

FREE to read on Kindle Unlimited The Key to Erebus

Check out Emma's exciting fantasy series with hailed by Kirkus Reviews as "An enchanting fantasy with a likable heroine, romantic intrigue, and clever narrative flourishes."

The Dark Prince

The French Fae Legend Book 1

Two Fae Princes
One Human Woman
And a world ready to tear them all apart

Laen Braed is Prince of the Dark fae, with a temper and reputation to match his black eyes, and a heart that despises the human race. When he is sent back through the forbidden gates between realms to retrieve an ancient fae artifact, he returns home with far more than he bargained for.

Corin Albrecht, the most powerful Elven Prince ever born. His golden eyes are rumoured to be a gift from the gods, and destiny is calling him. With a love for the human world that runs deep, his friendship with Laen is being torn apart by his prejudices.

Océane DeBeauvoir is an artist and bookbinder who has always relied on her lively imagination to get her through an unhappy and uneventful life. A jewelled dagger put on display at a nearby museum hits the headlines with speculation of another race, the Fae. But the discovery also inspires Océane to create an extraordinary piece of art that cannot be confined to the pages of a book.

With two powerful men vying for her attention and their friendship stretched to the breaking point, the only question that remains...who is truly The Dark Prince.

The man of your dreams is coming...or is it your nightmares he visits? Find out in Book One of The French Fae Legend.

Available now to read for FREE on Kindle Unlimited.

The Dark Prince

Acknowledgements

Thanks to my wonderful editor, Kezia Cole, who always makes me think and doesn't let me get away with anything!

For *To Break the Rules* I must give a very special thank you to Rebecca Vijay and her friends, Candace Andrew, Flora Xavier and Chandrabhanoo all of whom pitched in with discussions and brainstorming on all aspects of Indian culture. Their help and advice ensured that Lucia/Aashini was the courageous and fully rounded figure you've come to know. Rebecca especially will no doubt be relieved her messenger inbox isn't pinging with constant questions about everything from make-up, to weather and what Indigo smells like.

An extra special thank you also to Elise Marion for reading for me and reassuring me I was getting it right. As an established historical romance writer herself, I recommend you check her out.

To Victoria Cooper my cover designer for all your hard work, amazing artwork and above all your unending patience!!! Thank you so much. You are amazing!

To my BFF, PA, personal cheerleader and bringer of chocolate, Varsi Appel, for moral support, confidence boosting and for reading my work more times than I have. I love you loads!

A huge thank you to all of Emma's Book Club members! You guys are the best!

I'm always so happy to hear from you so do email or message me :)

emmavleech@orange.fr

To my husband Pat and my family ... For always being proud of me.

Made in the USA
Coppell, TX
10 December 2020

43993991R00177